DESTINY'S SONG

By the time Xavier finished singing, it was dark outside. They must have been in the church for nearly two hours. All that time Destiny was transfixed by her own private Allgood concert. But it wasn't a concert really. He was singing to her spirit and it seemed they were both oblivious to anything outside of themselves.

For a long time, they just stared into each other's eyes. Suddenly she knew she wanted to kiss Xavier more than anything else in the world. He must have read her mind because at that precise moment, he got up and walked down the stairs.

He walked toward her and Destiny couldn't move. She just stared into his eyes and felt herself being devoured by them. He stood in front of her and touched her chin. She rose as if on command and felt the intense piercing gaze of his eyes penetrate her to her very core.

Destiny's breath stopped as their faces grew nearer and nearer. She could smell the moist-sweet aroma of his breath as his lips pressed against hers. She began to lose herself in his embrace. And this time there was no mistaking it. His hands were slowly moving over her body.

BOOK YOUR PLACE ON OUR WEBSITE AND MAKE THE ARABESQUE ROMANCE CONNECTION!

We've created a customized website just for our very special Arabesque readers, where you can get the inside scoop on everything that's going on with Arabesque romance novels.

When you come online, you'll have the exciting opportunity to:

- View covers of upcoming books

- Learn about our future publishing schedule (listed by publication month and author)

- Find out when your favorite authors will be visiting a city near you

- Search for and order backlist books

- Check out author bios and background information

- Send e-mail to your favorite authors

- Join us in weekly chats with authors, readers and other guests

- Get writing guidelines

- AND MUCH MORE!

Visit our website at
http://www.arabesquebooks.com

DESTINY'S SONG

Kim Louise

ARABESQUE
BET
BOOKS

BET Publications, LLC
www.bet.com
www.arabesquebooks.com

ARABESQUE BOOKS are published by

BET Publications, LLC
c/o BET BOOKS
One BET Plaza
1900 W Place NE
Washington, D.C. 20018-1211

All Kensington Titles, Imprints, and Distributed Lines are available at special quantity discounts for bulk purchases for sales promotions, premiums, fund raising, educational, or institutional use. Special book excerpts or customized printings can also be created to fit specific needs. For details, write or phone the office of the Kensington special sales manager: Kensington Publishing Corp., 850 Third Avenue, New York, NY 10022, attn: Special Sales Department, Phone: 1-800-221-2647

First Printing: December, 2000

10 9 8 7 6 5 4 3 2 1
Printed in the United States of America

for leon

ACKNOWLEDGMENTS

I give thanks to *The Most High* for imbuing my soul with the desire to write. I also have to, need to, MUST thank someone who has been a colleague, a writing coach, but most importantly a friend: Lisa Jackson. Girl, if it hadn't been for you, Destiny would be singin' the blues! I also want to thank Pam for always believing in my writing, Loree whose beautiful story inspired part of this book, kamillah for researching African-American history on the Great Plains, Deborah for being the writer I've always looked up to, Steve for understanding when his mother was busy writing, my mother for being the most creative person I know, and my dad for being the greatest storyteller in the world.

Prologue

The van looked diseased. There were rust spots splattered across its white exterior in hundreds of small, reddish brown blemishes. The inside was also in a state of deterioration. Breaks and cracks in the gray vinyl seats exposed tufts of sponge padding. The latches on the windows were either broken off or inoperable and the "Watch Your Step" sign in the van had faded until there was nothing left but the faint impression of an old warning.

A middle-aged man in a wrinkled sheriff's uniform was in the driver's seat. He seemed to deliberately drive the van with all the haste of a sloth just to annoy the passengers. The van hit a pothole, and Rico Freeman was jostled as the van trembled and clattered over the uneven road.

Rico took careful inventory of his surroundings. There was a total of eight prisoners, including him. They had all been awakened that morning by the bellowing sounds of the armed guards.

"Roll up!" they had shouted—the traditional wake-up call for those who were being released from jail. Only Rico and the rest of the prisoners in the van weren't being released, just transferred to a minimum-security correctional facility. The guards' inappropriate use of the phrase *roll up* was another in a long series of taunts employed to remind Rico and the others that they were no longer considered human. *But soon,* Rico thought, glancing behind him, *I will again be a part of the self-existent world.*

Another deputy sat in the back. His nightstick was taut against his leg and his gun was secured in its holster. Rico figured the man to be in his late fifties, possibly early sixties. Rico smiled and returned his gaze to the front. Rat was right, he thought. *They give these transfer jobs to the old geezers.*

Rico laughed out loud. He couldn't believe how easy this was going to be. Just as he expected, the deputy in the back questioned him.

"What's so funny?"

Rico remained quiet. He almost blew it by laughing again. He tried to keep a straight face, but it was too hard. His exhilaration compelled him to smile. *Wait until we pass the airport,* he kept telling himself. *Just wait.*

Some of the other prisoners had turned around, perhaps hoping to get a look at an altercation.

"I said, what's so funny?"

Rico continued to stare ahead silently with a smile that broadened with each block. The deputy who was driving glanced repeatedly in the rearview mirror. When Rico heard the deputy in the back get up, he was ready. Just as Rat had said, it would only take from the jail to the airport to unscrew the two bolts underneath the seat, even with handcuffs on. Once the bolts were out, the metal support rod they held in place was perfect for bashing heads. Rico just hoped that Frampton and T-Bone, who were sitting behind the driver, were as successful at removing the bolts as he had been.

Well, Rico thought, gripping the rod tightly, *there's no better time to act than the present—especially when your destiny awaits.*

One

Destiny picked up the red notebook from her nightstand. The label read "Destiny Chandler v. Rico Freeman, Doc. 284, Page 549." She opened the book and scanned the information she had copiously collected over the past year. Letters from Rico, log sheets of his phone calls, pictures of broken windows, and copies of repair bills. She had hoped that keeping a thorough record of Rico's protection order violations would be enough. It wasn't.

Her lawyer had called a week ago to inform her that despite her intensive record keeping, she would have to testify against him. And because no one was ever around to witness his violations, it would be her word against his. Destiny had hoped desperately that things wouldn't come to that, but they had. And now her court date was less than an hour away.

Destiny pushed the notebook away in disbelief. How could this kind of tragedy happen to her? She racked her brain trying to figure out what she had done to deserve her predicament. She was deep in thought when the phone rang. Right away, she knew it would be her best friend, Jacq.

"Hi, Jacq."

"Girl, did you call Psychic Friends or what?"

"I just knew you would call."

"I wish I could be there with you, but . . ."

"I know, I know, your new job."

"Yeah, girl, and it's kicking my butt."

Destiny chuckled. "They always do."

Destiny Chandler and Jacquelyn Jackson had been friends since junior high school. In their twenty-year friendship, Destiny had never known Jacq to keep a job much longer than six months.

"So, what you doin' now?"

Destiny looked over at the red notebook that contained the traumatic details of her recent life, and shook her head.

"I'm trying to figure out what I've done to deserve all this."

"You shouldn't have whooped it on him so tough."

At that remark, Destiny almost smiled. Jacq could always make her laugh. But stalking was not a subject she could laugh off.

"I'm serious, Jacq. I can't figure it out." Destiny took a deep breath. "I work hard. I've been with the Arts and Humanities Council for ten years. I give back to my community. When the council started a tuition reimbursement program, I jumped on it. I wasn't out there playing in the streets; I was studying. And if I do say so myself, I'm probably the best photohistorian in Nebraska."

"And you said all that to say . . ."

"They say that what goes around comes around. After all the good I've tried to do, I don't understand why someone is so intent on making my life horrible. And it is *not* my whip appeal!"

Jacq almost laughed, but stopped herself because she knew her friend was serious. "Destiny, I know what you're saying, and I'm sorry about that comment. You know, girl, I was kidding earlier, but I'm serious now. You could have been Sarah, Rénee, or Shaneequa, and it wouldn't have made a damn bit of difference. Because it's not you; it's *him*. He's just pure-d crazy. So stop trying to blame yourself."

Destiny wanted to believe her friend, but was too anxious about the trial to think straight.

"Maybe you're right," Destiny conceded.

"Look, it's almost time. You need something to set your mind right. Have you listened to that Allgood CD I left over there?"

"Jacq, the last thing on my mind has been music, especially that hippity hoppity mayhem you have an affinity for."

"Des, I told you. This brotha is different. He's so different, they don't even have a category for him yet. He's inventing it as we speak."

"Uh-huh." Destiny feigned attention.

"I'm telling you, girl, he is the bomb, truly. And his stuff is just what you need to clear your head and lift your spirit. Imagine, a supa-fine brotha tellin' you that you are the most beautiful creature ever born, and meaning it."

"I sure need *something* to steady my nerves. I'm not a wreck now, but I've got a feeling it's coming."

"Then pop that CD in your car stereo and listen to it on the way to court. You'll see what I mean."

"All right, all right. And you do something for me. Call me when you get off."

"Are you kiddin'? I'm coming over."

This time, Destiny did smile. "Thanks, Jacq."

"Ain't no thang."

Destiny hung up the phone and tried to collect herself. She stood and smoothed out the navy blue coatdress she was wearing. She thought it made her look confident, but not domineering. She picked up the red notebook and headed for the door. Just then she remembered the CD. She walked to the stereo and pulled the CD from the rack.

On the front of the CD was a picture of the counter of an old-fashioned ice cream parlor. On the counter was a black, oval-shaped plate with an ice cube, a block of chocolate, and a mound of whipped cream all melting toward the center. The words *Allgood's Molten Hot Shop* were written in gold across the top.

Destiny turned the CD over in her hand and gasped. Allgood was leaning against a wall looking serene and exotic. His shoulder-length dreads hung freely. The dark locks framed his face like a lion's mane. An incandescent light coated prominent features—eyes closed and peaceful, high, well-defined cheekbones, generous lips that looked firm yet sensual, and mocha-brown skin.

There's something about a man with a five o'clock shadow, Destiny thought. Her eyes lingered on the precise cut of All-good's subtle facial hair. *Damn,* she thought to herself. *He is fine.*

Destiny tucked the Allgood CD and the red notebook under her arm and walked, more confidently than she felt, out of her apartment.

By the time Jacq arrived at Destiny's apartment, Destiny was packing so quickly and intently that she didn't hear the doorbell. She was startled when she heard Jacq calling her from the living room.

"Des!"

Destiny dropped the white laced camisole she was packing and spun around. Jacq came traipsing into the bedroom.

"I used your spare key to get in. Didn't you hear me ringing?"

"Sorry, Jacq. I guess I didn't."

Jacq looked at the packed luggage, Destiny's open chest of drawers, and the underwear on the floor. A look of panic jumped onto her face. "Damn, Des. Did they let him go?"

Destiny smiled. It was the first honest smile she had allowed herself to have in more than a year.

"No, girl. They decided to keep him for three years."

Jacq whooped. She grabbed her friend and hugged her tightly. Destiny squeezed back. She truly loved Jacq for being there through her entire ordeal with Rico. When Destiny had needed to talk about Rico's vile accusations and wild, erratic behavior, Jacq had listened. When Destiny needed a place to stay while Rico went on his drinking binges, Jacq opened the door to her home. And when everyone else had scorned her for staying with

Rico for four years, Jacq patiently helped her discover when to leave in her own time, and never called her stupid or foolish like some of her ex-friends. It seemed as though Jacq had been holding her for a long time.

"So why are you packing?"

Destiny sat down on her queen-size, four-poster bed and looked at the walls of her bedroom. Her own photography hung there, along with paintings and poems by some of the artists at the council. Now the very things that used to bring her comfort were uncomfortably familiar.

"I've got to get away for a while. This whole situation with Rico has just worn me out. I need time to rejuvenate and re-capture my life."

"What you need is a man. A real man. Not that imitation of life you just experienced. I'm talkin' a bona fide, gen-u-wine, real deal, make you cry when you doin' it, *man*."

Destiny shook her head. It never failed. Somehow, Jacq could always turn a conversation to sex.

"Look, the last thing I need right now is to be doin' it with somebody. I just want peace."

Jacq worked her neck and threw up the palm of her hand. "Good sex always makes me peaceful."

Destiny laughed. "You are certifiable."

Jacq picked up Destiny's camisole and handed it to her. "That's why ya like me. So, where are you goin' with this in such a hurry?"

"Atlanta."

Jacq sat down on the bed beside Destiny. "Atlanta? Girl, I thought you were going to say on a cruise or to the beach. Hell, even in the woods would have been more restful than Atlanta. What's in Atlanta?"

Destiny looked at the large candle sitting on her dresser. "Remember my candle story?"

A mischievous spark of realization crawled across Jacq's face. "Oh, snap! You're going to see *him?*"

"Slow down, Jacq. I know where your gutterish mind is headed, and you're wrong. Davis and I are good friends."

"Yeah, uh-huh. Good friends who were engaged to be married."

"That was a long time ago. Anyway, Davis is working on a special project. He won't be home much, and he's letting me stay in his condo while he's working."

"I'll bet that project won't be the only special thing he works on."

Destiny allowed herself to laugh again. Despite her situation, she wondered if there would be any sparks between her and Davis. Jacq was right. They had been engaged. If only he hadn't succumbed to the allure of a player's lifestyle, she would be Mrs. Davis Van Housen today.

Jacq looked into her friend's eyes. The more Destiny tried to turn away, the more Jacq got in her face. Destiny knew she had been found out.

"Okay, okay. So maybe I was thinking about it."

"I knew it."

"But it's only a mild curiosity."

"I knew that crazy Rico hadn't wrecked your stuff." Jacq glanced at the lingerie in Destiny's suitcase. "That's why you packing all those hoochie undies."

They roared with laughter again. Destiny couldn't remember the last time she felt so free.

"When do you leave?"

"Tonight. I have an eleven P.M. flight."

"Girl, you wasn't kiddin' about gettin' outta here. How long are you stayin'?"

Destiny thought about that. "I'm not sure."

"What about your job?"

"I'm taking an artist's sabbatical." Destiny saw the look on her friend's face and decided she'd better explain. "It's kind of like a leave of absence, only you're supposed to be working on your art. But I just want to power down."

Jacq nodded her understanding. "What are you going to do for money?"

"I've got a nice-size rainy day savings. And if needed, I've got some 401(k) money."

"Sounds like you've got a plan, missy," Jacq said, smiling playfully. "I'll let you go, on one condition."

Destiny smiled back. "What's that?"

"That you call a sister once in a while. You know how I worry."

"It's a deal."

"I tell you what," Jacq said, glancing at Destiny's strewn wardrobe. "Let's celebrate ol' school style, and then I'll help you finish packin'."

"That sounds wonderful."

"Cool. I'll go make us some fried bologna sandwiches like we used to eat back in the day, and you put on some Emotions."

Destiny had given up pork and beef years ago. "Now you know I don't have any bologna."

Jacq walked into the living room. "I know. On the way over, I stopped at the store and picked up some ninety-nine-cent bologna, some Miracle Whip, and some Wonder Bread. I felt a celebration comin' on."

Destiny called out after her friend, who was already headed toward the kitchen. "I guess I'm not the only one who called Psychic Friends today."

Destiny looked around her, satisfied. There was hardly anyone on the plane and no one sitting beside her. She could take up as much space to relax as she wanted. Wanting to be comfortable, Destiny chose black velour pants and a matching ribbed turtleneck to wear during the plane ride, despite a scolding from Jacq.

"You never know who you might meet," Jacq had warned, and suggested that she change into the leopard-print duster she saw hanging in her closet.

This fashion advice came expectedly from the woman who owned a credit card for every major department store in the country and had the clothes to prove it. Destiny, who only had one credit card for emergencies, possessed a distinctively more modest wardrobe and was quite comfortable in Levi's and Hanes Her Way tank tops. Despite her friend's coaxing, Destiny opted for comfort.

She was disappointed that Davis wouldn't be able to pick her up from the airport. But it was just as well. She would rent a car and take a leisurely drive into the city. She had heard that the Atlanta skyline was impressive day and night. This way, she could take her time in finding out.

Destiny stretched her long legs out as far as they would go under the seat in front of her. Normally, she would fall asleep during plane rides, but tonight she was too excited.

She leaned back in the seat, thankful that Jacq had gotten her to the airport in time. For a while, she thought she would have to catch a later flight. Somewhere between Jacq's bologna sandwiches and their dancing and singing, they had lost track of time.

But it was worth it. Celebrating with Jacq brought back memories she'd forgotten she'd had. They played all the "jams" as Jacq called them. "Best of My Love" by the Emotions, "Got to Be Real" by Cheryl Lynn, "Ring My Bell" by Anita Ward, and "Sophisticated Lady" by Natalie Cole were just a few on the hit list. Jacq called it a lady soul party.

Destiny almost laughed out loud remembering Jacq's singing. "Get it, girl. Work it, girl. Get down on the funk. Aw, sookie sookie, now. Go, Destiny, it's ya birthday, it's ya birthday!"

The two soul sisters had danced around Destiny's living room like teenagers. They shouted props back and forth to each other while the oldies but goodies blasted from the bedroom.

"Remember this one?" Jacq did the Gigolo, wiggling her arms back and forth.

Destiny hunched her shoulders as she turned from side to

side popping her fingers. "Yeah, how about the Smurf?" she said.

"Got you beat," Jacq snapped, and whipped her arms quickly up and down into the Prep.

"Not yet," Destiny answered, and Smurfed into the Freddy Krueger. After a few moments, they were both laughing uncontrollably and slumped down onto Destiny's rattan sectional, exhausted.

Destiny took a reflective look at Jacq. It's funny, she thought, ever since they became friends, people always asked if they were sisters. And sometimes not just sisters, but twins. She and Jacq had never seen the similarities themselves. Like now, Destiny wore her hair in the thin corkscrew twirls of sisterlocks; Jacq's hair was permed and straight. Destiny's complexion was golden brown; Jacq's was more like a buttery toffee. Destiny's compact frame consisted of easy contours; Jacq's physique had more curves than the Indy 500. But just last week when they were having espressos in a coffee club, their server all but insisted they were identical twins.

Their only explanation for this strange phenomenon came right after they first met. They were both varsity cheerleaders for the Lewis and Clark Junior High School basketball team. After staying late for practice one evening, Jacq asked Destiny if she could get a ride home with her.

"Sure. My mom won't mind. Besides, you just live a few blocks away."

The uniform-clad teenagers walked up to Mrs. Edna Chandler's gray Chevy Citation and got in.

"Mom, this is Jacq."

"Oh, my God!" Jacq shouted from the backseat.

"What's wrong?" Destiny and her mother asked, turning around.

Jacquelyn Jackson stared wide-eyed and openmouthed at Destiny's mother. After a few seconds, she spoke.

"You look just like my mother. You could be her identical twin."

So although they couldn't see the similarities in themselves, they both agreed that their mothers were doppelgängers, and that fact helped to solidify their friendship and to make them feel special when people mistook them for twins.

The two friends played more music, sang more songs, ate more bologna sandwiches, and danced more dances. When they finally realized what time it was, they were halfway through Destiny's CD collection.

"Jacq, look what time it is!"

Jacq glanced at the handmade clock on the wall and moaned. "Girl, I'm too tired to move." Destiny tugged on her friend's arm and belted out her best James Brown impression.

"A-get-up-a, get on up!"

They laughed some more and went into Destiny's bedroom to finish packing.

Even though Jacq drove like a bat out of hell, the ride from the apartment to the airport seemed to take forever. During that time Jacq took the opportunity to quiz Destiny about her decision to visit Davis.

"I'm kinda mad at you."

"Why, because I sing *and* dance better than you?"

Jacq took her eyes off the road just long enough to roll them at Destiny.

"No, cow. Because you never said anything about talking to Davis *or* this trip."

"Oh, that."

"Why you wanna keep it on the hush?"

Destiny thought to herself before answering. "I don't know, Jacq. I guess I just haven't been real sure of myself lately. So I didn't want to say anything until I was certain that I was going."

"And when were you certain?"

Destiny looked out at the night. "Just now."

Jacq gave Destiny a cockeyed look. "Okay, so who called who then?"

"I called him."

"I knew it, ya skeeza."

"I just needed somebody to talk to. Someone who doesn't know anything about my situation with Rico."

"And . . ."

"And we talked. I didn't tell him about Rico, but I did tell him that I need a break from the Arts and Humanities Council, which I do. He suggested I come down there. Actually, he sent me a ticket."

"Ooo, you go, girl. Now what does he do again?"

"He provides consulting and information technologies to various businesses. His company is called Van Housen and Associates."

Jacq often wished her friend would simply speak plain English. "He's a computer geek," Jacq quipped. "On a serious tip though, he must be bankin' some mad Benjamins."

"You amaze me. If it's not sex, it's money."

"In this case, I think we're talkin' 'bout both!"

Destiny refused to laugh. She was determined to keep her thoughts in the right place. She did not want to get her hopes up. Whatever happened, she reasoned, would happen.

They reached the airport in record time. Jacq pulled up in front of the United terminal and put the car in park.

"Aren't you coming in?" Destiny asked.

"You know I hate anything to do with good-byes."

"I know," Destiny replied, getting out of Jacq's black Mazda Miata. Although Jacq couldn't hold on to a job for long, she somehow managed to keep her sports car payments up.

Jacq helped Destiny get her luggage out of the trunk. The two women hugged for a long time and then slowly pulled away from each other.

Destiny smiled at Jacq with tears in her eyes. "Thanks for everything, Jacq."

"Ain't no thang," Jacq replied with tears in her eyes. "Now go on before you miss your flight."

Destiny picked up her luggage and hurried into the terminal. She stopped at the first flight schedule monitor she came to and scanned it for Flight 308. When she found it, she almost jumped for joy. The schedule said Flight 308 was departing at 11:35. She hadn't missed it. In fact, it was late, so she had a little extra time.

After checking her bags, Destiny walked to the gift shop to buy something to read. During her fervid packing with Jacq, she had forgotten to bring reading material. She was about to pick up *Heart & Soul* magazine when the *Essence* magazine stopped her dead in her tracks.

She froze as her senses leaped to life. It was him, Allgood, looking fine as chilled wine. With only a few moments remaining before her plane departed, Destiny bought the *Essence* and headed toward the boarding area.

She touched the cover of the magazine delicately as if she were stroking his cheek. Jacq was right, she thought. There was definitely something about Allgood that made a woman want to forget every man she'd ever met. Darned if she knew why, but ever since she had heard Allgood's songs, it was as if she was falling in love with someone she'd never met.

Destiny leafed quickly to the table of contents, found the page number for the Allgood article, and, hurrying, flipped the pages to it. "Whoa," she said, then looked around to see if anyone near had heard her. Luckily, the surrounding passengers didn't seem to notice.

The full-page picture of Allgood was mesmerizing. He was standing against a lush backdrop of cobalt-blue, crushed-velvet drapes, which flowed into large folds on a concrete floor. He wore a matching blue crushed-velvet suit. The shirt was open to the navel and the pants clung to long, powerful legs. The look on his face mingled eagerness and tenderness. He stood with his arms outstretched as if he were urging the love of his life to come walking into them.

When Destiny's heart began to dance with excitement, she told herself she was being silly. After all, it was just a picture. But Destiny felt something as she read the article. And what she felt was an undeniable bond. She knew it was ridiculous, but it was true. By the time she had read half the article, she wondered if she was experiencing some residual feelings for Rico and projecting them onto this Allgood person.

Nevertheless, Destiny read the article with feverish intensity. The author wrote about Allgood's growing number of fans, his comparisons to the artist once again known as Prince, and his love for old school music. She got goose bumps when she read the description of his sensual energy on stage. When the flight attendant handed her the complimentary peanuts, Destiny couldn't eat. Her stomach was a-flutter with butterflies.

She pushed the peanuts aside and continued to read. The author wrote dripping details of Allgood's reverence for women and his struggle to find the right one. She also told of Elise Kent, his first love, their fleeting affair, how saddened he became when they broke up, and how he never saw her again. When Destiny read this, her arms ached to hold him.

She tried to make herself stop, tried to turn down the intensity of her emerging feelings, but it was too late. When she got near the end of the article, she was completely convinced that Allgood was the perfect man. She felt a long, deep sigh coming on when she was startled by the last details of the article. "Allgood is currently designing a recording studio and working on a new album, *1000 Words,* in his home in Atlanta, Georgia."

Destiny slammed the magazine shut. *Okay,* she told herself. *I've indulged myself too long. Yes the man is gorgeous, but this infatuation must be some sick leftover from a bad relationship.* "Get a grip," she said out loud as a flight attendant was walking past her seat.

"Excuse me," the flight attendant replied.

"I'm sorry," Destiny offered. "I was just thinking out loud."

The flight attendant put on his plastic smile. "Is there anything I can get you?"

"No, I've had enough already," Destiny answered, and spent the rest of the flight gazing out the window into the murky night sky.

Two

After a four-hour flight, Destiny found herself exhilarated in the largest passenger terminal complex in the world, the Hartsfield-Atlanta International Airport. She thought she had died and gone to African-American heaven. Her people were everywhere. They were flight attendants, clerks, supervisors, and managers. They were bosses and bosses' bosses. She was thoroughly impressed. Coming from Nebraska, she was refreshed to see so many people that looked like her, everywhere.

No wonder so many people called Atlanta "The Black Mecca." Destiny had picked up her luggage and had gone directly to get her rental car. When she got there, she was also surprised to see that all the employees were African-American. Something about the city already felt like home.

She was again impressed when she got into the 1999 Grand Prix and turned on the radio. Immediately, the sound of Mint Condition enveloped her to the tune of "You Don't Have to Hurt No More." Like a magnificent precognition, she knew instantly she had made the right choice in coming.

Destiny reached into her carry-on bag and took out the envelope that had contained her plane ticket. Along with the ticket, Davis had sent her a picture of himself posing like a Mack Daddy in front of a champagne-colored Lincoln Navigator, a map with the route from the airport to his condo, and a key. At the bottom of the map he had written, "Just in case I'm not home when you get here." *That's just like Davis,* she thought.

He doesn't miss a work-beat for anyone or anything. But she kind of liked the idea of being alone for a while. It would give her time to power down and settle in.

As Destiny maneuvered the car through the airport and to the highway, she found herself deep in thought. She wondered if Davis had anything special planned for them to do together. She hoped he wasn't really as busy as he had indicated he might be. Perhaps between the time she talked to him last and now, he had found a way to rearrange his schedule so that they could spend more time together.

She was also beginning to think that maybe she had made a mistake in telling Davis that she was purely interested in rest and relaxation. It would be nice to have at least a few exciting diversions. Otherwise, she knew her mind would easily drift backward to Rico sitting in jail and the dreaded day he would be released.

But Destiny wasn't one to sit around and wait for an escort either. She didn't mind entertaining herself, and sometimes she preferred it. Besides, she was in Atlanta now, the city of possibilities. She made up her mind right then and there that she would see the city of brown angels even if she had to do it all by herself.

Buckhead was one of the largest suburbs of Atlanta, and it was home to some of the most affluent African-Americans in Atlanta. The houses and condominiums were clustered in tight rows, and each residence seemed a small variation on a theme: affluence.

The directions on the map were perfect. Destiny made it to Davis's condo without taking a wrong turn. When she arrived, his garage door was open and a night-light was on as if it had been waiting for her all evening. *I wonder what covenant he broke with that one?* she asked herself as she drove in.

Destiny parked the rental car, removed her luggage, and walked into the open garage. She saw a small note addressed to her taped to a button on the wall.

Destiny,
   Welcome to The ATL! I hope you remembered to bring the key I sent you. The refrigerator is stocked and so is the bar—help yourself. As you can see, I'm working late, so I'll check on you in the morning. I should be home by 9:00 A.M.

                                    Love, Davis
P.S. Please press the button this note was attached to and close the garage door; don't want the neighborhood in an uproar.

Destiny obliged. After closing the garage door, she took the key from the envelope, opened the door, and went inside. She wasn't surprised by the opulence of Davis's condo. She knew him well enough to know that he would only have the best, but she was impressed. The décor definitely said "money." Destiny knew that if Jacq were there she would probably say, "Just open your legs *now,* and be ready when he comes home!"

Her cursory examination took in bright hardwood floors in a living room chock-full of oversize furniture. The love seat, sofa, and matching chair were so large, Destiny imagined sitting on them and being swallowed completely into their busy brown and black patterns. The finishing touch in the room was the wide oak trim around the ceiling, floor, and windows.

Yep, he most definitely had some mad Benjamins, as Jacq would say. She set her bags down and gave herself a nickel tour. The man's home could be in *Architectural Digest.* Large living room, high ceilings, color-coordinated everything. And every modern appliance imaginable, with a color scheme of mother earth tones.

The spiral staircase was to die for. Destiny climbed it as if she were a heroine in an old movie. There were three bedrooms upstairs and two baths. The master bath was the size of her bedroom in Lincoln. She didn't see any more notes so she presumed she could take either of the two guest rooms. She decided to take the one farthest from the master bedroom. That way Davis's comings and goings wouldn't disturb her, and hers wouldn't disturb him, if he were home.

The guest bedroom she chose was like a small studio apartment—complete with a full-size bed, two nightstands, a chair, a desk, and a nine-drawer dresser. Destiny plopped her bags down and smiled.

Suddenly it was as if an immense stone had been hoisted from her shoulders. The reality of the moment set in and felt good. She was in Atlanta, a thousand miles from Rico, who was locked up and couldn't possibly get to her to continue the damage he had done to her life. And she was in Davis's home—a man she had once loved with all her heart and soul.

She needed to celebrate. Not a party like she and Jacq had had earlier, but a special celebration for herself. She went to the boom box on the oak dresser and turned it on. She took out the Allgood CD from her purse and popped it in. The music covered her over like a warm blanket. It was mellow-smooth, like she felt at that moment.

Destiny's body became a testament to free-flowing motion. She danced and swayed. Perhaps all those jazz dance lessons at the Arts and Humanities Council hadn't gone to waste, she thought. She let the rhythm take her. She twirled and dipped. She sashayed and sauntered. Allgood sang, "Come on in to your place, baby." Destiny responded, "Your place, baby." Allgood crooned, "It's your place, Momma." Destiny danced and sang, "Your place, your place, baby." She was so enthralled with the music and with the motion it stirred in her that she never noticed the man standing at the top of the stairs, watching her.

Everything was going according to plan, almost. The code for the software conversion was being written and rewritten to specifications. It just wasn't going fast enough. Davis Van Housen's first taste of corporate empowerment strategies was slowly turning sour.

He had always been a self-made, do-it-yourself man. When businesses contracted for his services, he usually did all the work. From planning through implementation to evaluation, Davis was always a one-man show.

When he took the assignment with Integrated Marketing as project leader, he thought he was stepping into territory he could handle. Getting things done through others, that's the message of empowerment. All he had to do was coordinate a fifteen-person programming team of IM employees. Sounded simple enough. Little did he realize, the corporate culture of the company made it nearly impossible for their employees to work together cohesively.

It took all of Davis's professional strength to keep from taking over the project completely. But it was a massive project, which involved refurbishing a large and antiquated computer system. He would have to clone himself at least ten times to meet his deadline. Again, Davis thought, *I'll have to find a way to ride in on my white horse and save the day.*

The only thing keeping him going at this late hour was Destiny. The thought of her sleeping in his home gave him the energy of ten men. It also gave him the resolve he needed to work as facilitator—and not dictator—of the conversion process. Ever since Destiny had accepted his invitation, he had been on a natural high. Even members of the programming team had noticed it. After their last project meeting, Bill Goodman, who was becoming more of a friend to Davis as the project went on, questioned him about his change in demeanor.

Bill reminded Davis of Johnny Cochran. He had small, hooded eyes with crow's-feet flowing like small tributaries from the corners of his eyes. His full mustache and sepia-toned skin added to their resemblance. "You've been riding high these past few days. Did you buy a new car or something?" Bill asked.

A sly smile slid across Davis's face. "No, but she reminds me of my Jeep, though."

"Oh," Bill said knowingly. "That explains that power stride you've been using. You've got a new light in your life."

"Nope," Davis said, clearing the conference table. "More like an old flame . . . from back home."

Bill, who was usually quite reserved, slapped Davis on the back and picked up his task planner from the table. "I feel a long dinner break coming on."

Davis and Bill finished clearing the conference room and headed to Abruzzi's, where Bill got an earful of Davis's relationship with Destiny. Over two orders of fettuccine Alfredo and sparkling water, Davis told how he and Destiny became high school sweethearts.

"At first, I wasn't even interested in her. I was trying to get next to her friend Frieda. Man, Frieda was this fly redbone with scarlet hair and freckles. She wouldn't give me the time of day. But I was on a mission. I called, I wrote love letters, I went to Frieda's house. Every time I tried to push up on Frieda, Destiny was always somewhere around.

"I don't know how it happened, but Destiny started to look better and better. I'm telling you, it was just like that song, 'You Make Me Wanna Leave the One I'm With.' The next thing I knew, man, it was me and Destiny."

"How long were you together?"

"That's the thing, man. It was just a year—which I guess is a long time for a teenager. But in that year, we loved so hard. In every relationship I've been in since then, I've tried to recapture what Destiny and I had together. I've come close, man. Very close. But no one really compares."

The waiter came by and refilled their water glasses. The two ate in silence for a few moments—each digesting both the food and the conversation.

"Why did you two call it quits in the first place?" Bill asked.

Davis stared out the window. He had thought about their

breakup many times over the years and asked himself how a decision could be right and wrong simultaneously.

"I decided I wanted to play the field."

"Oh, that."

"Man, I was eighteen, just out of high school, headed for the army, and horny as hell. Actually, it was my first taste of army life that led me to break up with her."

"But you just said . . ."

"When I got to basic and saw the opportunities we had to make time with beautiful women, all those beautiful, single women, my eighteen-year-old hormones said, 'Woof!' "

"So you played on her."

"No. Never. When I came back home from basic, I told her straight up that I just wasn't ready to settle down. She was pretty torn up about it. But I couldn't lie, not to her."

"Man, the way you were talking, I thought she was the love of your life."

"She was. We were engaged."

Bill was stunned. "No shit?"

"No shit."

The waiter walked past, leaving their check on the edge of the table.

"Man, it's a wonder she even talks to you now."

"We're cool. I think. I hope she respects me for being honest. Anyway, before I went back to the base, I saw this candle at a boutique store. It was so beautifully crafted that it reminded me of Destiny."

Davis could see the candle clearly in his mind. "It was orange and black and about twelve inches high. And cone-shaped—molded to resemble a volcano. The neat part was these two-toned swirls of wax that erupted out of the top and flowed in drips down the sides. Just the way the colors mingled fascinated me."

Davis paused for a moment, then continued. "When I gave it to her, I told her that the candle was a symbol of our love."

"You romantic dog."

"I also told her that the candle flame was like a phoenix that flies into fire and is reborn from its own ashes. Then we kissed, and I told her that if our love was meant to be, nothing could stop it. And that someday it might be reborn of its own ashes just like a phoenix."

"Whew! How old were you, man? Eighteen? That's some heavy shit for a teenager."

"It wasn't me, it was Destiny. She just has that effect on people. We kept in contact off and on over the years. But when she called last week, it was like an answer to a prayer. A prayer that I've been saying over and over since high school and didn't realize until now."

"Sounds like she's got you in the zone, my man. When does she arrive?"

"Actually," Davis said, checking his Rolex. "She's probably at my house now."

Bill was shocked. "Then what are you doing here?"

"I've got to tie up some loose ends."

"Sounds like you've got some loose ends with her that need tying. You better get on it."

"I know. The phase two reports are nearly completed. But she knows my schedule is hectic. And now that I've got another client, my schedule is going to be even harder to juggle."

"You're under contract with another company besides IM?"

"Not a company, a musician. He wants to set up a digital recording studio in his home. He's paying big bucks for my musical and technical expertise."

"What do *you* know about music?"

Davis raised his water glass and tipped it toward Bill. "Oh, I tap the ivories now and then. Used to have big fun back in the day. I would play the piano and Destiny would sing."

"No shit?"

"Yeah, and she can sing her ass off."

The two men glanced at their watches and knew it was time to leave. They paid their bill, leaving the waiter a ten-dollar tip, and walked back to the Integrated Marketing office building.

Bill was quiet and reflective while Davis hummed a tune from his past.

There were just some nights that were pitch perfect—when the moon is truly in the seventh house, Jupiter sho-nuf aligns with Mars, and all the music in the universe converges in one shared heartbeat. Xavier Allgood had just had that kind of night. He felt as though the ancestors were present and the angels had showered down their blessings.

It was the best kind of night—not hundreds of howling fans, but a few people in a small jazz bar who tranquilly seemed to enjoy listening to his music. He couldn't think of a better perfection. And the band, his crew, was smokin'.

Even when he had deviated from the program and rode the vibe he got from the audience into an extended rendition of "Paradise Rising," the crew stayed with him. Together, they re-created the song with the audience. The experience was so intense, he lost himself in the performance. Before Xavier realized it, he was inseparable from the music, and indistinguishable from the audience. Xavier, his crew, and the audience became one.

It was such a delicious performance, the crew was reluctant to go home afterward. Something in the night made them want to hang out and savor the moment. But Xavier had other plans. With his adrenaline intact, he wanted to use his energy to tackle his latest challenge—automating his new music studio.

Working on his recording studio was close to becoming an obsession with Xavier. He had had his fill of controlling forces in mainstream studios. They were too stifling. And it was that kind of controlling force that kept his first CD sitting on a back shelf for a year before it was released.

This time would be different. This time he would maintain creative control over the entire process. That's why it was so important for him to have a top-quality consulting firm to help him identify the best use of music technology for his studio.

He believed that the fans that made him successful deserved the best.

Luckily he had found a company owned by a brother who was not only a top-notch service provider, but was turning into a good friend. They discovered quickly that they worked well together and shared the same vision of how to merge music with technology.

After the concert, Xavier sat down with his crew while they were depressurizing from the performance, and he used their kinetic energy to finish the specs for the studio. He could hardly recognize the basement of his house in the plans. It was a good transformation. He was eager to share his final product with Davis Van Housen, his consultant.

Playing to the hometown crowd always left the crew cheerful and talkative. Tonight, backstage at The Fuse Supper Club, was no exception. In fact, it was exceptional. After showers and fresh clothes, the crew was pumped. While Xavier concentrated on his studio plans, he heard their comments as if from a distance.

"Did you hear that applause?"

"Did you hear them singing along?"

"How many times did they stand?"

"Earth to Zay, come in, Zay," called Sammy, the bandleader and elder of the group.

Xavier realized he had spent the entire after-session in deep thought about his studio.

"Man, I'm sorry. I'm zoning out. I was definitely away from here. As a matter of fact, I was home," Xavier said.

"Well, you missed all the compliments we gave you," Sammy said.

"And the suggestion to take this party somewhere else," Tyrica said, adding her two cents.

"That sounds like the bomb. But you'll have to give me a

rain check. I really need to drop off these specs for Davis. Sorry, y'all."

Sammy's look was smug. "We understand. Once you get your studio built, you can get rid of us and create that high-tech crap they call music these days."

Xavier was surprised by the echos of "Uh-huh" and "Yeah" by the members of his backup band. Even the quiet one, Shade, piped up in agreement.

"Are you serious?" Xavier asked, concerned.

"Of course we're serious," Sammy responded. "Computers are putting everyone, especially *real* musicians, out of business."

"I know that's right," Tyrica, Xavier's backup singer, chimed in. "Pretty soon all an artist will need is a mike to sing with and a box for the music and background vocals to come out of."

"Y'all are whacked," Xavier admonished. "I will never, ever use a box or technotronic gizmo to replace the real deal. You can't touch anyone's soul with a box." Xavier paused for a moment to reflect. Then he continued. "If I can't touch someone's soul, then I might as well quit now."

"Humph," Sammy grunted.

"And y'all know I'm not about to quit now."

"So why all the gadgets?" asked Sammy, an ordained minister who played the meanest bass in the city.

Xavier glanced approvingly at his plans. "Because . . . I want the freedom to create my music without constraints or quotas or deadlines."

"Or session charges!" Tyrica finished.

"That too," Xavier agreed. "Basically, I want control of my own vibe. If I feel like slamming a track at three in the morning, I want the space and the technology to do it. Am I being unreasonable?"

"Guess not," Sammy conceded, packing his guitar in its case. "So, what are you waiting for? Get out of here and take that computer guy, I mean that consultant, your plans."

* * *

Xavier was pumped. Shortly after the concert, he left the bar with schematics in hand and made a beeline for Davis's condo. On the way, he thought about how well the plans were coming together.

He also mused over the band's concerns of abandonment. At first, he didn't think they were serious. But reflecting on it now, he could understand their disquiet. He had been spending inordinate amounts of time on the project. And it had become the number one item on his list of things to talk about. But he hoped Sammy and the crew knew that he could never turn his back on them.

When Xavier pulled up into Davis's driveway, he saw a light on in the house. *I thought Davis had to work tonight,* he said to himself as he stepped out of his all-terrain vehicle. Xavier came in through the back door as he always did and was just about to holler, "Yo, G. It's me!" when he heard himself singing a duet with a woman.

He closed the door behind him and followed the sound of the music. It was coming from upstairs. As he started up the stairs, the most enchanting woman he'd ever laid eyes on stopped him midstride. She could not have been more captivating if she had been performing on stage and he had been chained to the only seat in the house. Xavier was completely transfixed.

She danced like an angel and sang like an angel's daughter. He felt humbled by her honest interpretation of his song. He knew that somehow, someway, his music had touched her. And that's all he had ever wanted—connection to someone, somebody, who could feel what he felt. He climbed the stairs stealthily, trying hard not to alert her to his presence. He felt guilty about his covert behavior. But his heart wanted him to stand on Davis's spiral staircase and watch her dance forever.

At that moment she turned around, startled. A look of alarm quickly washed over her face. The last thing he wanted was to frighten her.

"You can jam," Allgood said, trying to put her at ease.

"Oh my God," Destiny said, and covered her mouth, clearly frightened.

The next thing he felt was a sudden, blunt force on his upper chest and then himself tumbling down the stairs. As his body rolled into a bend in the staircase, his head lightly grazed one of the oak banisters that lined the steps.

Xavier thrust his right arm and leg out just in time to prevent his head from striking the other side of the staircase. His tumble came to a halt only a few steps from the bottom. He laid there for a few seconds, too dazed to right himself.

"Oh my God, Davis! I'm sorry."

Her angel's voice was not so angelic anymore as a ringing sound had started in Xavier's ears. It distorted her voice and made it sound like something from Looney Tunes. He felt soft hands helping him to sit up and then they quickly let go.

"You're not Davis!"

Xavier's head was a little foggy from the scrape. "Right now, I'm not sure who I am." He lifted his head to get a good look at the woman responsible for his disorientation. He heard her gasp and decided he'd better assure her that he was not an intruder.

"Don't worry. I'm not a burglar. I'm a friend of Davis's." Xavier rubbed his head where it had grazed the staircase.

It was a while before she spoke. She just stood there aghast, which was just as well until the ringing in his ears subsided.

"Th-that's going to be quite a bruise," she said finally. Then Xavier felt the soft hands on him once again.

"Can you stand?" she asked.

"Yeah," he said and stood up with her help. She walked him over to the couch and helped him sit down. "I'll get a cold towel for your head."

"Thanks," Xavier replied.

While the woman went into the kitchen, Xavier's mind cleared enough for him to remember having a discussion with Davis about a friend that was coming to visit.

"You're Destiny, aren't you?" he asked as she handed him the towel.

"Yes," she said, smiling.

"I'm Allgood, Xavier Allgood." He extended his free hand and for a moment he wasn't sure if she would take it. And then she did. Her hand was warm despite having just been in cold water, and it was as soft as newborn skin.

Xavier touched the towel to his temple. "I guess we've gone about this the wrong way. I usually like to know a woman first before she knocks me off my feet."

Destiny smiled. "I'm sorry about that. I really am. It's just that I've been kinda jumpy lately and when I saw you on the stairs, my reflexes took over."

The scrape at Xavier's temple was beginning to throb. He held the towel closer, hoping it would help. Instead it shot a thin bolt of pain across his forehead. He winced.

"Here, let me see." Destiny sat down close to Xavier on the couch and took the towel. "It doesn't look as bad as I thought it would. But I think you're gonna need to put some ice on it to keep the swelling down."

She replaced the towel and Xavier took it from her.

"How did you know my name and how did you get in here?" she asked.

She had a low, silky voice, and when she spoke the syllables of her words walked themselves tenderly over his body. "Davis told me you were coming. And he and I barge in on each other all the time. I was so wrapped up in my own thing," Xavier said as he looked over at the schematics scattered at the foot of the staircase, "that I forgot you might be here."

Destiny walked over and gathered the papers.

He watched her swift, deliberate movements. "I'm sorry if I startled you," he said.

Destiny handed the papers to Xavier. "I'm sorry I overreacted."

"Not at all. Reflexes like that could save your life. You never know about people nowadays." Xavier examined this wonder woman who had toppled him. She looked like she could hold her own.

They were both quiet for a moment. Suddenly Destiny seemed far away. He wondered what she was thinking. Whatever it was, it didn't interfere with her beauty at all, but it made her look just a little sad. He thought to himself, if Destiny were his woman, he would make sure she never was unhappy or frightened about anything.

"You really do have a lovely voice," he said.

Destiny smiled broadly. "Thank you."

"Sounds like we make beautiful music together." He couldn't resist trying to make her smile again. But she didn't. She just looked him deeply in the eyes. Xavier felt her gaze as soft as a caress. As if on cue, the throbbing in his temple began to subside and the ringing in his ears stopped.

Destiny's face softened into recognition. "It's really you," she said, blinking her vibrant jet-black eyes.

"I'm afraid so," Xavier admitted, and he captured her eyes with his. He heard a small gasp from Destiny's temptingly curved mouth. It sounded almost sensual. He studied her facial features one by one. The fringe of her long lashes cast playful shadows on her cheeks. Her eyes were so definitively almond-shaped, he wondered if she had a grandmother or grandfather of Asian descent. He sensed a growing energy racing through his bloodstream.

"Let me get you some ice," Destiny said, rising.

"Thanks," he said, watching her walk away.

She returned with an ice pack and a wondrous smile. Xavier thought she could power an entire city with her smile.

"I owe you one," she said, handing him the ice pack and taking the towel.

"Really? How's that?"

"Your music helped me to cope with something I was going through recently. You caught me on the tail end of a celebration just a few minutes ago. Anyway, I just want to say thank you."

"You're welcome, Destiny."

Xavier liked the way his mouth felt when he said her name. *What a lovely woman,* he thought to himself. *A lovely woman who belongs to Davis,* his conscience told him.

"You know what. I should leave. I'm overstaying a welcome that doesn't exist." He looked at Destiny again with his piercing eyes. "I know we just met, but I would like to ask you a favor."

"A favor?" she asked.

"Yes." Xavier rose from the couch and handed her the plans for the studio. "Will you ask Davis to call me about these first thing in the morning?"

"I can do that."

Xavier, mesmerized by her beauty, wondered what else she could do. Before he realized it, his mouth spoke his thoughts. "You can do other things, too."

"Excuse me?" Destiny asked.

"You sing and dance very well."

Xavier walked toward the front door. Destiny thought she hadn't seen a walkaway like that since Denzel Washington's exit in *Devil in a Blue Dress.* When he reached the door he turned abruptly as she walked behind him. Suddenly they were a finger-width apart and Xavier didn't seem to mind. Destiny, on the other hand, was all a-flutter. They were so close, she could almost taste his breath. It was ambrosial and airy on her lips—which she dared not lick for fear of losing her tongue in the moist recesses of his mouth.

"Y-Yes," she stammered, gazing up into his dark brown eyes.

"Lock the door behind me," Xavier said, mischief settling on his face. "You wouldn't want any strangers to barge in on you."

Destiny flushed as she felt the blood finally returning to her cheeks. "I will."

And with that, he was gone. Destiny summoned her last remaining strength to peek out the window. When she did, she saw a large, black all-terrain vehicle back out of Davis's driveway and cruise down the dark street.

Destiny stood watch at the window for a few more minutes with the memory of Xavier Allgood simmering in her mind.

The sounds of the morning pushed their way into Destiny's slumber. The birds were singing as if to welcome the sun. Nature's alarm clock, Destiny thought. Sitting up, she yawned and stretched out the kinks of a pleasant night's sleep. Her slumber was filled with images of Xavier Allgood. Like an eternal loop, her dreams replayed their last moments together.

In her nighttime fantasy, Destiny watched from the window as he drove away. She tried to keep her silhouette out of the window frame so he wouldn't discover her staring out into the night after him. She just wanted one more glimpse to make it real. One last glimpse so she could believe she had just met the man of her most recent daydreams. She held the vision of him backing his car out of the winding driveway for a long time. She wanted to store up the feeling it gave her.

Destiny glanced over at the large clock on the nightstand just as the numbers showed eight o'clock. She stepped out of bed and headed for the shower, wondering if Davis had made it home.

After she finished dressing, she walked to where Davis's present sat propped against the wall. She took it out of the box and laid it on the bed.

The photo of the abandoned building was a stark contrast of black and white, old and new, strength and frailty, birth and death. Its size contributed to the sense of enormity implied through the close-up. Destiny just hoped that Davis remembered that the building was where they had their first date.

She had suspected that transporting the large, framed photograph on the plane might present some difficulty. She had packed the photo in a large box and marked it "Fragile." When she checked it along with another piece of luggage for the trip, the woman at the counter processed it without breaking her rhythm.

Destiny looked at the picture now and tried to imagine where Davis could put it—perhaps in the guest bedroom where she was sleeping. The room was sparsely decorated. The picture would add an interesting ripple to Davis's austere décor.

She placed the photograph in the armchair and stepped back from it. It almost looked like the North Side Recreational Center that she remembered. It had the same arched front door, the same smoky glass windows, and the same long staircase leading up to the door. But there was something different about the building, too. It looked sad and weary. Time had seen fit to allow shingles to be blown off the roof and the paint to crack and peel. The concrete steps were broken in some places, along with a few of the windows. Yet in the midst of the deterioration, the spirit of endurance and survival resonated on the front door that looked almost new. Destiny believed that she had caught the essence of that spirit in her photograph.

She picked up Davis's picture and headed downstairs. She touched the railing softly, remembering the place where Xavier stood watching her. She smiled, recalling his good nature about the entire incident. His freshly showered aroma came back to her as keenly as if he were standing before her now. And the way the muscles in his arm tightened when she helped him up . . .

By the time Destiny reached the bottom of the staircase, her body temperature was about three degrees warmer than it was at the top of the stairs. She propped the picture up against the Japanese-style coffee table and fanned herself with her hand.

"Come here and let me see how beautiful you are." Destiny heard Davis's familiar voice coming from the kitchen. She walked into the spacious kitchen, and there in a gray designer suit was Davis Van Housen. He opened his arms and Destiny walked toward him with open arms of her own. The two embraced tightly.

Davis stepped back slightly and gave Destiny an appraising look. She assumed that his smile meant she passed, and Destiny gave him a sizing up also. He looked the same. He was still tall and slender. He still kept his curly hair cut short. And he still had the longest eyelashes Destiny had ever seen on a man.

"Des, it's good to see you." Davis rested against the counter.

"You, too, Mr. Big-Time Analyst. And your home is gorgeous!"

"Aw, you know," Davis said, shrugging his shoulders. "Have to impress the clients. They don't want to do business with you unless they feel you don't *have* to do business with them."

Destiny nodded. "You're right about that.

"Thanks for opening your home to me, Davis. You don't know what it means for me to be able to stay here."

"Anything for you. And you don't have to be in a rush to leave either. I'm not seeing anyone. So it's not like I have a woman that might be jealous of your being here."

Davis's eyes locked onto Destiny's. She wasn't sure what he meant by his comment, but she was not going to read anything into it. She shyly averted her eyes.

"An eligible bachelor like yourself . . . I'm shocked that some woman hasn't captured your heart by now."

Davis rose a shrewd eyebrow. "I'm very particular about my women," he said.

Davis turned around and took a sack from the counter. He set it on the kitchen table. "Hungry?"

Destiny watched as Davis took out Egg McMuffin after Egg McMuffin.

"After working all night, all I really want to do is go to bed. But I'm starving and I don't feel like cooking."

"I could have made breakfast, Davis."

Davis crumpled the empty sack and put it into the garbage can under the sink. "No way would I ask you to cook on your first day here." Davis handed Destiny a McMuffin with mischief playing in his eyes. "Now tomorrow is a different story."

Destiny rolled her eyes. She took the sandwich, wondering if he remembered she was a vegetarian. She unwrapped the sandwich and, lo and behold, it was an English muffin with egg and cheese. No ham.

They sat down at the large oak table. "I know that look," Davis said, finishing off his first bite. "You thought I forgot."

Destiny took a bite of the sandwich. She shook her head no. Davis cocked his head to the side in disbelief. "You didn't?"

"Well, I just wondered if you would remember."

Davis's eyes bore holes of warm remembrance into Destiny's soul. "Destiny Chandler, I remember more about you—about us—than you'll ever know."

Destiny felt parts of her heart, frozen from her last relationship, begin to thaw. She wasn't sure how to respond or even if she wanted to respond. The room grew uncomfortably quiet. As she was getting up the nerve to reply to Davis's comment, a deep, luxurious voice resonated from behind them.

"Well, good morning. Hope I'm not intruding."

"What's up, music man?" Davis said, turning his intense gaze away from Destiny. "Cop a squat. Have some Mickey D's."

Xavier Allgood came into the kitchen and seated himself next to Davis and across from Destiny. She found his closeness intoxicating. The polar ice caps on her heart went into nuclear meltdown.

"I'm sorry to come by so early. I just wanted to apologize to you for last night."

"I don't know why you're apologizing. I haven't even looked at the plans yet."

"No," Xavier countered. "It's not that. Man, I forgot that you had company. So I came in through the back like I always do and walked in on Destiny. Scared her, actually. I'm sorry. From now on, I'll knock."

"What do you mean, you walked in on her?"

"I heard music playing upstairs. So I went to investigate. When I got to the top of the stairs, there she was. Apparently she didn't hear me come in, because when she saw me, she . . . well . . ." Xavier touched his fingers to the small scrape on his forehead.

"Don't tell me my homegirl cracked that cranium."

Xavier strummed his fingers on the tabletop. "She caught me off guard, man. See, what happened . . ."

"Nope, nope. Don't try to play it off."

"Davis, it was an accident," Destiny interjected.

Davis was not assuaged. He was holding his stomach, bent over with laughter. "Wait until I tell the tabloids about this," he said after his laughter abated.

Xavier leaned back in his chair and shook his head. His movement caused Destiny to take inventory. Today he smelled of an enchanting musk. The aroma wafted through the room like a sweet breath. His linen suit made him look sophisticated. At the same time, the unstructured white cotton gave him a casual appearance.

Unexpectedly, she felt the need to intercede on his behalf. "What really happened is he caught me singing and dancing like I was in a Puff Daddy video."

"Naw. What I saw was classy. They don't dance like that in any video I've ever seen."

"Or probably made for that matter, if I know Destiny."

Xavier considered Davis's words for a moment, and then it hit him. "You know, that's true."

"You're damned skippy it's true, right, Des?"

Destiny was afraid to admit she hadn't seen any of his videos. She didn't think she had seen any Puff Daddy videos either, but Jacq talked about him all the time.

"I'm sorry. I can't remember ever seeing any of your videos. Once you've seen one video, haven't you've seen them all?"

Apparently Destiny said something wrong because suddenly Davis and Xavier were looking at her as though she had giant caterpillars crawling out of her ears. Then Xavier's expression slowly changed from puzzled to inspired, as if an invisible person had just whispered something sweet in his ear.

Davis wasn't too sure about that look on Xavier's face. "Looks like you just swallowed a cat."

"Quite the opposite. I just realized that whatever I do next,

I've got to raise the bar. Ideas for this new CD have been floating around in my head for a while, but they're just ordinary. What I want is something extraordinary."

Davis started laughing again.

Destiny folded her arms across her chest in protest, but it was too late. Suddenly they were all laughing. Davis grinned proudly at Destiny.

"I can't get over it. My girl, kicking butt and taking numbers. Don't worry, man. Your secret is safe with me."

Xavier frowned and looked questioningly at Destiny. "You're not a martial arts expert, are you?"

Davis spoke up before Destiny could respond. "Naw. Destiny's forte is in the lens."

Xavier looked intrigued. "Camera lens?" he asked.

"Oh, that reminds me!" Destiny said, standing. "Davis, I brought you something." Destiny walked into the living room and retrieved the picture. She returned to the kitchen with it and held it up.

"This is exactly what I'm looking for," Xavier remarked. He walked over to Destiny's photograph. "Destiny, where did you get this?"

"Are you kidding," Davis said smugly. "I can tell right away that this is Destiny's work. She's a brilliant photographer."

"What?" Xavier said, looking in Destiny's direction.

"Thanks for the compliment, Davis. I believe the more truthful thing to say is that I know a good subject when I see one."

Xavier's face lit up. "Do you have more work here?"

"I have some things," Destiny said cautiously. "But if you mean a portfolio, that's in Lincoln."

"Judging by this, I won't need to see much else."

Davis interrupted. "What have you got in mind?"

Xavier took a seat. "You know I've been working on my next CD?"

"Yes," Davis replied.

"I'm not sure if I told you, but it's called 'One Thousand Words.' I had an idea to use a metaphor to describe my evolution as an artist. I want to use a montage of pictures in everything, videos, concerts, paraphernalia, you name it. But I want the montage to be unique. Something that speaks to transformation and redefinition and change." Xavier got up and walked over to the picture. "Something like this." Xavier paused as if contemplating a great feat. "How about it, Destiny?"

Destiny was unsure of what he meant. "How about what?" she asked, handing the photograph to Davis.

"How about becoming my personal photographer? It would just be for my next project. Just while you are here visiting Davis."

Xavier took one more look at the photograph. "I would really like you to do it."

"Great idea, man. Destiny is an awesome photographer. Actually, I kind of like the idea of the two of us having a little piece of the project. It will give us more time together."

Somewhere in the back of Xavier's mind, he was thinking the same thing.

Destiny was appalled. "Whoa. I came here to rest. If I want to work, I'll go back home to the Arts and Humanities Council."

"Arts and Humanities Council?" Xavier was intrigued. "What do you do, may I ask?"

Destiny didn't get a chance to answer. "She was an artist in residence for years," Davis said. "She used to go into schools and community organizations to teach the history of photography."

"Now, I sit behind a desk and administer arts programs. I haven't done a project like the one you're proposing in years."

"I think it's time to call in my marker," Xavier offered.

"Your marker?" Destiny echoed. Their eyes locked. Then, quick as her own heartbeat, Xavier turned away. At first when he suggested that she be his personal photographer, she allowed herself to hope for a second that he was looking for an excuse to be with her. But it was obvious that Davis had mentioned her line of work to him and that's what sparked his interest.

Davis's brow furrowed. "What marker?"

"According to Destiny, my music somehow helped her through an unusual time in her life. She said she owed me one."

Xavier Allgood turned out to be the most persistent man Destiny had ever met. He absolutely would not take no for an answer.

Finally, Destiny agreed to help with the project. The three of them sat around Davis's kitchen table long enough to finish off the Egg McMuffins. Then the two men excused themselves. Xavier mentioned going to an interview at a local radio station. Davis, after working twelve hours straight, went to bed. Destiny spent the remainder of the day imagining all the ways she would like to photograph Xavier Allgood.

Three

"Girl, where have you been? I was gonna write yo ass off fo sho." Jacq always turned ultra-ghetto when she was upset. "You didn't eeeeven leave me a number where I could call you, heifer. I woulda axed for one if I'da known you'd pull some jack-leg shit like this!"

"Calm down, Jacq," Destiny said into the phone, trying to pacify her friend. "I'm all right."

Jacq would not hear it. "How in the hell was I supposed to know that? You could have been in a plane crash, or a car accident!"

"I know, I know, Jacq. I'm sorry."

"Sorry!"

"Look, I'm calling you now, aren't I?"

"Have you checked your calendar recently? It's been two weeks! You could have called."

"I know, Jacq, but I was sort of detained."

The tone in Destiny's voice told Jacq there was a man involved. Suddenly she forgot all about her friend's oversight.

"Ooo, you skank! You done went down there and got your bootie spanked, didn't chew?" Jacq didn't wait for Destiny to answer. "How was it? And when are you gettin' some more, 'cause you need it, girlfriend."

Destiny didn't know how to tell Jacq what happened or where to begin. She couldn't believe it herself actually. But somehow, it was true.

"Jacq . . . are you sitting down?"

"Yeah, girl. And I want *all* the details."

"No," Destiny replied. "It's not like that . . . it's . . . it's . . . better."

"What could be better than getting your nasty on?"

Destiny couldn't stand it any longer. She fought herself desperately to keep from blurting it out.

"I met him."

"Davis? I thought you already knew Davis."

"No, not Davis," Destiny said, more calmly than she felt. "Him."

"Him who?"

Destiny couldn't bring herself to say it. The past two weeks seemed like some surrealistic fantasy. *"Him,"* she repeated.

Jacq was beginning to get annoyed. "Him who? Damn it! Who?"

Destiny cleared her throat and took a deep breath. "Allgood."

"Whachewtalkinbout, Destiny?" Jacq responded as if she hadn't heard correctly.

Now that Destiny had said it, it finally seemed more real. "Allgood. I met him."

Jacq was stunned. At first she wasn't sitting when Destiny had asked. But now she was. "Allgood, *Allgood?*" Now she was repeating *her*self. "How? Did you go to one of his concerts?"

"No."

"Then what are you talking about?"

Destiny settled into the big comfy chair in Xavier's basement. The tan recliner molded and contoured around her body like a velvet comforter. She couldn't remember ever feeling leather this soft. The lambskin chair was so relaxing it surprised her. She was amazed at how tranquil she felt. Almost homey. *I could get used to this,* she thought, and prepared herself to tell Jacq the details of the two weeks she'd spent in Atlanta.

She started by telling Jacq how she discovered that Allgood lived in Atlanta. Then she told Jacq of her arrival and that Davis wasn't home when she got there, so she had let herself in with the key he had sent.

"You didn't tell me he sent you a key."

"Because I knew I'd never hear the end of it."

"You know that's some serious shit when a brotha gives you his key."

"See what I mean."

"Okay, girl. Go 'head."

"So, anyway," Destiny continued, "I went in and looked around. Davis really does have a nice home."

"Will you get to the Allgood part!"

"I am, if you'll be patient."

"Go on, girl."

Destiny felt schoolgirlish telling her friend the play-by-play details. But she couldn't help herself. Destiny went on. "I staked out one of the guest bedrooms . . ."

"*One* of the bedrooms?"

"Will you let me tell you what happened?"

"I said go on."

"The guest room had a CD player in it, so I played that Allgood CD you let me borrow."

"So that's where it went!"

"Will you hush!"

"Damn, girl. Don't be so sensitive. Now will you tell the story?"

"I felt so good being here. I was overwhelmed. I felt like celebrating. What's the name of that Toni Braxton song . . . 'Breathe Again'? That's how I felt. Like I could breathe again. So I started dancing and singing with the music."

"Didn't we party enough?"

"I'm never going to get this out."

"You know I'm playing with you. You sound different. I'm just trying to get the old Destiny back."

Destiny felt different too. But she wasn't ready to admit that to Jacq yet. "So there I was, dancing and singing like Debbie

Allen or somebody, oblivious to everything, when I feel like somebody's watching me."

"Remember that song by that guy Rockwell?" Jacq uttered a pitiful imitation of Michael Jackson. "I always feel like somebody's watching me!"

Destiny laughed, feeling a little punch-drunk. "Anyway, I turned around and it was Allgood." Destiny remembered the way he smelled like he had just stepped from a shower, and she inhaled deeply. "He was watching me from the top of the stairs."

"In Davis's house?"

"Yep."

"What did he do, break in?"

"No, silly. Davis works for Allgood."

"That still doesn't explain how he got in there."

"People don't lock their doors in this neighborhood. That whole key thing with Davis was engineered chivalry. Actually, I thought it was kind of cute."

"Sounds kinda stupid to me. But what's up with Allgood? You mean you met him? You actually met him?"

"Yes! Unfortunately I didn't realize it was him until after I knocked him down the stairs."

"What!"

"Jacq, he frightened me. What would you do if you thought you were in a house alone and then realized there was someone right next to you, watching?"

"I guess you have a point," Jacq admitted.

"After all I went through with Rico, there's no telling what a mix of reflexes, impulses, and adrenaline will do to me." Destiny paused to reflect. "Anyway, that's why I haven't called you in two weeks. He saw the photo I brought for Davis, and ever since then I've been creating a storyboard for his photo montage." Destiny paused when a small shiver went up her spine. "We've been almost inseparable since then."

"Damn. I can't believe it. My homegirl, doin' the nasty with Allgood."

"Now I know why Baptist preachers say, 'Y'all don't hear me.' I am not sleeping with the man!"

Jacq was dumbfounded. She could not understand why Destiny would give it up to Rico, a sho nuff waste of booty, and not to Allgood, the finest brotha on the planet. "Why not!"

Destiny couldn't allow herself to consider that question seriously. If she did, the answer would clearly be because Xavier didn't seem interested. Besides, she knew their relationship was strictly professional.

"Because we are working together on a project. We have a business arrangement. We are not seeing each other romantically."

"What's romance got to do with it? This is Allgood we're talking about. You better go on and tap that ass while you're in the vicinity."

Destiny laughed. *Same old Jacq,* she thought.

"Well, if you won't make yourself at home, then I sure will. Now that I got connections."

They both laughed this time. But underneath that laughter, Destiny was beginning to think that Jacq was right. Besides, who would know? And she had played the role of straightlaced woman for such a long time. Perhaps it was time she let her dreads down.

"So where is Mr. Superfine now?"

"He went to pick up some Mexican. I'm just waiting for him to come home."

"Home? You're at his tilt? Girl, if you don't get some now, you might as well sew it up and forget you had one."

"You are just too profane for me. His new studio is in his house. I spend a lot of time here."

"If it ain't nighttime, it don't count."

Destiny hooted. She was really starting to enjoy the idea of approaching Xavier. After all, he could only say no. And according to Jacq only dead men turned down a free piece. She was just about to tell Jacq of her plans to "get with" Allgood when she heard the upstairs door opening.

"He's here. I better go."

"Tell that man if he wants some *real* honeydew, it's in Nebraska. And her name is Jacquelyn."

"You are too much."

"Quick," Jacq said. "Give me Davis's phone number before you go."

Destiny gave Jacq Davis's number, and in case of an emergency, she gave her Xavier's number. She hung up the phone just as Davis came into the basement.

"Davis!" Destiny said, startled. "What are you doing here?"

"Zay sent me."

"Who?"

Davis shook his head and walked over to where Destiny was seated. "Allgood," he said and sat down next to her in the big fuzzy chair. "We—his friends, that is—call him Zay, short for Xavier."

Destiny thought about that. The name Zay was okay, but she much preferred Xavier. She thought it sounded more like the gentleman he seemed to be. "Well, X-a-vier was supposed to bring dinner back here. We've been working awhile and I'm starved."

"Enter moi. Zay called me and told me that he was going to be detained. He asked if I wouldn't mind taking the most beautiful woman in the universe out to dinner."

Destiny beamed like a lighthouse. "He said that?"

"Actually, I added that last part myself." Davis deliberately bumped his shoulder up against Destiny. "The chance to take you to dinner was an opportunity I couldn't pass up."

Destiny tried to hide her disappointment by smiling at Davis's playing. She hadn't been playful with a man in so long, she hoped she hadn't forgotten how. Rico was rarely playful. He was all business. She bumped Davis back. "Let's go."

It took a moment for Destiny's eyes to adjust to the light, or lack thereof. Torches of all shapes, sizes, and colors illuminated the entire dining room. The shadows of their flickering lights moved hauntingly against the mahogany wood walls and high, wood-beamed ceilings. Destiny could smell the honeysuckle and peach blend of the aromatic flames. And she could feel their warmth as she and Davis approached the host's station.

"Welcome to Xanadu. Are there just two of you this evening?"

"Yes," Davis responded.

"Very good. Right this way."

The host showed them to a table on the terrace, and Destiny sat down, slightly concerned. "Davis," she said, looking around, "I feel like I'm underdressed." Everywhere she looked, the designers Gucci, Giorgio Armani, Donna Karan, and Versace affirmed their presence. From what Destiny could tell, she was surrounded by people of old wealth who were more than comfortable wearing money.

Davis, who rarely went anywhere or did anything without wearing a suit, flicked a piece of imaginary lint from the cuff of his shirt. "You're so radiant, you can pull off a casual look in a place like this. Don't worry about it."

Destiny glanced at the table. It was beautifully set with a smoke-gray tablecloth accented by bright red napkins, lemon slices in long-stemmed water glasses, and fresh flowers.

"Thanks, I think," she said, raising a brow.

The waiter came to their table and presented them with menus. "Good evening. My name is Tobias and I'll be your server tonight. Would you like to start with something to drink?"

"Des?"

"Actually, I'll just have ginger ale."

"Fine, and for you, sir?"

Destiny noticed how confident and self-assured Davis looked in the ambient light.

"I'll have a glass of vin rosé," he answered.

"Thank you. I'll be right back with your drinks."

Destiny fingered the large brandy glass in the middle of their table. It looked as though someone had drizzled amber, indigo, magenta, and gold paint down the sides of it. There was a small votive candle burning inside.

"I've never known you to pass up the chance to have a good glass of wine, even when we were in high school."

Destiny's mind flashed back to her many arguments with Rico when he was in a drunken rage. Since then it had been difficult for her to take pleasure from something that had been a part of what made her so miserable for the past few years.

"I don't drink as much as I used to."

"Well, that must mean that you quit, because you didn't drink all that much before."

They both chuckled.

Destiny leaned forward. "How's your mom and Lena?"

"My mother has not changed a bit. Still a pistol. Lena's fine. I talked to her the other day. I told her you were coming down. She said to tell you hi."

"Please tell her I said hello."

"I will. You know she's eighteen now?"

"No!"

"Yep. She just had a birthday and is about to graduate from high school."

"Davis, I remember her when she used to cling to your leg like there was no tomorrow." Destiny unfolded her napkin and draped it across her lap. "Now you know that's bad when I have to travel a thousand miles to catch up on people that live in my own city."

"She won't be in Lincoln much longer. She's been accepted to Spelman."

"Oh, I know you'll love having her here."

"Yeah. I miss my little sister." Davis leaned in closer. "What about your folks? How are they?"

"Like your mom. They are as ornery as ever. They haven't changed either. They're retired now, so they're not at home much."

"I remember how they like to travel. Please give them big hugs for me."

"I will."

Davis glanced around for the waiter.

"So, tell me, how do you like Atlanta, or as residents like to refer to it, the ATL?"

"So far what I've seen is very nice."

"A lot different from Lincoln, Nebraska, huh?"

"Much. I've never seen so many people. Especially black people. I just love it."

"Now you know why I stayed."

The waiter came back with their drinks. "Are you ready to order?"

Davis shrugged. "We haven't even looked at our menus yet."

"That's fine. May I tell you our specials this evening?

"Please," Davis said.

"They are stuffed cabbage leaves, chicken and zucchini in mustard sauce, lemon shrimp and asparagus, and scallops and broccoli with pasta."

"Umm," Destiny purred. "The scallops and broccoli sound good."

"I'll have a rib eye steak, medium-well, with a baked potato and Italian dressing for my salad."

"Very good." The waiter took their menus and headed back toward the kitchen.

Destiny lifted an eyebrow and slightly dropped her head. "Come here often?"

"Occasionally," Davis said, placing his napkin mechanically over his lap. "So, Des, we really need to finish playing catch-up."

"I know." Destiny raised her glass and tipped it toward Davis. She knew he was dying to fill her in on the events of his life. "You first," she said and sipped her ginger ale.

Davis sat forward in the leather seat. "Well, let's see." He paused several seconds. *Probably to make me wait,* Destiny thought. Some things don't—can't—change.

"Since I started my consulting firm, I've had ten Fortune 500 companies as clients. Their referrals and repeat business have kept me busy for the past several years. And this conversion thing! It's a consultant's dream."

"From what I understand, conversions are more like nightmares."

"Only if you don't know what you're doing." Davis picked up his glass and rocked it gently. Destiny watched the sanguine liquid swirl against the sides of the glass. "On a more personal note, I almost got married once." Davis took a sip of wine, then looked straight ahead at Destiny. "Once since you. But she didn't measure up." Davis tipped his glass toward Destiny and took another sip.

"Well, I just created a mentoring program at the Arts and Humanities Council. I finally made the transition from artist to administrator."

"Really?"

"Yeah. So instead of focusing exclusively on my own work, I help other artists develop their talents and skills."

"That sounds nice, Des. Waiter!"

The waiter approached their table. "Bring a glass of vin rosé for her," Davis instructed.

Destiny's brow wrinkled. "No, no. I don't want any wine, Davis."

"But I hate to drink alone. And besides, we're celebrating."

"We are?"

"Yes," Davis said as he took another sip from his glass. The waiter looked from one person to the other, unsure of what to do. "It's a reunion of sorts."

Davis's sentimentality touched a soft spot in Destiny's heart. But right next to it was the rock-hard place that Rico left. Destiny had the experience of a man trying to make decisions for her once too often. "Davis, I have what I want to drink right here." She pointed to her glass and cast a stoic look toward the waiter.

The waiter smiled and left their table once more.

"I guess your job isn't the only change you've made."

"What do you mean?" Destiny asked, sipping her ginger ale.

"I thought you were about to make a scene. The Destiny I remember would never do that."

The waiter returned with Davis's salad and a basket of bread. Davis stared down at the ring on the waiter's little finger as it passed before him. It was an impressive gold nugget. "Excuse me," Davis said. "I couldn't help but admire your ring. May I ask where you got it?"

"It was a gift from my uncle Sol."

"Sol Pastioni?" Davis asked.

"That's right."

"Thanks, man."

When the waiter left, Destiny was puzzled. "What was that about?"

"When you're in business for yourself, you never really stop working. The key is to market yourself within your span of contact." Davis sat back in his chair. "The way I play it, anyone that comes within three feet of me is a prospective customer."

"What would a waiter need with a systems analyst?"

Davis laughed, his hearty chuckle chopping the air. "He wouldn't, but whoever gave him that ring might. When I saw that nugget on his finger, I figured that he probably couldn't afford something like that, even working here. Someone had to have given it to him."

"Damn, you're good."

"Yes, I am," Davis responded. "It also helped that Tobias looks exactly like the owner of the restaurant, minus the gray. Turns out Sol is his uncle—I took a chance and"—Davis made a twisting motion around his little finger—"it paid off."

Destiny shook her head. It seemed Davis had also changed. He was a lot shrewder than she remembered. "Now what are you doing?"

Davis had taken out one of his business cards and was writing on the back of it.

"Sometimes I write a customized mini-sales pitch on the back of my business cards. I'm writing one for Sol. Basically it says that I can show him how to save up to twenty-five percent in administrative costs by automating his work processes."

Maybe he hasn't changed after all, she thought. Since she'd known him, he had always put his work above all else. Even, it seems, above the supposed celebration of a reunion *of sorts.*

Davis put the business card at the edge of the table and started into his salad. Destiny took some bread from the basket and pinched off a small piece. Davis watched her eat for a few moments.

"What kinds of artists do you work with?"

"All kinds," Destiny said, finishing off a mouthful of warm bread. "Painters, sculptors, writers, storytellers, other photographers."

Davis finished the last of his wine. "Do you miss doing your own work?"

"I miss doing it full time. I still do it, though. But now I do less commissioned work and do mostly my own research and documentation." Destiny spread butter on her remaining piece of bread. "I guess what I miss most is collaborating with other people."

By the time Tobias came back with their dinner plates, Destiny's stomach was rumbling. All the bread did was make her hungry for a real meal. She dug into her food and watched in silence as Davis explained to Tobias who he was and what he did. Then he gave him his business card and asked him to see that his uncle got it.

He really was good at selling himself, Destiny thought. When Tobias left their table, Davis quickly shoveled large forkfuls of food into his mouth. "Doing business always makes me ravenous."

Destiny didn't say anything. She simply remained quiet and fixed her attention on the flame on the small votive candle at their table. There was a breeze, and it threatened to snuff the fire out. After struggling for several minutes, the candle flame faltered and finally blinked out.

Xavier was baffled. He couldn't figure out why he hadn't been able to get the image of Destiny's dancing out of his mind—even after two weeks. He had seen other women dance before. He had heard other women sing before. Tyrica was one of the best singers he'd ever heard. But something about Destiny haunted him. Just like her name, Destiny.

As he lay in bed, he tried to put thoughts of her out of his mind, but he couldn't. Finally, he reminded himself that she was off limits. Destiny was here for Davis. And he respected that.

Xavier had forgotten the tsunami of feelings a woman could cause. Not since Elise had he felt that captivated and alive. Elise. Now there was a subject, he thought. Slowly his mind played back their brief affair.

He had met her at Brisko's, the hottest nightclub in Buckhead. He was sitting at the bar with two friends when he saw her on the dance floor. She was smokin'. Much too much for the guy she was dancing with. Something about her seemed to flow with the music. He waited until ten minutes before closing time to ask her to dance.

Their two-step was electric, like a small, erotic current pulsing through his body. And he had to have her. Xavier and Elise left the bar together and drove directly to Embassy Suites. They made love the entire weekend. And just that quickly, he fell in love.

They repeated their liaison every weekend for a month— same time, same hotel. Xavier even paid extra so they could have the same suite.

One night Elise didn't show. When Xavier called the number she had given him, it was disconnected. He went back to Brisko's night after night. But he never saw or heard from her again.

It had been two years, but ever since then, Xavier had avoided serious romantic entanglements. Now that his CD was out, countless women had professed their love and devotion, but he was not swayed. He had no intention of being abandoned again. So he numbed himself against any attraction. That was until now. Now, no matter what he did, his mind, body, and spirit called out for Destiny.

He reasoned that the only way he could keep his feelings in check was to remind himself repeatedly that she was Davis's girl. Even though Davis hadn't come out and said so, Xavier could tell by the way he talked about Destiny there was something between them. Something Xavier could understand and would honor.

He hoped his crew would understand, but now more than ever, he would have to immerse himself in his project. Keeping his mind occupied was the only way. For the first time in months, Xavier went to bed yearning for the comfort of a woman. And he realized, frustratingly, that no other woman besides Destiny would do.

Four

Davis's condominium provided a clear view of the sunrise from his deck on the second floor. Although Destiny favored sleeping in, she awoke early to experience the dawn of the new day.

Early fall in Georgia was pleasant and invigorating. There was just enough warmth in the atmosphere to make her skin glow. Yet the full and frequent breeze in the air kept the humidity and heat at bay.

Destiny sat back in the Empire-style deck chair and propped her bare feet on the ottoman. She wore a pair of white cotton shorts and a blue-and-white, oversize T-shirt that she made during a tie-dye class given by one of her friends. She had sprayed her sisterlocks with water and scrunched them with her hands so that they hung in tight curls against her head.

More than once, she fought the urge to run and grab her camera. The velvety sky was painted with brush strokes of topaz, claret, and persimmon. The colors appeared to lie one on top of the other until the result was a flourish of abandon flung against the stratosphere. Destiny thought it was a picture well worth taking.

She watched in awe as the bright, gold sphere rose slowly above the horizon. The sounds of daybreak increased with the rising of the sun—birdsong, a dog's bark, the occasional close of a front door, cars starting up and backing out of driveways. Even amid the varied noises of morning, Destiny felt at peace.

She closed her eyes and let the gradual warmth of sunup surround her. Before long, she drifted off into a contented sleep.

Her dream began as it always had since she arrived in Atlanta, with her enclosed in the softness of fluffy white sheets. Then she would turn over and see the most beautiful man on the planet lying beside her. The resonance of his voice would calm her by declaring his love. But for some reason, she couldn't quite make out what Xavier Allgood was saying this time. He seemed to be in a conversation with someone else. His words weren't clear, and she strained to hear them.

"Here she is."

"Man, I can't believe she got up and came out here. She's usually in bed until ten."

"That must be why we haven't been able to meet before noon."

"Well, you'll have to get your photography questions answered later."

The two men took seats on the deck near the slumbering Destiny.

"In the meantime, I've been meaning to ask you how that new software program worked out."

"Terrible. I had the hardest time just getting it loaded onto the computer. I kept getting a message saying the installation was unsuccessful. Then when I stripped it down to just the bare essentials, I finally got it installed."

"You had to strip it?"

"Yeah. Only now, the program won't execute any songs that have more than three instruments on them."

"I was afraid of that. I'm going to have to upgrade your computer again."

Destiny finally made out the words in her dream. They definitely weren't declarations of love. She stirred in the chair and opened her eyes. She was waking up, but the voices continued.

"Morning, sleepyhead."

Destiny sat up sluggishly and rubbed her eyes. The two figures seated adjacent to her came into view by degrees until she made out the faces of Davis and Xavier smiling at her.

"I didn't know a woman could snore that loud," Davis said with a smirk.

"Forget you," Destiny retorted playfully. "I know I don't snore." Then she thought about her remark and wasn't sure. "Do I?" she asked.

The two men emitted a combined blast of laughter. Destiny stood and gave herself a full stretch. "Laugh all you want. See if I care," she said and left the deck to freshen up.

Once again the three had breakfast together in Davis's kitchen. This time Davis wasn't too tired to cook and prepared three veggie omelets stuffed with onions, broccoli, and Monterey jack cheese.

Despite the excitement scurrying throughout her body, Destiny was able to eat her breakfast. She was beginning to feel more comfortable being around Xavier as the days went on. However, she was always stunned at how good he looked in his clothes. He must have a personal tailor, she thought, checking out his bronze, crinkle-friendly linen jacket and what appeared to be drawstring pants. A white T-shirt topped off the uncomplicated look.

Davis, on the other hand, was out of character. He was dressed unusually casually in gray gabardine pants and a coordinating gray polo. He had apparently given up his suit for a less formal style. Something he hadn't given up were his wing tip shoes. He was almost never without them. As for Davis's clothing, Destiny wondered what the occasion was.

"I hope I'm not being too presumptuous, but I thought we could go to the bazaar. I saw it advertised on television. There's supposed to be more than one hundred vendors there. And it's so . . . well . . . eclectic, it sounded like something Destiny could get into."

"Well, Davis, man, I'll check you later then." Xavier headed toward the kitchen door. Destiny's heart capsized. She wasn't ready to end the cozy feeling of being in Xavier's presence. "Why don't you come with us?" she heard herself say.

Xavier turned to her with a half smile. "You know they say three is a crowd."

Davis stood in front of the half mirror. He smoothed his mustache and ran his fingers down his goatee. "Who the hell are *they?* Besides, Zay, you and I really need to break this studio project down into bite-size pieces. This would give us the opportunity to refine our plans." Davis turned to Xavier and Destiny, who were watching him while he worked the mirror. "How do I look?"

Destiny couldn't resist. "We're going to a bazaar, and you'll definitely fit right in."

Davis looked wounded. "Do you see how she treats me?"

Xavier snickered. "I see."

"Oh, you should see the way he treats me. He didn't even meet me at the airport." Destiny flashed Davis a teasing smile. "Some host you are."

"Oh, pshaw!" Davis tried to wave off Destiny's complaint. She would have none of it.

The two continued their mock argument out the door and into Davis's car. Once in the car, Davis was focused almost exclusively on Xavier's studio project. Destiny was all but shut out of their discussion. When there was a slight lull in the conversation, Destiny broke in.

"Are you two finished ignoring me or should I continue to pretend that I'm somewhere else?"

"Yeah, man, we have been kinda rude," Xavier agreed.

"I'm sorry, Des. It's just that I've been so tied up with other things, I haven't had time to work through the plans with Zay. I'll be more considerate." Then Davis smiled like a mischievous kid. "But not much."

Destiny reached over and poked Davis in the head. "Oh, you!"

* * *

Destiny found that the bazaar was just as its name implied, strange, weird, and definitely bizarre. The Wilton Civic Center had been turned into one giant room filled with vendors that looked like they had emptied their basements, attics, and garages and were now offering those items for sale.

Destiny expected Davis to take one look at the large number of odd wares and insist that they get their admission fee back. But instead, his reaction was quite approving.

"Wow! Look at all this stuff." Davis scanned the room and placed a hand on his chin. "I wonder how they keep their inventories." Davis started walking in the direction of a woman sitting behind a table filled with old books. "If you'll excuse me. There's no rest for the self-employed."

Destiny and Xavier looked at each other in astonishment.

"Has he always been like that?" Xavier asked Destiny.

"For as long as I've known him," Destiny responded.

"I guess that's what makes him so good at what he does."

Destiny smiled and nodded. "I guess so."

"Well, that must mean it's just us then."

Destiny felt her smile broaden. She was too thrilled to say anything coherently. She felt Xavier's eyes on her and warmed at the thought of spending time with just him.

"There's so much here," Xavier said, looking out into the mass of vendors, tables, people, and stuff. "Where should we begin?"

Destiny saw some vases that caught her eye. "How about over there?" She motioned toward a table on the far side of the room. Xavier nodded and they walked over. The flower vases were of varied sizes. Each was covered with a mosaic of small, multicolored tiles held in place by thick, textured grout.

Destiny picked up a small vase and ran her fingers over the tiles. They were cool and smooth to the touch.

"That one's just fifty dollars," an elderly gentleman said. He was sitting behind the table unwrapping more vases and setting them out for her to see.

"Thanks," Destiny said. "I'm just looking."

"Do you make these yourself?" Xavier asked.

"Yes, he does," replied an elderly woman seated next to the man. "You wanna know how he makes 'em?"

"Hush up, Martha."

"He goes to flea markets like this one and buys the cheapest dishes he can find. You know, stuff for twenty-five and thirty cents."

"Martha, I'm warning you." The man glared at his wife, frowning.

"He gets the vases at the same time. For maybe two or three dollars. Then he breaks up the dishes into little pieces, grouts them onto the vases, and charges a whole buncha money for them."

"Quiet, you saboteur! Don't pay any attention to her. She hasn't had her nap today, and when she misses naptime, she's liable to say anything."

Destiny laughed heartily. "I'll take two," she said.

"Thank you, thank you," the man said. He waited while Destiny chose the two she wanted. Then he wrapped them for her and placed them in a bag. "That will be one hundred dollars," the man said.

Xavier looked at Destiny, concern pulling his mouth into a frown. "Are you sure?"

"Definitely."

Destiny paid the man and took her purchase. As she and Xavier walked away, it was obvious that he didn't understand what had just happened. "Those vases probably cost him all of five dollars to make."

"That's true, but she was desperate for her husband to sell something."

"Were we listening to the same woman? She sounded like she was trying to dissuade you from buying."

"On the contrary. In her own way, she was telling us about her husband's work and how important it is for him to sell something."

"You think so?"

"I know so. Otherwise, she would have sat there and said nothing."

"Women! How do you possibly expect us to figure you out?"

"I'll let you in on a little secret," she said with a smile.

Xavier bent closer to Destiny. "What?" he asked.

"We don't really want you to figure us out at all. Part of the fun is to keep you guessing."

Xavier's eyes widened from her response. "I'm not sure how much fun that is."

The two maneuvered their way through row after row of tables. Each table offered a different display of items for purchase. By far the most popular item appeared to be books. Destiny stopped counting the book tables after she reached fifteen. But there were also dolls, figurines, paintings, sculptures, posters, jewelry, and a host of other things Destiny would classify as bric-a-brac, knickknacks, and whatnots. Most of the items were older than she was, she guessed. Now and then she would linger at a table with items that reminded her of some of the artists' work back in Nebraska. She couldn't believe what some of the vendors were asking for the things they were selling.

Destiny noticed that Xavier lingered over the jewelry tables. Looking at him now, she noted the large turquoise ring on the middle finger of his right hand, the jade ring on the small finger of his left hand, and the cowrie bracelet and necklace he was wearing. She watched him as he examined a copper bracelet.

"How much is this?" he asked the woman seated behind the table.

"Seventy-five dollars."

"I'll take it."

As he paid for the bracelet, Destiny was taken by the most beautiful watch she had ever seen. It was small and delicate. The face was about half an inch in diameter and a perfect square. Tiny chipped diamonds were crusted around the face. There were also chipped diamonds set into the band. The light from the civic center caused the diamonds to sparkle like a million tiny flashes.

Destiny looked at the woman seated behind the table. "May I?" she asked, pointing toward the watch.

"Sure," the woman said.

Destiny picked up the watch slowly and gently placed it around her arm. She held her arm away from her and glowed at the sight of it. The brilliance of the diamonds danced off the gold tones in her skin.

"You wear it well," Xavier said.

"It's gorgeous, absolutely gorgeous!" Destiny would hardly dare to ask, but she just had to know. "How much is it?"

"Because it looks so good on you, I'll part with it for fifteen hundred dollars."

Destiny took the watch off of her arm slowly and placed it back onto the table. "I've already spent more than I expected to." Even though Destiny thought the watch might actually be worth a thousand dollars, she wasn't about to spend that kind of money. "Oh, well," she said. "Are you ready to look at something else?"

Xavier looked as though he was about to say something when Davis popped up out of the blue. "I believe congratulations are in order," he announced.

"How many vendors here are now your clients?" Destiny asked, smiling.

"Yeah, man, inquiring minds want to know," Xavier added.

"None," Davis replied smugly.

"None?" Destiny and Xavier asked in unison.

"That's right. You see, while I was talking to the woman with all those books, the sponsor of the event happened to be walking by. He heard part of my sales pitch and asked me to come into his office." Davis clasped his hands behind his back and started rocking slowly back and forth on his heels. Destiny watched the smile on his face get broader and broader.

"I thought I was in trouble for soliciting, but then I figured wouldn't everybody be? Well, it turns out that the sponsor has been setting up a database program to keep track of all the vendors at this event—things like who sells what, and the number of days they've paid, how many tables each vendor needs, where each vendor is set up, where they're from, and stuff like that. But he lacks some of the technical virtuosity to pull it off. Voilà! Van Housen and Associates to the rescue!

"I thought that I would check in with you guys to see if you were ready to go. If you are, I'll tell Mr. Fletcher that I will come back another time to discuss the particulars. If you're not, I can go back and have a quick meeting with him to actually demonstrate on his computer system some of the services I can provide."

Destiny and Xavier shot quick looks at each other. Destiny shrugged her shoulders. Xavier glanced in her direction again and then back to Davis. "Go get 'em, dog." The two men exchanged a dap and Davis trotted off in the direction he had come from. "I won't be long. Thanks for understanding." Davis's voice trailed off, and once again Destiny was left in Xavier's company.

The two walked in silence for a few moments before either of them spoke. "Tell me more about what you do. I mean, do you do other things besides take pictures?"

Destiny picked up a heart-shaped candy dish. It reminded her of one her family had when she was a child. "Yes," Destiny said, turning the porcelain dish over in her hand. "Actually, I'm a photohistorian."

"Umm, I'm not sure what a photohistorian does, but I like the sound of it."

Destiny checked his face to see if he was kidding. He was smiling but his comment appeared to be genuine. She quickly turned her attention back to the candy dish and returned it to the table. She looked up at Xavier and mirrored his smile. "There are generally two types of photohistorians: those that study the origins of photography and those who have collections of photos on a specific subject or era."

Xavier stopped to examine a mantel clock. "Which type are you?"

"Actually, I'm a hybrid. I've studied and continue to study the origins of photography. I also have a collection."

"I see," Xavier said. "Tell me about your collection."

"Well . . . it consists of photos that document African-Americans on the Great Plains."

"Really? How many photos do you have?"

"I have more than one hundred pieces in my collection. I say pieces because in addition to photos I have other things like illustrations, newspaper articles, and posters. Sixty-two of the items in my collection are actual photographs."

The two had reached the end of one aisle of tables and were headed toward another when Destiny spotted a concession stand. "I'm thirsty. Are you?" she asked. She looked at Xavier and thought she saw a twinkle in his eye. "Yes," he said, holding her gaze.

If this is a game of chicken, I'm going to lose, Destiny thought and looked away. With the intensity of Xavier's smile still warming her, she walked with him toward the smell of hot dogs, relish, and popcorn.

"What would you like?" he asked.

"Lemonade, please"

"Make it two," Xavier said to the young man behind the counter.

"That will be four dollars," the young man said, staring at Xavier. "Hey, aren't you that singer?"

Xavier smiled and paid the four dollars. "Yes," he said.

"Man, my girlfriend is crazy about you. She's always comparing me to you and I keep telling her, 'You don't even know the guy.' But she won't listen." The young man handed Destiny and Xavier their drinks. "Wait until I tell her you've got a girlfriend," he said, nodding to Destiny. "Now maybe she'll cut me some slack."

Destiny was about to protest, but Xavier took her arm. "Here's hoping she goes easy on you, man." Xavier tipped his cup and the young man nodded in their direction. They walked over to a nearby bench and sat down with their purchases and drinks.

"Why did you do that, Xavier? Now that guy thinks we're a couple." Destiny admitted to herself that she kinda liked that idea.

Xavier took a sip of his lemonade. "I learned a valuable lesson about the private lives of public people when I first became famous. Sometimes you must dispel myths and lies at all costs. And other times it's better to let people come to their own conclusions. The key is knowing which time you're living in at the moment."

"I take it this was one of the times where you let people come to their own conclusions."

"Yes. Most of it is deciding which path will cause the least amount of damage."

Destiny sipped quietly on her lemonade. The drone of the people milling around in the large room echoed off the walls. Now and then Destiny could pick out a few words, "Oh, look at this!" "Genuine." "Authentic."

"You didn't finish telling me about your collection," Xavier said. "Why the Great Plains?"

"Well," she said, adding her voice to the many around her, "I think the Great Plains experience is one of the most underresearched areas of African-American history. And my family has lived in the Midwest for many years. I was curious about my own heritage and became fascinated with the idea of the history of the Great Plains in general."

Xavier sounded reflective. "I guess I never thought much about our people being on the plains."

Destiny sat up straight. "Are you kidding? John Wayne wasn't the only person to go west with the covered wagons!" They both laughed and then Destiny's expression became more serious. "That's why it's important for this kind of work to be done. Like you said, there's a time to dispel the myths and lies."

Xavier raised an eyebrow and Destiny sat back against the back of the bench. *I guess he liked that,* she thought.

They spent the rest of their time at the bazaar walking and talking. Occasionally, they would stop when some unique or unusual item caught their attention. But mostly they were engaged in conversation.

Destiny talked some more about her work with the Arts and Humanities Council. She told Xavier about her views on public history and public memory. She explained how important it was to her for African-Americans to leave a living legacy for the future. He listened closely when she told him about her efforts to work with oral historians in preserving the past.

Destiny listened as Xavier talked about songwriting and what it would mean to him to have his own studio. He told her about how fortunate he felt to be working with Davis. He explained that one day while he was autographing CDs in a music store, he saw a man in a line of about a hundred women.

"When the guy finally got up to the front of the line, he handed me a CD and a business card."

"No!" Destiny said.

"Yep," Xavier responded. "That's how I met Davis. He told me that if I ever wanted to automate my recording process to give him a call."

Destiny doubled over with laughter. "You mean he stood in line just to make a sales pitch?"

"Sure did. And it just so happened that I was about to move in that direction. The other thing was, I just liked his style." Then Xavier paused and looked Destiny squarely in the face. "He knows exactly what he wants and goes directly for it."

Destiny felt heat from the pit of her stomach rise to her neck and cheeks. She lowered her head, but only for a moment. When she looked up into Xavier's eyes, she could feel the raw stirrings of passion coming to life within her. It seemed as though his face was getting closer and closer to hers. Then an alarm of panic went off in Destiny's body and she moved away.

"I wonder if Davis will be as successful with the bazaar sponsor as he was with you."

Xavier joined her at her side. "I wonder," he said softly.

They walked over to a table filled with license plates. Destiny was astonished. "Some people will buy . . ."

"Destiny," Xavier said, turning her around to face him.

"Yes," she said while her heart made quick thunder in her chest.

"There you are!" Davis's familiar voice cut through the crowd. "I thought I was going to have to have you two paged." Destiny turned to Davis, the exhilaration of the past few seconds dwindling into nothingness. "How did it go?" she asked, a lot more enthusiastically than she felt.

"Yeah, man," Xavier added. "Is he on board or what?"

Davis puffed out his chest. "If I could do the Tarzan yell, I would."

"Congratulations, Davis."

"You are something else," Destiny replied.

"Are you two ready to go? I'm starving!"

"I am," Destiny answered quickly.

"Me, too, sort of. Will you two wait right here? I think I saw something back there that I wanted. It will only take me a minute."

"Sure," Davis said. "We'll be right here."

The note read,

I apologize, Destiny, but there's a small "fire" at the office. I'll be back as soon as I can. If you care to venture out on your own, the keys to the Navigator are on my dresser. See you soon. Love, Davis

She was actually relieved. After her first few weeks in Atlanta, Destiny felt as though she was going to need a vacation from her vacation. In addition to her photo schedule with

Xavier, Davis had taken off two days from work. They had gone all over the city, shopping and visiting some of Davis's friends. They had even found time to squeeze in a movie.

When they would finally get back to Davis's condo, it would be the middle of the night and Destiny would be exhausted. Even so, they stayed up an extra hour just talking. And Destiny found that being with Davis was as easy and familiar as if they had never broken up. She remembered how his fast pace complemented her slow and cautious approach to things. As tired as she was when she finally went to bed, she was also refreshed and exhilarated.

She had wondered, though, if the nights would be awkward for them. She had thought that perhaps Davis would try to initiate some form of intimacy. But he was a gentleman, almost to Destiny's disappointment. Even though Destiny would have turned him down, it would have been nice to know that she was wanted. Now, she wasn't quite sure.

So when she found Davis's note the next morning, she took it as a sign that Davis was committed to having a platonic relationship, which was fine by her. The scars from her last relationship hadn't healed completely. But something told Destiny that coming to Atlanta was just the remedy to help them heal.

She decided to start her morning slowly. She went downstairs and used Davis's juicer to make herself a glass of orange and papaya juice. After that she opened the drapes to let the sun in. The rays streamed straight through the beige cotton dress she wore, warming her.

She turned on some music from the colossal stereo system in the front room and played some Jamiroquai. Then she began her morning tai-chi routine.

She moved slowly and in a relaxed fashion. She made circular movements with her arms, yet kept her body in perfect alignment. Soon, Destiny could feel the energy flowing synchronously throughout her body. It revitalized her and relaxed her at the same time. She was so relaxed that she failed to see Xavier checking her out from the window.

He went around to the back and came in as usual, this time announcing himself.

"Hello," he called in full voice.

Destiny paused her morning ritual.

"In here," came her voice from the living room.

Xavier walked through the kitchen and into the living room.

"That's beautiful," he said, as she continued her fluid movements. "I thought you didn't know any martial arts."

Destiny came to the end of her routine. "I don't . . . except for this one." Destiny took in a deep cleansing breath and released it.

"Davis is at work," she said. She walked over to the stereo and turned down the volume.

"Actually," Xavier said, moving close to Destiny. "I came to see you."

Destiny could hear her heart beating a rhythm to rival the one coming out of the speakers. She hoped the sound of her voice wouldn't betray her emotions.

"To what do I owe this visit?"

She knew her eyelashes were batting flirtatiously, but she couldn't help it.

"We've been doing a lot of planning and what I want to do is help you get a sense of who I am as a musician."

Destiny examined the way he wore his brown Polo shirt and khaki jeans and believed she knew exactly who he was as a man.

"Should I get my camera?"

"No," he said, smiling.

"Okay. I just need to get my purse," she replied, climbing the stairs.

"By the way," she asked when they were outside. "Where are we going?"

"Where the magic happens," was Xavier's response.

Five

Non-Stop Music Studio was larger than Destiny could have ever imagined. After she signed in at the front desk, she tried to prepare herself for the world within the walls of the large building, but nothing could have prepared her for this.

The foyer was exquisitely decorated with marble walls and black-tiled floors. There were mirrors everywhere, except on the ceiling. The entrance was more atrium than hallway and the roof was more skylight than ceiling. You could see all the way to the top of the forty-story building and then through the glass ceiling to the clouds above.

Most impressive were the gold records that lined the walls. Xavier watched as Destiny read several on the way to the elevator. Her breath caught in her throat when she saw the one titled *Allgood's Molten Hot Shop.*

"You must be very proud," she said.

Xavier smiled humbly. "I'm very blessed," he said softly.

They walked down the long corridor to the elevators. Now and then passersby would pleasantly acknowledge Xavier. Some even gave Destiny a curious glance. She felt her bosom swell with pride to be in Xavier's company. His air of importance was rubbing off on her. Destiny felt important, too.

"Where are we going?" she asked when they got to the elevator lobby.

"I want you to meet some friends of mine."

Xavier pressed the up button.

Once on the elevator, one of ten, Xavier pressed the button labeled THE SKY SET.

Destiny was intrigued by the name. "What's The Sky Set?"

"You'll see," Xavier said.

"You are stretching my trust in you. Davis should have told you I hate surprises."

"This isn't so much of a surprise as it is a distraction. For some reason, you seemed like you needed one."

Destiny sighed and decided that Xavier was right. She needed something to take her mind away from where it had always seemed to wander for the past four years. Besides, this was Non-Stop Music Studio. Maybe she would meet some stars.

The elevator stopped several times on the way up to the thirty-ninth floor. Everyone who got on knew Xavier and greeted him warmly. Each time he returned the warm greetings, and each time he made no effort to introduce her. Not that he had to, but it would have been nice. *It's just as well,* Destiny thought. *It's not like we're seeing each other or anything.*

The elevator finally opened on The Sky Set, and the name did not disappoint. The floor was primarily one large mirrored room—what appeared to be a rehearsal hall. In the back of the room was a sound room filled with electronic mixing boards and sound equipment.

In the middle of the room, four musicians were tuning their instruments and three others were setting up microphones.

"What are you doing here?" a sable-skinned woman asked. The woman was hunched over a Fenway keyboard adjusting knobs and pressing what Destiny imagined was middle C.

"I came to see what you guys do when I'm not around."

"And now you'll never know," offered an older gentleman—much older than Xavier or anyone else there. The man came over to where Destiny and Xavier stood watching and extended his hand.

"I know he won't introduce me properly. I'm Reverend Samuel Webb."

Destiny shook his hand. He had a mighty grip and dry, rough

hands with calluses. "I'm Destiny Chandler," she said, smiling at the man.

Xavier playfully rolled his eyes. "This," Xavier stated strongly, "is Sammy Jam, the baddest, phattest, bombest bass player on the planet."

Sammy walked back to where the others were in the middle of the room. "That's Mr. Jam to you, son."

Xavier laughed along with several of the others. Sammy picked up his bass guitar, strummed a few chords, and said, "Nice to meet you, Miss Chandler."

Xavier introduced the rest of the band. He started by pointing to the woman on the keyboard, "That's Shade. The man with the drumsticks is Brian Bam-Bam. Over there are the voices from heaven, Tyrica Glover and the twins LeRoy and LeRon Johnson. And then there's Dutch, who plays lead guitar. Collectively, I call them my crew."

"Hey, everybody," Destiny said, proud to meet them all.

"You singing, Zay?" Tyrica asked.

"No," Xavier said, guiding Destiny back to the sound room. "We just came to listen."

Destiny and Xavier took seats and watched as the band began to warm up. In the process, Xavier told Destiny stories about each of the band members. Most were handpicked by the record company. Based on the type of music Xavier played, the record company negotiated with those whose talents were best suited for the job. The only members who were added were Sammy and Dutch.

"Sammy came with the package," Xavier added. "No Sammy, no Allgood. We go back too far. Besides," Xavier said, sending a smile toward the mature bass player, "Sammy's the father figure in my life."

"Oh," Destiny responded, understanding his attachment.

The sound of the band's playing filled the sound room. Xavier turned a few of the dials on the mixer and adjusted a few more levers.

"What's Dutch's story?" Destiny asked curiously.

Xavier sat back in his chair and his smile broadened. "Dutch is a special case. We held open auditions for a lead guitar player. After a morning of listening to men and women who were all decent players, Dutch comes in. And without saying a word, he plugs in and proceeds to do the best rendition of 'Purple Haze' I've ever heard in my life. I mean the man was like Jimi Hendrix incarnate. By the time he got to the 'Star-Spangled Banner,' we had a contract out and ready for him to sign."

Destiny took a good look at Dutch. He was a tall, thin reed of a man who looked more like Nat King Cole than Jimi Hendrix.

"Does he always wear sunglasses?" Destiny asked.

"Always. I think he even sleeps in them."

Destiny and Xavier chuckled.

"The most unusual thing about Dutch is that he doesn't talk much. He shows up when he's supposed to, plays the hell out of his guitar, and leaves. We don't even know his last name."

Destiny whooped. "You're kidding!"

"I'm telling you, lovely, Non-Stop makes his checks out to Dutch. No last name. Just Dutch."

Did he just call me lovely? Destiny wondered to herself. She pretended to be listening to the band, but she was replaying Xavier's last words to her. *Hmmm*, she thought, *probably some kind of pet name for women.*

"What do you think?" Xavier asked, dislodging her from her thoughts.

"I think they're great." And she did. Even though it was obvious that they were warming up, Destiny could tell right away that they were all outstanding musicians.

"I am truly fortunate that they let me work with them," Xavier said thoughtfully.

Destiny was outdone. Here sat one of the greatest talents in the music business and he was so modest about his own abilities. She searched his face for signs that he was being facetious. She found none. Instead she saw deep admiration and gratefulness in his eyes. He turned to her and spoke softly, seriously.

"I appreciate remarkable things and exceptional blessings."

Destiny looked away self-consciously. Xavier turned his attention back to the crew. Tyrica spoke into her mike as the band began playing an up-tempo melody. "And now, a crew original, 'Funk Syndrome'."

Xavier and Destiny listened to the fast-paced song. Each member got his or her own solo. And the background singers blew Destiny to the back of the room. Tyrica was a true diva. Her soul-stirring voice gave Destiny goose bumps. And LeRoy and LeRon performed like a perfect harmonizing machine. Destiny quickly realized that each member of Xavier's band was a star in his or her own right. They were all talented enough to have solo careers in the business.

"They are so bad," Xavier complimented. "During the concerts, sometimes I want to just let them jam for as long as they want to. But I know the audience has come to see me, so that might not be too cool. But still . . ." Xavier's voice trailed off as the crew settled into the song. The track was hot now. Destiny could tell they were really getting into it.

Xavier turned to Destiny. After studying her for a few moments, he offered his commentary. "That's what we call being in the zone."

Destiny smiled and nodded. It must be quite something to see these artists in concert, she thought.

The crew reached the end of their song. Destiny and Xavier applauded from the sound room. Sammy Jam spoke into the microphone in front of him. "I know it's your day off, but why don't you sing a little something, Zay."

"Nah," Xavier responded.

Sammy rubbed his short, salt-and-pepper hair. "You know we can practice that new arrangement of 'Your Place'."

"Sorry, my voice is on vacation," Xavier said, stroking his chin. "But I tell you what, if you really want to practice that song, why don't you ask Destiny to sing it?"

Destiny whipped her head around, astounded. "What!"

Sammy offered a partial smile. "You sing, sweetheart?" he asked.

Before she could yell no, Xavier answered for her. "She sings like sweet Sunday morning, Reverend Webb."

"That so?"

"No!" Destiny blurted.

The crew snickered at Destiny's intense response. All except for Dutch, who simply raised a cool eyebrow.

"But I heard you," Xavier insisted. "You have a beautiful voice."

"No, I don't," Destiny said between clenched teeth. She couldn't understand why Xavier was trying to embarrass her. If he had asked for her to show them some of her photographs, there would have been no problem. But sing in front of people, that was out of the question.

"Well, while you two argue, we'll finish rehearsing. They charge by the hour, you know," Sammy said, putting his bass back on.

Destiny and Xavier spent the rest of the morning watching the crew rehearse.

After rehearsal, they all went out for lunch. Destiny got to know the members better. Sammy Jam was truly the patriarch of the bunch. His fatherly advice popped up numerous times throughout lunch. Shade was a little on the shy side, but very friendly. The twins were a barrel of laughs. Destiny had never known any one person to be so quick-witted. And there were two of them. Her jaws ached from laughing by the time lunch was over. Brian Bam-Bam was the biggest flirt Destiny had ever met. His clever come-ons were thwarted by Sammy on more than one occasion. Tyrica reminded Destiny so much of Jacq that the two hit if off famously. And just like Xavier had said, Dutch was quiet throughout the entire lunch.

In the company of artists, that's where Destiny had felt most comfortable all her life. That's what made her job at the Arts and Humanities Council so rewarding. Destiny had a large extended family of artists back in Nebraska. By the end of lunch,

Destiny felt like Xavier's crew was a new addition to her family. She also felt like maybe she was an extended part of theirs.

That evening, in the rear guest bedroom of Davis's home, Destiny lay on the bed in a short black nightgown, bathed in the light of ten votive candles. The warm shadows played off her chestnut-brown skin and made golden, flickering silhouettes on the walls.

She had just finished taking a luxurious milk bath and was stretched out on the queen-size bed enjoying a moment of relaxation. The aroma of the cinnamon- and honey-scented candles surrounded her. She inhaled deeply.

She lifted her arms over her head into a long and much-needed stretch that released the remaining tension in her body. Then she reached over to the CD player on the nightstand and pressed play.

Xavier Allgood's velvety falsetto voice floated out of the speakers, as smooth as Godiva chocolate. Destiny drank in the sound of his song as it relaxed her even more. She felt each tone settle on her like a rhythmic stream of soft kisses—every note a gentle massage to her body and soul.

Destiny soon closed her eyes and before long drifted into what began as the best night's sleep she had had in months.

At the same time, Xavier Allgood sat behind a keyboard in his Tudor home and played a song that reminded him of Destiny.

So much about her was indelible to him now. The way he could see her warm heart in her eyes. The way she always smelled like an alluring combination of lilacs and sandalwood. The way he could hear the ocean in her voice. The way her bottom lip curled in slightly when she laughed. The way his body generated a hot spot wherever they intentionally or unintentionally touched. The way she gave off the most soul-stirring energy he had ever felt.

He had imagined them together a thousand times and in his mind he had made love to her a hundred different ways. Every time he actually saw her, there was a split second in his mind when she was in his arms, in his bed, in his soul.

"The way the happiness in her laughter makes me want to fly," he said out loud. He wondered if her skin tasted as creamy as it looked. If it would be sweet in his mouth. He imagined that causing a mere moan from her lips would satisfy him for days.

Xavier worked his fingers expertly across the ivory keys until the notes he played sounded like "Lovely Destiny. Lovely Destiny. Lovely Destiny."

Destiny and Xavier had spent the entire day together. From one end of the city to the other, Xavier had taken Destiny to all of the out-of-the-way places, unusual one-of-a-kind places, not the touristy and trendy upscale ones that Davis had taken her to.

Their first stop had been a curio shop on the outskirts of town. There had been knickknacks and figurines galore. Destiny had grown up in her grandmother's house and was surrounded by these small statues. Going into the shop felt like a homecoming. Destiny wondered how Xavier could have known that she would instantly fall in love with the shop.

Their next stop was an eclectic artist's cooperative and residency gallery. This time Destiny found herself surrounded by things that reminded her of the Arts and Humanities Council. There were extraordinary sculptures and abstract paintings. The next place he took her was a quaint candle shop in the center of the city. When they went in, Destiny wondered if Davis had told Xavier their candle story. She glanced at him as they walked around and saw no sign of recognition on his face. He seemed to genuinely think that she might be interested in the place. And to Destiny's surprise, she was.

At first, she thought it was because of her candle at home and the memories—and promise—it held for her. But the more she thought about it, she realized that it wasn't about the candle at all. No, it was actually about her own rebirth and the fire of her spirit, her heart, that was coming back to life. The candles in the shop were painstakingly crafted, and their aroma was heavenly. Destiny had to fight a strong urge to reach out and touch each one. Slowly she realized she was gaining her old strength back, becoming herself again—only better.

Destiny was overjoyed. She turned to Xavier to thank him for a wonderful day. When she didn't see him, she thought he had somehow wandered ahead of her. She went searching but couldn't find him. Perhaps some fan had spotted him and asked for his autograph. Destiny continued looking around the candle shop, but Xavier was nowhere to be found. Finally, she decided she would step outside and wait for him.

When she walked outside the door, she stepped into a dark and damp alley—an alley that looked vaguely like the one behind her house in Lincoln. *This can't be right,* she thought to herself. "This must not be the way we came in," Destiny said and turned to go back inside the candle shop. When she pushed on the door, it was locked. She was just about to knock on the door when she heard a voice that filled her with horror.

"You don't want to go back in there, baby girl."

Destiny spun around, panic-stricken. Although she knew that it couldn't possibly be, it was. Rico was standing across the alley staring at her like a demented madman.

Screaming, Destiny pounded on the door in hopes that someone on the other side would hear her. But the door remained locked. She pushed and shoved and tried to force the door open. Still nothing. All the while the sound of Rico's voice moved closer and closer.

"I think about you every day. You are my first thought in the morning and my last thought at night. But in between those thoughts, there's nothing. I can't live my life without you, you know."

As Rico came closer, a paralyzing fear swept over Destiny.

She closed her eyes and began to scream. "Ah! No! No! No! No more! Leave me alone! No more! No more! No more!"

When she opened her eyes, Davis was holding her. He began rocking her back and forth and whispering. "It's all right. You were dreaming. Calm down, baby. I've got you now."

Destiny was so relieved to find out she was dreaming that she grabbed on to Davis and held him as tightly as she could.

After attempting to work on his remodeling plans for an hour, Xavier gave up. No matter how he tried to distract himself, his mind slowly maneuvered back to Destiny. He wanted to know so much more about her, he wanted to hear her angelic voice again, and besides that, his body ached to hold her.

As he thought about her, he tried to remember Davis's original news flash that Destiny was coming. He and Davis had been browsing in Circuit City. Davis was showing Xavier some of the equipment and software programs that might be useful in his digital studio.

"The sky is the limit, man. Almost any program you can imagine has been written and is available for purchase. And if you can't find it, I can build it for you."

"I'll bet you charge a little sumthin', sumthin' for that."

Davis held his fist up for a dap. "You better believe it."

Xavier responded with a hearty rap on the fist. "Well, you know me. It'll be special or it just won't be. So when can we get started?"

Davis picked up a couple of bargain CDs from a large box. "Well, normally, I would say today, but I've got a lady friend coming to town, so I may not be available for the next couple of days."

Xavier noticed the twinkle in Davis's eyes.

"I see, and by the look in your eyes, it's kinda serious. Am I right?"

Davis returned the bargain CDs to the bin. He paused and looked at Xavier reflectively. "It was once. And it could be again. At this point, I'm not really sure, but I'm willing to give it a try."

Just then several women who recognized Xavier began closing in on them. Xavier spent the next thirty minutes signing autographs and answering questions about his upcoming album. Xavier hadn't realized it until now, but Davis never really said that he and Destiny were actually an item. He had merely suggested that they might become an item if the circumstances were correct.

Could this be it? Xavier thought. *Could I have finally found a loophole through which to approach Destiny?* He decided there was no time like the present to find out. He would go over to Davis's house and be the honest man his mother raised him to be. He would confess his feelings for Destiny and let the chips fall where they may. Either he would jeopardize his friendship with Davis or pave the way to pursue a relationship with Destiny. But either way, he couldn't torture himself any longer wondering whether there was a chance for him and Destiny to be together.

Xavier drove on autopilot to Davis's house. He had just pulled his Hummer into Davis's driveway when he heard the most awful screams. Xavier leaped out of the tank because there was no mistake . . . those were Destiny's screams. Ignoring his vow to himself to knock before entering, he pushed open Davis's front door. As he entered, he heard the screams again coming from upstairs.

Xavier bounded up the stairs three at a time and walked quickly toward the back guest room. When he got there he was halted in his tracks. He saw Destiny in bed wearing a beautiful black negligee. It made her honey-chocolate skin look radiant. But what froze him into place was that she was completely absorbed in what appeared to be an incredibly passionate kiss with Davis.

Luckily, Destiny and Davis were too involved with each other to notice Xavier standing there. And before they had a chance to see him, he carefully slipped back downstairs and out of the house.

* * *

The Nebraska State Penitentiary was tucked away on the outskirts of Interstate 80. It was carefully positioned between the state's largest cities—Lincoln and Omaha. The facility was modest by big-city standards. However, the growing prison population was forcing the state legislature to consider building a bigger and better facility somewhere else.

Until a new facility could be built, however, inmates had to contend with overcrowding, ration shortages, and quick tempers. Among those with quick tempers were Tony Frampton, a man called T-Bone, and Rico Freeman.

Although these men had each entered the prison on separate occasions and did not know one another previously, it didn't take long for them to find one another. They became the closest thing one could have to friends in jail. Soon they discovered that their desire to be out of jail was strong, and it became the glue that kept them close.

Their reasons for wanting to get out were very different. Frampton was addicted to crack cocaine. And unlike big-city jails, drugs were not so easy to come by in the Nebraska prison. T-Bone had an extreme case of claustrophobia and was prone to frequent and frightening anxiety attacks during the night. Rico's claim to the outside world was encapsulated by one word: *Destiny.*

"She never really gave me a chance, man," Rico stated, talking more to himself than to anyone else. He actually seemed to stare through the two men sitting opposite him.

"They never do."

"I did the best I could do."

"Man, shit."

"We were just getting started. Four years ain't no time."

"I hear ya."

"We can't let it go that easily. It's too late for that." And then, as if two people lived in the same body, Rico flipped his own script. "Man, forget that! She started this war, I didn't. But you know what comes after that, Bone?"

T-Bone had heard Rico say it so many times in the past few weeks that he finished the sentence without thinking. "But you damn sho gonna finish it."

Rico absentmindedly twirled a few strands of his patchy beard and nodded his head in agreement.

Six

Thought I had seen it all before
Thought there was no more me to explore
Thought my fate was singularity
Thought there wasn't any magic left for me

Then miracle, blessing gift, divine
Like a sweet, sensual chocolate valentine
Your enchanting sacred fire stepped into my soul
Ignited this slow burn that's making me whole

Now I search my body for signs of you
Seized by your will like some luscious voodoo
I'm living you like a habit in this hallowed place
Feelin' you like a soul breeze through my lonely heart
  space

Seven days later
I'm a man, brand-new
Might as well be a mountain
Seven days after you

Xavier worked in his future studio driven by an unfathomable force. The urge to write, produce, create, was so strong that even though it was 4:00 A.M., he had no thoughts of sleep.

It always happened. Whenever he found his emotions in turmoil, the songs came. The songs that made women scream at concerts, earned him Grammy nominations, and kept him sane. Like a tsunami, he could feel them coming in, wave after wave. And he would do the only thing he knew how—ride them until they were gone.

First, there was the song he wrote because no matter what he did and despite what he saw at Davis's house, he knew he was falling for Destiny.

If I could write a thousand words to say
How much you mean to me in every way
I'd set them all to music, oh so clear
A symphony that's just for you to hear
And then I'd blend the music and the rhyme
To a perfect melody like yours and mine
Your light will lift my head and raise my voice
I pray to God that he'll make me your choice

After that, there was the song he wrote just because he was considering her name.

Saw you with my third eye
Watched you dance in the sky
Your moves were true to the night
Our cosmic fate was my sight
Can't push or pull it away
No force will make it obey
No sleep since you came to me
Your heart is my destiny

And then he did the unthinkable, something so out of character that it took him completely by surprise. As much as Xavier appreciated order and planning and everything in its own place and time, he turned on the track-recorder in his studio and just sang. Whatever came to mind. No practice. No rehearsal. He simply belted out a stream of consciousness torn straight from his heart. When he finished, he was drained and exhausted. He could no longer think straight. He took one look at the clock on the wall, which read 7:00 A.M. Before he all but collapsed at his piano, he managed to scribble a name for his creation on the tape label. He wrote, "Destiny's Song."

Davis settled into bed, unsure of what just happened, but he was definitely glad that it did. Since Destiny first agreed to spend some time with him in Atlanta, Davis felt as though his ensemble would finally be complete.

For all his adult life, he had been the epitome of urban professionalism. He held an advanced degree from Morehouse College. Contracted with Fortune 500 companies as a programmer no less. And, to top it all off, he was, as one of his part-time honeys called him, dashing.

The only thing missing was a good woman—a wife. And not just any wife. She had to be beautiful—stunning, really. She also had to be intelligent, resourceful, determined, and ambitious. Destiny, Davis thought carefully, was all of those things.

And now that she was in an administrative role at the Arts and Humanities Council, she was in a perfect position to slide into a good fit in his life. He couldn't imagine himself explaining to any board of directors that his wife was a photographer. But a program director at an arts and humanities council, now that was something he could be proud of.

Yes, things were most assuredly falling into place. And that kiss . . . well, that said it all. He still wasn't sure how it happened. One minute Destiny was screaming in his arms from a nightmare, and the next his tongue was in her mouth.

But she had been so hard to resist. She looked broken and pitiful when he came into the guest bedroom. When he put his arms around her shoulders, she clung to him like a child who had been lost and had just found her way home. And then she looked up at him with such sadness in her eyes that all he could think to do was kiss it away.

When they broke free of their brief encounter, they stared into each other's eyes momentarily. They both averted their eyes. Davis didn't want to seem as though he were coming on to her.

"Are you better now?"

Destiny arranged the covers around her. "Yes. I'm sorry. It was a horrible nightmare."

"Really?" Davis smiled slyly. "I thought it was kind of nice."

A small smile made its way across Destiny's face. "You know what I mean, Davis."

Davis stood up, seeing that Destiny seemed recovered. "I know," he responded. "Just wanted to see if I still have it."

"Have *what?*" Destiny quipped softly.

"The ability to make you smile, even when you don't want to."

Destiny smiled again.

"So what was it about, your nightmare, I mean?"

"Never before breakfast."

Davis frowned. "What?"

Destiny nuzzled down into the bed and back into the pillows. She looked as if she were pulling on a memory from far away. "My father always said it was bad luck to discuss your dreams before breakfast. So," she continued in a barely audible voice, "if you want to know about my dream, you'll have to wait until morning."

Davis began to walk softly out of the bedroom. He could still hear Destiny mumbling from sleepland. "After the pancakes and sausage that Jacq would say I should let you cook."

When Destiny sounded as though she had drifted back to sleep, Davis closed the bedroom door and went out into the hall. As he walked toward his master bedroom, he heard a noise coming from outside. He went downstairs to investigate.

When he got down to the bottom of the staircase, he saw a pair of headlights shining into the living room. As he walked closer to the picture window, the intensity of the lights diminished. By the time he got to the window, the lights were gone and there was only a faint shadow of a car in the distance. It must have been someone turning around in the driveway, Davis reasoned, and he went back upstairs to bed.

Unlike Destiny's earlier nightmare, Davis's dreams that night were sweet and filled with office parties and company dinners where his new wife made him the envy of all his colleagues.

Destiny felt exhilarated and confused. First, she was beginning what she believed would be a wonderful photographic experience while she was on vacation. Second, she was sure that she was falling for Xavier, but she just shared a passionate kiss with Davis.

Maybe Jacq was right. Maybe she had been too hasty about leaving. She wasn't even out of the courtroom yet, and already she was packing for Atlanta. All before her head could make sense of what was going on. So for the past few weeks, her body had been on autopilot.

She just hoped that her body wasn't getting her into trouble. And why she had agreed to work with Xavier, when all she really wanted was some peace and downtime, was beyond her.

Nevertheless, she looked in the mirror and was pleased with what she saw. Her long legs were hidden in free-flowing, wide, napkin cloth pants. The matching shirt and calf-length shank were sleeveless and showed off her muscle-toned arms. The entire outfit was cream colored, which contrasted with her dark skin and jet black locks.

Destiny was checking her makeup when Xavier rang the doorbell. Since she had arrived, she hadn't heard the doorbell. Despite what Xavier said about not intruding, he still hadn't knocked or done anything to announce his presence until now. Destiny laughed on the way to the front door. Davis's doorbell was not really a bell at all but an excerpt from an Anita Ward song, *"You can ring my bell, ring my bell."*

Destiny tried to contain herself, but when she got to the front door and opened it, she couldn't hold back any longer and let out a deep belly laugh. Xavier, looking perplexed, stepped inside and smiled as Destiny proceeded to laugh uncontrollably.

"I would ask if it was something I said, but I haven't said anything yet."

Now Destiny had crossed over from the land of the silly to the land of the ridiculous. Between chuckles, she tried to regain her composure and explain why she was laughing.

"It's just that . . . Davis is so serious . . . and his doorbell . . ."

"Davis has a doorbell?"

At that remark, they both were laughing, and Destiny tried to continue through her laughter.

"His doorbell sings . . . it sings 'Ring My Bell'."

Now Destiny was laughing hard, too hard. She saw Xavier's smile turn to puzzlement, but she couldn't stop. For the first time in months she was laughing, really laughing. And that made it even more humorous, because what started her laughter wasn't really that funny. But it was as if the floodgates were opening and she was powerless to stop them. Wherever this was going, Destiny would just have to ride it out.

Xavier became concerned. "Hey, are you laughing or crying?"

Destiny discovered she was doing both. Xavier led her to the couch, and after she sat down, she realized that now she was only crying. Xavier hugged her and looked into her eyes. That's when she started to recover herself. *I can't break down like this. I can't!* she thought. Slowly her sobs subsided and Xavier wiped her tears.

"You definitely should talk about it."

"I don't know what happened. I think I've been under too much stress at my job."

"If it's *that* stressful, you should quit. Plus that didn't look like stress you were releasing. It looked more like pain and anguish."

Destiny looked into Xavier's eyes with no doubt in her mind. She was in love. As Jacq put it, "feet first and ass up," but there was no mistaking it now. Her kiss with Davis had been a misplaced reflex action to all the turmoil in her head and soul. But here, she sighed, was the real truth.

"From your sigh, I take it that you don't want to discuss it. But you should discuss it soon. You seem to be okay now. But whatever it is, it's no good to you where it is—hidden and buried. Bring it out into the open, where it will either breathe or die."

Destiny nodded.

"Take it from me. One way or the other, you can't run from it. You eventually get tired and it will start to overtake you. Face it while you still have the strength."

Destiny wanted to cry again, but didn't. She knew she needed a distraction to get her mind off things.

"I think we should go now," she suggested.

Xavier still looked concerned, but quickly conceded to her wishes.

"Cool," he replied, and they walked out of Davis's house and into Xavier's solid black Hummer.

Destiny had only seen Hummers on television. She had never imagined anyone actually driving one. The uniqueness of it lifted her spirits. She found herself amazingly elated when Xavier sped down the street.

"Do you always drive this fast?"

"Not always."

"Why now?" Destiny asked as she pushed back her locks, which were blowing around her face.

Xavier popped the clutch and sent the large all-terrain vehicle sailing into third gear. "You look like someone in need of a thrill."

At that, Destiny chuckled. She felt her anxiety subsiding. Xavier glanced over several times at Destiny, who was smiling as if she had just swallowed a big secret.

"What's that half smile for?"

"I was just thinking about a close friend of mine and how she would respond to a comment like that."

Xavier made his way through the inner city of Atlanta. It wasn't until he had driven past Brookville Cemetery that he realized that he hadn't gotten on the interstate. Maybe some part of him was purposefully extending their time together. It would take them at least thirty minutes longer to get to his house this way.

"Looks like you've got the other half of the smile," Destiny offered. "Or were you someplace else entirely?"

"No, I'm definitely here."

With all of her thoughts of hesitation about the man, Destiny knew she wanted him. And she was beginning to think that even if he had no feelings for her, she still wanted to give herself to him.

But then again, the thought of being involved, no matter how slightly, with another uncaring man frightened her. And her improving mood suddenly took a downturn.

Somehow Xavier sensed it. He glanced over toward the passenger seat and saw the expression on Destiny's face. He couldn't fathom the cause of such sadness, but he knew one thing. He would do anything to erase it. Before he could think better of it, he changed lanes and headed south away from his house and toward the Board district.

Destiny, startled by Xavier's abrupt lane change, felt compelled to comment.

"Are you sure you know where you're going?"

"I do now," Xavier replied, and seemed to drive even more determinedly through the heavy Atlanta traffic.

"Hello."

"Hey, cow."

"Jacq! I was just about to call you."

"I know. I'm psychic, remember? I thought I'd save you some time on your phone card." Jacq snickered. She knew Destiny didn't use a phone card. "What's up, girl? I know you've got something to tell me. And my name ain't Linda Tripp so you can give me the righteous 411."

Destiny did have something to tell her friend. But since she had arrived in Atlanta and first laid eyes on Xavier, it was difficult for her to begin to discuss her experiences. Her emotions were so stirred up that she wasn't sure if what was happening was real or a dream.

"Well? I'm tryin' to save you some money, and you're tryin' to spend mine."

"Sorry, Jacq. I guess I got lost for a moment. You're right. I do have something to tell you."

Jacq listened quietly on the other end. She could tell by the sound of Destiny's voice that whatever she was about to say wasn't exciting news. Either Xavier was absolutely terrible in bed or she still hadn't gotten any.

"I just had the most romantic experience of my entire life."

Romantic? Now that was a word Jacq had not expected to hear. This sounded serious. She remained silent and let her dear sister-friend tell her tale.

"We were supposed to be going to his house to finish the storyboards. When he picked me up I had a laughing fit over Davis's doorbell, of all things. Anyway, after a few moments of uncontrollable laughter, I started crying for no reason."

Jacq felt compelled to step in. "You are the most intentional person on the planet. You are the only sister I know who goes window shopping with an agenda. If you were crying, it had to be for a reason."

"That's just it, Jacq. This spur-of-the-moment trip to Atlanta and now this agreement to be Xavier's photographer, it's not me. I mean, I always know what I'm doing and why I'm doing it. And now, it's like I'm just going with the flow. It's causing me to do and feel things that I shouldn't."

"So what happened when you started crying?"

"He was so nice, Jacq. I mean, he was right there. He just stepped in, as if there was a fissure opening up in me and only he could close it. I swear, Jacq, it was like abracadabra or something. But he was there and that made it all right."

"Hmmm. That *is* romantic."

"Oh, that's not the romantic part."

Jacq remained silent, letting Destiny continue in her own time. After a few moments, she resumed. Jacq had no more complaints about the cost of the phone call.

"He took me to the Non-Stop studio. That's where musicians go to hang out, network, make deals, and practice without distraction. That's where the members of his backup band hang out. Anyway, we stayed there all morning. The band is great, especially Sammy Jam. He's the father figure of the group. Along with being the greatest bass player I've ever heard, he's also a Baptist minister. Can you believe that?"

"Kinda like a play-step-godsister, huh?"

"Girl, you are certifiable."

"I know, I know. G'on, girlfriend."

"Okay. So Sammy has all of these programs with him that he had printed up for Sunday's service and asks Xavier to drop them off at the church for him."

"Oh yeah, this is quite romantic. I don't think I can take much more."

Destiny ignored Jacq's comment and continued her exciting tale. "So we left and went to the church. I met Sammy's wife, Verle, there. She was leaving when we arrived, so she asked us to lock up when we left.

"Xavier put the programs in the office and gave me a tour. And Jacq, it was like he became a different person in the church. Actually, church isn't an appropriate word. It was more like a cathedral with high ceilings and elaborately golden, handcrafted ornamentation throughout. And in it, Xavier wasn't Allgood anymore. Not Allgood the entertainer. Not Allgood the shy genius like in the magazine article I read. Not even Allgood the Mac Daddy like his fans probably want to believe. He was Xavier, the awe-inspired servant of a higher power. And I was caught in his aura like a deer in headlights."

Damn, Jacq thought, knowing that Destiny was finally getting to the romantic part. Jacq, who had been sitting at a desk in the living room of her apartment, took the phone into her bedroom and stretched out on her bed to settle in for the story. Unbeknownst to her, Destiny was doing much the same thing on the bed in Davis's guest room.

"He saved the best for last when he took me to the organ loft. And when I say organ loft, I mean organ loft. I've never seen pipes so magnificent and shiny. Xavier approached the organ almost as tentatively as you would approach a new lover."

"Not me!" exclaimed Jacq. "My motto is *bam, bam, bam, bam,*" Jacq imitated an actor in the movie *Boomerang.* She waited for a response from Destiny. When there wasn't one she feigned an apology. "Sorry."

"No, you're not. But I love you anyway."

"Love? Whachewtalkinbout love for? Destiny Sharice Chandler, your nose is wide open, ain't it?"

"Stop being ridiculous. Just because I'm talking about something romantic—"

Jacq interrupted her midsentence. "Oh, hell no. Don't go there. I *know* you. The only time you start poppin' that I love you yang is when you're in love, ya damnself. Why don't you just start singing the Barney song?"

"What!" Destiny protested.

"Aw, you know." Jacq did her best impression of Barney. *"I love you. You love me. We're a happy family!"*

Both women roared with laughter. Then there was a long silence, which Destiny finally broke.

"Damn, Jacq. Do I sound that bad?"

"Only because I know you. So I know the signs. I'm sure he doesn't know. Guys are so easy to fool anyway. I wouldn't worry about that."

"I'm not so sure."

"What do you mean?"

"I'll finish the story, and then you tell me."

Jacq listened closely as Destiny finished the story.

* * *

Xavier sat at the organ and ran his hands over the keys. Then he looked up at Destiny with those piercing jet black eyes. "Sometimes the need to write, sing, and create is as powerful and urgent as breathing."

And then, as if he were asking for her hand in marriage, he said, "Let me sing for you."

Destiny couldn't say anything. If she had opened her mouth, somehow she knew she would have fainted right then and there. So instead, she just walked down the staircase and sat out in one of the pews.

He started playing a song she had never heard before. Destiny didn't know how he did it, but it was a writhing combination of jazz, gospel, and blues. It sounded sad but hopeful, warm and distant at the same time. Familiar and fleeting like a favorite meal you only eat once a year.

She felt suspended in time, like the second hand on every clock in the world had stopped and the only thing that existed in the universe was the experience they were having in that church.

His playing became more intense until he added his voice into the mixture. But he wasn't singing or humming. It was more like a sensual scat that flowed over Destiny's body like urgent sea waves. His voice was actually touching her—caressing her skin. Through the music, she felt his fingertips stealthily stroking her body.

And then Xavier started singing—every slow love jam Destiny could imagine—his and everyone else's.

Xavier sang from that organ loft, but he stepped into Destiny's soul.

"Girl, that *is* romantic. I think he was tryin' to tell you somethin'."

Destiny sat up. "What—that he can seduce women at will?

That it's time to put another notch in his belt." Destiny paused, then retorted, "I don't think so."

"What if he loves you, too?"

Destiny would not allow herself to entertain the thought. "Impossible," she responded.

Destiny slid from the bed to the floor and sat in a yoga position. "Well, all good things must come to an end. So let me finish telling you what happened so you can"—Destiny did her best impression of Jacq—"get yo reality check on."

Jacq once again fell silent and listened to her friend.

By the time Xavier finished singing, it was dark outside. They must have been in the church for nearly two hours. All that time Destiny was transfixed by her own private Allgood concert. But it wasn't a concert really. He was singing to her spirit and it seemed they were both oblivious to anything outside of themselves.

When the songs ended, Destiny could feel herself slowly returning to the real world. It was as if he was easing her back gently with the descent of the music. When he finished, there were fresh tears in her eyes, and from what she could tell, his too. In the short time they were there, he had made himself a permanent part of Destiny's existence.

For a long time, they just stared into each other's eyes. Suddenly she knew she wanted to kiss Xavier more than anything else in the world. He must have read her mind because at that precise moment, he got up and walked down the stairs.

He walked toward her and Destiny couldn't move. She just stared into his eyes and felt herself being devoured by them. He stood in front of her and touched her chin. She rose as if on command and felt the intense piercing gaze of his eyes penetrate her to her very core. She could see a thin covering of sweat on his head and neck. It made his face glisten in the golden light.

Destiny's breath stopped as their faces grew nearer and

nearer. She could smell the moist-sweet aroma of his breath as his lips pressed against hers. She began to lose herself in his embrace. And this time there was no mistaking it. His hands were slowly moving over her body.

"I was ready to surrender. I knew that if he wanted to go back to his house or even a hotel, I would have gone. All he had to do was say the word. And then I heard her. Xavier heard her too. His head snapped to attention like he was in the army. A woman, who looked and dressed like she just stepped out of an *Essence* catalog, was standing in the front doorway calling his name.

" 'I thought that I recognized your car,' she said and walked toward us.

"Xavier looked at me, then looked back at her. He let me go real quick and said, 'Destiny, this is Elise.' I don't remember much of what happened after that."

Seven

Rico fell into the stereotypical "exercising inmate" persona like it was an old and familiar role. The physical exertion and strenuous routine went a long way to channel the anger, frustration, and stress of being on lockdown.

Quickly it became poignantly clear to Rico why animals pace in their cages in the zoo. The steady movement is something, *anything,* to stay focused. To remain sane, and to be ready for the first opportunity to change a prisoner's condition, and escape. The pacing becomes a powerful diversion from captivity—a way to direct pent-up energy before it becomes a person's undoing.

Rico took his diversion in doses of sit-ups and push-ups—three hundred each, every day. It was a quiet and intense activity that allowed him to focus on his goal. Nothing he did would rid his mind of her. They had somehow merged into one person.

When Rico looked in the mirror, it wasn't his own face he saw, but Destiny's. And every moment he was apart from her, he wondered what she was doing. As he prepared for his morning schedule of alternating sit-ups and push-ups, his memories of Destiny were almost overwhelming. They washed over him in tidal waves, at times nearly knocking him over or stealing his breath. He simply could not exist without her.

His separation from her was like having an arm or leg torn from the socket and knowing the gaping wound would never heal. It would always bleed. It would never scab over. It would forever cause him unbearable pain. Rico knew that the only way to stop his pain would be to get Destiny back. Even if that meant breaking the hell out of the correctional facility.

As always, Rico recounted every event of their relationship while exercising. From the first meeting to the last time he saw her. By the time he had gone over their entire relationship in his mind, he would reach the end of his exercise routine.

Rico began to count his sit-ups: one, two, three, four . . . And then he was back at his old job as a recently hired drug and alcohol counselor for New Kemet Recovery Center. The directors of the center considered him a young upstart, still wet behind the ears. He had to bust his ass just for them to take him seriously. And it didn't help matters that his ideas were unique, different, radical even. Rico's approach to recovery was so divergent from anything the center had done in the past that there were rumors of Rico's possible removal by the board.

So when he started his art therapy program, he knew he had to prove himself once and for all. He wanted the program to produce dramatic results, the kind of results that would eliminate any remaining doubts the board may have had.

There were several arts organizations in the city. Most seemed unfamiliar with, and uninterested in, an arts therapy program. It wasn't until he went to the Nebraska Arts and Humanities Council that he found someone willing to work with him. That person was Destiny Chandler.

When he approached her with the idea, she admitted that she had only read about such programs and had never coordinated one. But she also told him she believed art could be a catalyst for the physical as well as the emotional healing of an individual.

By the end of their first meeting, Rico was convinced that Destiny was the one he wanted to work with. He also came to the conclusion that he wouldn't mind seeing her on a more informal basis.

As an artist-in-residence, it was Destiny's job to partner with the staff and develop a program that would suit the recovery center's needs. After several meetings with her, Rico believed that they finally had come up with a program that would produce the results he needed.

Destiny and Rico created a six-week program. During the first two weeks, Destiny came in for an hour to present a condensed version of Photography 101.

During the second week, everyone in the recovery program was given a disposable camera. Then the entire group went on an excursion to Neale Woods nature center in north Omaha. During the outing, the patients were encouraged to take a picture of anything they wanted anytime they felt a strong urge to drink or use drugs or anytime anything reminded them of drinking or using drugs.

After the outing, Destiny had the pictures developed and a few days later returned to the center with the patients' photos. In the fourth-week debriefing session, she provided the patients with journals and asked them to write about why they took the pictures they took, what was going through their minds when they were taking the pictures. Then she had them brainstorm ways in which they could use the recovery reminders to offset the addiction triggers. The result was incorporated into a recovery plan in which the patients could use powerful images and associations to fight their addictions. The patients spent the fifth and sixth weeks in sessions where they discussed their findings. What the patients discovered about themselves and the world around them was substantive enough that rumblings of Rico's dismissal from the board ceased.

It wasn't a cure-all, but it was ammunition. And Rico knew from personal experience that sometimes for an addict, the more resources you have to fight your disease the better.

Through the process of working with Destiny on the arts therapy program, Rico lost himself. After a while, Destiny was all he knew and all he wanted to know. He thought at first that it was just his addictive personality taking over, but he soon convinced himself that he really and truly loved her.

That's when the dates started and the courtship that would have won Rico a thousand Oscars began. "I swear, all the things you have to pretend to be just to get a woman to notice you," Rico said to no one in particular. He continued counting sit-ups and reminiscing.

If Destiny wanted a straightlaced dolt who catered to her every whim, then so be it. But soon the pressure of being an impostor became too great. Unlike the participants in the program who now had helpful mental images to help curb their cravings, Rico had taken no pictures during the outing. So instead of having visions of those things that would buffer him from his addiction, he began imagining what it would be like to take one drink.

Just one drink, like normal people, he imagined. Everybody else could do it—drink socially and then quit. Rico hadn't had a drink in six years. Maybe just one drink would put his mind at ease about this role he was playing for a one-woman audience.

Rico's better judgment kept him from taking that one drink for a while. Instead, he would go out to bars with friends, something he hadn't done in the years of his sobriety. He would order juice or pop. But nothing with alcohol.

After that, he went to gatherings at his friends' houses, something else he had avoided. When it was time to make a beer run, Rico would volunteer. "I'm not drinking any," he would announce to those of his friends who knew him from before. Some would nod slowly and then look away, as if to say it was just a matter of time. But Rico knew he was just trying to get some of the fun of his other life back.

Once while going out to buy a twenty-four-pack for a football game, Rico found himself staring at a pint of vodka. The next thing he knew, a sweat had broken out across his brow and the beer he was carrying nearly slipped out of his hands. In a panic, Rico set the case of beer down where he stood and dashed out of the store.

He drove quickly to a park located in downtown Lincoln. He

sat there for twenty minutes with his head in his hands. For six years he had pretended to be someone he wasn't—a non-drinking person. Add to that three years with Destiny where he had also pretended to be sweeter than honey and more chivalrous than Billy Dee.

Lying causes conflict, Rico thought. *And conflict makes me drink.* "Too many lies!" he said, stepping out of the car. He strode purposefully across the street, more confident and scared than he had been in a long time. He headed toward a brick building that was as familiar to him as his own breath. Several of the men standing outside of the building greeted him.

"What's up, man? Long time!"

"Hey, now!"

"My man, where you been?"

Rico ignored them all. He couldn't really see or hear them. The gentleman's mask he was wearing kept his senses dulled. But all that was about to change. He walked up to the counter, money already in hand. "Give me a pint of vodka," he said.

"Mr. Rico," the man behind the counter said. "What you wanna go and buy some vodka for? I heard you got a nice job and a good woman now."

"You telling me my money's no good here? Because if you are, I know plenty of places that will take it!"

"Calm down, man." The man behind the counter walked over to the shelves behind him that were full of liquor.

"As a matter of fact," Rico said, slamming a ten-dollar bill on the counter, "make it a fifth."

"One hundred and one, one hundred and two." Rico continued counting sit-ups and smiling about his memories. The night when he bought that fifth, he got plenty lit. Plenty. By the time he went home, he had visited all his old hangouts, reacquainted himself with his old drinking buddies, and managed to feel up three women.

Yep, the old Rico was back with a vengeance. How he had

missed the sweet burning of vodka as it went down his throat. The all-too-familiar feeling of warmth in the pit of his stomach gave him back the confidence to be the person he hadn't been in years. The only thing missing was Destiny. Strangely enough, he still wanted her. As much as he wanted his next drink.

"Hey, baby," he said, hanging from the doorway.

Destiny ran into his arms. "Oh my God, Rico. I thought something terrible had happened to you."

Rico watched with a smile as Destiny stepped back from him looking confused.

"Have you been drinking?"

"Hellll yeah," he slurred. Rico pushed past her and plopped down on the couch. "And it was glorious. I think I'm going to do it again."

"One hundred and twenty-four, one hundred and twenty-five." Rico wiped the sweat from his neck and face. "And I think I'm going to see you again, Ms. Destiny."

As often as possible, Xavier Allgood liked to remind himself of how lucky he was. He had money and respect in such abundance that at times he wondered if he was living someone else's life. More importantly, he was doing what he absolutely loved to do. He wasn't sure how many people on earth were making a living doing what they loved, but he would wager that the number was small.

Sometimes he gave thanks by attending Sammy's church services when they were in town. He always gave thanks on the road by adding at least one gospel song to his repertoire. Other times he donated the proceeds from some of his concerts to special programs for inner-city youth.

Today was different. Today he wandered from room to room

in the rustic, Tudor mansion he called home, and gave thanks for what he had been given. In each room, he stopped and was thankful for his surroundings—the Fulani statues in his living room, the Romare Bearden painting in his dining room, the prayer rug made for him by church members, the shelves of books in his library, the equipment in his music studio, clothes by Prada, jewelry by De Beers.

Special to his heart was his music. He had an extensive collection of CDs that ranged from Billy Eckstine and Billie Holiday to Erykah Badu and Busta Rhymes. As a tribute to his love for music, he had a musical instrument in each room, including an old blue guitar he kept in his studio. But by far, his most prized possession was an Excalibur crossbow that he kept above his bed. It was a sleek tool made from aircraft aluminum. It had a telescope mount for aiming and a trigger comparable to that of a rifle.

Xavier looked from the crossbow on the wall to his bed. It was large and empty just like his heart. He thought of all the women he had met on the road while touring who made it embarrassingly obvious that they would be willing to join him in his bed. At times there were so many and they came so fast that they were like blurs in his vision.

When he first got in the business three years ago, he had been flattered and excited by all the female attention. He even took a few women up on their offers. But after a while too much of a good thing numbs the senses. Xavier knew that his appreciation for beautiful women was intact, but he found his attention would wane if beauty was all a woman had to offer.

And then there was Destiny. Since the incident on the stairs, she was never far from his thoughts. The more time he spent with her, the more he wanted to spend with her. His first attraction to her was physical. When he had looked into her almond-shaped eyes as she helped him to his feet, he felt himself overwhelmed by the beauty he saw there. If eyes are truly mirrors of the soul, then Destiny's soul was compelling and magnetic.

As for her body—its delicious curves and golden umber skin—Xavier dared not even contemplate it. Being alone now, his desire could rise to a ridiculous level, which he could do nothing to abate. But what had pushed him over the edge of desire was her uniqueness. He had never met a woman before that expressed herself the way Destiny did, or who had the ideas that Destiny had. She wasn't starstruck at all, and she never asked about the business the way most people did. Xavier couldn't remember how many times he had been asked if he knew Janet Jackson or Will Smith, or if he could give someone a "hookup."

That kind of discussion got old quickly. But Destiny seemed genuinely interested in him and not his fame. And he couldn't forget her incredible rendition of his song. Only someone with deep emotions could truly get to where he was heading with that song. Destiny had gone there and beyond. He felt an instant attraction and connection to her.

But above and beyond all that, there was just something about that woman. It defied explanation or definition. But whatever it was, it had Xavier deliriously lovesick. As he took an appreciative survey of his surroundings, he hoped that one day he could also be thankful for Destiny Chandler.

Peachtree was packed with cars, most of which were driven by young blacks that seemed barely out of high school. And the cars they were driving were new and expensive.

Davis strolled next to Destiny on the busy sidewalk and remembered his first time seeing this spectacle, this parade of black prosperity. As he watched, the expression on Destiny's face reminded him of his own back in the day.

"What do you think?"

"I think I'm in the wrong business."

Well, Davis thought, *at least she's open to the possibility of changing careers.* That would fit his plans even better. "There's a lot of money to be made here," Davis said proudly.

Destiny smirked. "Or a lot of debt to go into."

Davis chuckled knowingly.

Destiny was unrelenting. "No, really. Aren't most of these people living way beyond their means?"

Davis raised an eyebrow and cocked his head to the side. "Are you insinuating something here?"

This time it was Destiny's turn to chuckle. "No, Davis. You've been playing the urban professional gig for some time now. But some of these folks," Destiny said as she pointed to a metallic gold Lexus going by with a very young black man at the wheel, "still have womb juice on them."

Davis stopped walking and frowned. "If you don't sound like Zay talking? Hmm . . . I think you two are spending too much time together."

Destiny winced as if she had been prodded in the stomach with a broom handle. "Zaaay," she said with emphasis, "and I haven't been spending too much time together, I assure you."

Davis took note of the expression on Destiny's face. The frown told him that he shouldn't worry.

The two walked quietly for a moment. The noise of the busy city swirled around them. Davis, who had lived in Atlanta for ten years, had become accustomed to the commotion. But he could tell that Destiny was a little unsure of it all. She hadn't talked much lately and although she said she came to Atlanta to relax, right now she didn't seem very relaxed.

He hadn't been able to spend as much time with her as he had wanted to. The demands of the project with Integrated Marketing were just too great right now. But seeing Destiny like this made him want to do something. And then, just as they were about to enter Underground Atlanta to go shopping, the idea hit him.

"Say, Destiny, Zay has a concert coming up in about a week. I'm sure he'll give us tickets."

Destiny opened her mouth to speak, but Davis cut her off before she could protest.

"I know you have been working hard lately, so this will give you a chance to get away from it all." Davis put his fingers to Destiny's lips when he saw her about to protest again. "Live music is the best way to relax and have fun. And I've overheard women talking about Zay. They say he's the King of Unwind.

"So, if your answer is no, I'm not gonna hear that, see."

Destiny shook her head. "All right," she conceded. "But please, don't make me stay to get an autograph."

Davis chuckled again. Nothing like a little mood music, he thought. He hadn't tried anything since the mysterious kiss the other night, but it had been on his mind. He would let Allgood, Mr. Mellow-Smooth, put this beautiful woman in the mood to be served up. And then that night after the concert, with Destiny ripe for plucking, he would make his move.

The last time Jacq had heard from Destiny, Destiny was spending more and more time with a man who was exponentially fine. But not the kind of time that she should have, Jacq thought. She remembered Destiny's sorry excuse for not hitting Allgood's skins.

"Jacq, I'm not sure if I'm completely over Rico."

"Girl, don't you know? The best way to get over someone is to get under someone."

Destiny gasped. "That's it. I'm not calling you anymore. Or if I do, I will not talk about Xavier. Let's talk about something else. How about *your* love life? Any new prospects?"

"Ain't you all up in the Kool-Aid? Well if you have to know, there aren't, but that's okay. I like being free and single."

"Since when?"

"Since I've been free and single." Jacq laughed. Destiny really did know her well. Jacq didn't want a long-term, serious kinda thing. But she did enjoy her male companionship. If she went too long without sex, she started to get crabby and lose focus. That was usually about the time when she changed jobs. Funny how that seemed to go together, Destiny thought.

"I know you would like to run up a nice long-distance bill,

but I've got to go. I want to make sure I get plenty of rest so that I look my best for my date tomorrow."

"Wow. Is Mr. Golden Voice taking you out?"

"No, silly. I'm going out with Davis."

"Whoa, a moment away from Allgood!"

Destiny felt a familiar warmth in her cheeks at the sound of that name.

"Actually, Davis is taking me to see Xavier in concert."

"Girl, what I wouldn't give to trade places with you."

Destiny smiled, remembering the article she read on the airplane and knew that if the concert was half as good as the article described, Destiny would be floating two feet off the ground for weeks.

"Well, you get your beauty rest, Des."

"I will."

"Later, girl."

"Bye."

Eight

Destiny didn't know why she felt so unsure of herself. She had spent all day shopping for the perfect outfit and now that she looked in the mirror, she was disappointed.

Destiny had swept up her sisterlocks and they fell around her face in a mass of dangles. The gold, studded earrings she wore complemented the gold threads that she carefully set into her hair. Her golden accessories matched her amber and black, ankle-length dress perfectly.

Destiny twisted in front of the full-length mirror. The dress shimmered in the light and clung to her body like a lover. The bottom of her dress swooshed over her black pumps and accented their gold trim. "Damn," Destiny said, staring at the scooped neckline. "I'm definitely overdressed."

Apparently Davis didn't think so. In a smoky gray Armani suit, he walked into the guest bedroom as Destiny stared at her reflection in the mirror, and sent her a barrage of catcalls.

"Damn, baby . . . I hope your man has got explosion insurance, 'cause, uh, from where I'm standing you are da bomb!"

Destiny laughed as he slowly came closer to her with each comment.

"You got it goin' all the way on. I mean . . . tell me your husband ain't married."

Davis began to bob and swagger like a Mack Daddy as he circled her.

"Pardon me, miss. I seem to have lost my phone number.

Can I borrow yours? My name ain't Elmo, but you can tickle me anytime. You must be Jamaican cuz cha makin' me crazy. Can I borrow a quarter? I want to call your mother and thank her."

Destiny giggled in relief. Maybe she didn't look as bad as she thought. She smiled at Davis as he slowly walked up to her and looked seriously and deeply into her eyes.

"Do you have a map?" he asked, taking her hands into his. "Because I keep getting lost in your beauty." Davis kissed the backs of Destiny's hands and seemed to wait for a reaction.

Destiny couldn't tell if Davis was serious or simply ending his playfulness on a dramatic note. In either case, she didn't want to be pulled into anything like the other night when she found herself in the middle of a passion-filled kiss with him. She still hadn't figured that out and now with this latest twist with Xavier, Destiny was more confused about her feelings than ever. She gently pulled her hands away from Davis's and gave him a shy look.

"So does that mean that I look okay?" she asked, hoping to steer the mood back to its previous lightheartedness. And it worked. Davis let out a belly laugh and shot her an approving look.

"I will be the envy of every man at the concert."

Not every man, Destiny thought, remembering the last moments in the church with Xavier. He had seemed so taken with Elise that Destiny knew the kiss they exchanged was merely Allgood exerting his star privilege to conquer whomever he chose without a care.

And perhaps, Destiny thought, that's why she had such a tough time getting ready for the concert. She wanted to make sure that she appeared to be none the worse for wear. She wanted to give the impression that she wasn't hurt by his dismissal of her and that she wasn't concerned about Elise.

"Starfleet Command to Voyager . . . come in, Voyager."

Davis's voice snapped Destiny to his attention. She felt guilty about zoning out and decided she would force all romantic feelings for Xavier out of her mind. Tonight, she was with Davis.

It was too easy to slip into the heart space owned by Xavier. Destiny would have to concentrate hard on being with Davis.

Davis extended his arm for Destiny's. "Shall we go?"

Destiny obliged and together they headed out of the condominium.

When they arrived at the auditorium, Davis was as excited as a schoolboy. At first, Destiny thought it was because of all the beautiful women she saw headed into the Orpheum. They came from all directions and were in all colors, shapes, and sizes. And from what Destiny could tell, she was not overdressed at all. These women were on a mission of glamour. It was as if they were all dressed up for their "date" with Allgood. And suddenly Destiny realized why she had such a hard time getting ready. She felt the same way.

Davis walked her briskly to the box office and presented their tickets. While they filed in line behind hundreds of other attendees, Davis smiled broadly and glanced repeatedly in her direction. The expression on his face reminded Destiny of the time he gave her his class ring to keep while he was in basic training. She knew he was up to something.

"All right, what is it?" she asked, hoping that whatever it was would not distract her.

"I should have known I couldn't keep anything from you." Davis put his arm around Destiny's shoulders. "I have a surprise for you."

"Davis, you know better than that. I don't do well with surprises."

Davis guided Destiny slowly to the entrance of the main floor and handed the usher their ticket stubs. As they walked in, Destiny could hear one of the songs from *The Miseducation of Lauryn Hill* playing in the background. She glanced at Davis, who remained strangely quiet, and frowned.

"Well . . ." she said, as the usher found their seats in the front row. "Is this the surprise? Front-row seats?"

Davis looked at Destiny as though he had just swallowed a secret. "Nope. This was a given."

Destiny would not be dissuaded. "What then?"

Davis sat back in his seat and folded his arms. "You'll see."

Destiny folded her arms too—in disgust. This was not starting off right. She had hoped that despite her feelings for Xavier, she would cast them aside to enjoy the evening. Davis was trying to ruin it with some silly surprise. *Well* . . . Destiny thought to herself, *not tonight.*

"Davis . . ." she started. But before she could finish her sentence, the house lights dimmed and hundreds of women screamed in unison. *Saved by the belles,* she thought.

Destiny noticed her heart quickening as she waited for the announcer to proclaim Allgood's arrival. There were more shrieks and screams. Destiny realized that if Davis weren't with her, she might be obliged to shriek and scream as well. She glanced around the auditorium. It appeared that she and Davis, along with about five other brothers, were the only ones sitting calmly in their seats.

The shrieks and screams stopped abruptly when the sound of Xavier's voice came softly through the speakers. His melodic tones floated through the auditorium and touched her from the inside out. She felt her recent frustration with Davis slide away. Destiny settled in for a massage of sound.

> *Steppin' in gots ta come with the clever*
> *Leaving you on the backside of never*
> *It's time*
> *That you give in to lovin' sublime*
>
> *I don't need to put you under pressure*
> *'Cause my love, girl, is too deep to measure*
> *You know*
> *That I'm the one that's kickin' your flow*

The house lights came up along with the curtain and more screams. And there on stage looking both strong and demure was Xavier Allgood. The band kicked in and Destiny watched with keen interest as they played. Her goal was to avoid looking at Xavier, but she lost the battle with herself. She gave in to find his eyes on her. She took a deep breath and, as if on cue, he began to sing.

> *Lay your hands on me*

The women squealed with delight.

> *Lay your hands on me*
> *Heal me with hope they can't see*
> *Your love is my destiny*
> *So, lay your hands on me*

After a few moments it was obvious that Destiny was in for a concert like none other she had ever been to. She was sure, like all the other women in the crowded auditorium, that Xavier was singing directly to her.

Xavier performed like the quintessential star. He took control of the audience with their permission. When he wanted them to listen, he sang quietly and softly. And when he wanted them to party hardy, he raised the sultry power of his voice and danced like a man with an inferno in his veins.

"Go, Allgood! Go, Allgood! Go, Allgood!" The chants rang all around Destiny and Davis. Through two sets and as many changes of clothes, Xavier had taken this adoring throng through a sensual journey of mellow-smooth music and seduction. It was most definitely ladies' night.

The musicians were hot, the backup singers were in full tune, and Xavier Allgood had won the heart of every woman in the audience. After each set, he was showered with roses. And every time, he kissed the tips of his fingers, extended them toward the audience, and then touched them to his heart. It was obvious he loved performing and he loved his fans.

Destiny had not been able to take her eyes off him since the curtain rose. She watched him now after a heart-thumping rendition of his hit song "Love Now" in which he brought the entire audience out of their seats to dance.

He was glistening with sweat. A woman seated next to Destiny, who had given Xavier roses twice that evening, now offered him her handkerchief. He accepted it, dabbed at the sweat on his brow, and handed it back to her, crooning, "Thank you, baby." She replied with an immodest "Anytime," and touched the kerchief to her face.

For a moment, Destiny thought that Xavier was looking at her, but she realized that he was looking at Davis. When he winked and said over the mike, "You ready, G?" Destiny knew something was up. She looked from Davis to Xavier as Xavier motioned for the band to lower the sound of their playing.

"Take it down, y'all."

"Ooh, ooo," Xavier crooned in falsetto. *"Take it down, down, down, down-down-downnnn."*

The band began to play very softly. The tempo melted into a slow instrumental groove that had so much funk and passion women were waving their hands in the air, fanning themselves, and springing from their seats like they had been lightly touched by the Holy Ghost.

"How's everybody feeling tonight?" Xavier's sultry voice oozed through the speakers.

More screams.

"Yeah, me too." He smiled appreciatively. "I want to tell you that there are some special friends of mine here tonight—Mr. Davis Van Housen and Ms. Destiny Chandler. Y'all show 'em some love."

Davis waved a hand in the air and Destiny smiled and listened to the applause. She hoped this wasn't part of Davis's surprise. When Xavier continued, she knew that it was.

"My man Davis has been helping me with my new studio. And I'm so grateful for his help that when he asked me to sing a special song for him and his lady friend, I couldn't refuse.

"Now y'all know how much I dig old school, right?"

Many in the crowd shouted in affirmation.

"Well, me and the band are gonna kick this old-school jam. Anybody remember 'Midnight Star'?"

At that question, the fans went crazy.

"We gonna do a little summin' summin' called 'Night Rider.' Sammy Jam, come on!"

The band jumped right into the groove. And Destiny paid full attention. The rhythm was familiar and comfortable, like a favorite blanket. She looked over at Davis, who was cheesing old-school style. "Surprise!" he said.

Destiny remembered the song from their days together and wasn't sure what to think. She appreciated the thought, but still she didn't want Davis to get any ideas. Destiny heard the now-familiar voice of Xavier coming toward her from all directions.

Xavier's slow grinds and hip gyrations drove the women crazy. There were a myriad of shouts from the audience.

"You go, boy!"

"Work it, Allgood."

"All right, now."

Destiny was impressed. Xavier knew how to work a crowd. And the music was a haunting groove of drums and bass mostly with Xavier's sultry voice weaving skillfully between the beats. She had to admit, Xavier's performance was working some kind of magic on her. Just then, Davis reached out and took her hand.

She turned to him in appreciation. "Thank you, Davis, for the song, but . . ."

"Don't say anything now. Just enjoy the music. We'll talk when we get home."

Xavier's loud pronouncement brought her attention back to the stage.

"Break it down right here!"

The band stripped the song down to just the barest musical

essentials, and Xavier slipped coolly into baritone. He directed his gaze toward Destiny and Davis.

"Night rider, baby. Night . . . rider, baby." Then he directed his attention toward the audience. "Anybody out there need a night rider tonight?"

Again the women hollered "Yeah!" right on cue.

Xavier paced across the front of the stage as if he were searching for something.

"I need somebody that needs somebody," he declared.

Instantly, hundreds of arms lifted into the air. In one second, Xavier had transformed the auditorium into a mass of sculptured nails, rings, and bangles. Some women in the front row shook their hands wildly in hopes of gaining his favor.

When Xavier stepped down from the stage, the fans went berserk. He had really stirred them into a frenzy now. If it hadn't been for a small retaining gate between him and the audience, Xavier would have probably been stripped of all his clothes, ridden hard, and put away sweaty.

Destiny watched him walk toward the opposite end of the auditorium. Women screamed frantically as he moved past them. He repeated his earlier statement.

"Y'all don't hear me. I said I need somebody that needs somebody!"

This time Xavier walked directly toward Davis and Destiny. For a moment, Destiny thought he was coming for her. She unconsciously extended her hand when he came near.

He took it as smoothly as he sang, kissed the back of it, returned it to her, and continued on his search. He and Davis exchanged nods as he passed.

He stopped in front of a woman who didn't seem to be as frenzied as the others, but her eyes sparkled at the sight of him nonetheless. Destiny recognized her and her heart sank. It was Elise.

Destiny hadn't even realized she was there. Not only there, but sitting so close to where she and Davis were sitting. Davis broke his stoic silence of the evening.

"I guess he found somebody."

"I guess so," Destiny said, slightly dejected.

She had done it again—allowed her hopes to be built up and then come crashing down. Destiny had had enough of these flying and falling feelings. She watched in misery as Xavier led Elise to the stage.

When Xavier returned to the stage with Elise, there was a stool for her to sit on, and the band picked up where they left off in the middle of the "Midnight Star" classic. This time his performance was centered on Elise as he did the things to her that all the other women in the audience wanted him to do to them. He touched her softly on the cheek and looked deeply into her eyes as he sang. Deep inside, Destiny would have given anything to trade places with Elise.

Xavier's voice sent its melt-in-your-mouth tones out once more and the audience fell silent with anticipation.

Then Xavier dropped to his knees and knelt at Elise's feet. He slipped off the blue sling-back heels she was wearing and kissed each foot gently. He then picked up the microphone and whispered sensuously, "Let me take you there."

For a split second, Destiny wondered what Jacq would do if she were here. Instantly, she knew that Jacq would probably stop the show by being the first person to run up onstage the moment he said he needed somebody. Then, Destiny guessed, Jacq would launch into some suggestive dance that would have the men in the audience making the kinds of noises the women had been making since the concert began. So, in effect, there would be no Elise onstage because Jacq would have taken it over.

Xavier laid a hand on each of Elise's knees and slowly parted her legs. As his head descended into the space between her knees, the music stopped, the lights went out, and the curtain came down.

This time the women rose to their feet and offered thunderous applause. Soon there were shouts of "encore, encore," and "more, more, more." Well, Destiny had heard enough. She turned to Davis, who seemed to be quite pleased with himself, as if he had just given the performance.

"Is that it?" she asked.

"I don't think so," Davis replied. "Just hold on for a second."

Sure enough, the curtain rose to the sounds of Xavier's band firing up again. It was a long concert. They had played for nearly two hours. *This must be the last song,* Destiny thought. The curtain rose to reveal Xavier standing onstage with his white shirt open. The thick curly hairs on his chest glistened invitingly with sweat. Destiny was relieved to see that Elise was gone.

At the first six notes of Xavier's last song, the crowd whooped and hollered—Destiny and Davis included. The old-school jam was unmistakable, "I'll Be Around" by the Spinners. The band was obviously feeling the exhilaration of the end of a good show.

Xavier's voice thundered through the speakers, and he clapped his hands in rhythm above his head. "Everybody get up!" Even those who hadn't risen before stood and clapped in unison. From the rising crowd, Xavier turned his attention directly to Destiny. She could feel his hot stare burning desire in her soul. It looked as if he was going to sing directly to her.

Xavier was well into the second verse before he turned his attention to the rest of the audience, which was singing along with him. Destiny could not figure out why he would stare so intently at her while singing that song. If he was trying to make a point, it shouldn't be to accuse her. He had been the one who had decided to end their relationship before it began.

The tease, she thought. She was bumped out of her thoughts by Davis, who was jamming to the song, oblivious to her fury. "Come on, Des," she heard him say from a place that seemed far away. "Party with me." Davis chivalrously spun Destiny toward him like a man who had seen too many Oscar Micheaux movies.

Destiny, who had tired of trying to read innuendos into Xavier's music, gave in. She and Davis danced vigorously in the aisle for a lengthy and spirited version of the seventies hit.

Xavier danced like a man with fire and precision beneath his feet. He bent down to pick up one of the roses that had been thrown on the stage and placed it between his teeth. The band started the music's steady descent to the end of the show.

As Xavier bid farewell and bowed like a prince before his adoring fans, the women seated in the front row dashed up to offer him more roses and other accolades. Xavier appeared overwhelmed by the outpouring of appreciation. A boyish smile beamed across his face as he accepted the gifts and offered thank-you's muffled by the sound of his name rising from the throng.

Destiny had to admit that he had given an outstanding performance. Possibly the best concert she had ever been to, with one exception. No matter how many other concerts she went to, or how many other times she saw Xavier perform, the private concert he gave her in Sammy's church would burn in her soul forever.

Before she and Davis headed out with the masses, Destiny stole one last look at Xavier onstage. He must have been waiting for her to turn to him, because he was already looking in her direction. He and Davis exchanged half nods while Destiny could do nothing else but drink in his gorgeous presence with her eyes. And be angry with herself for doing so.

She watched him exit the stage, and waiting for him in the shadow of the curtain folds was Elise. Destiny decided she had had enough excitement for one night.

"I don't want to go to the after-party," she told Davis abruptly. "Please take me back to your place."

Davis smiled coyly at her. "Whatever you say," he replied, wrapping his arm around her shoulders and ushering her out of the auditorium.

* * *

Xavier was distracted. He had just given what might be considered the best performance of his career, and he didn't care.
All he cared about was the woman who had been sitting in
another man's arms in the front row at his concert.

He had tried to explain to his crew that he wasn't going to
be any good for the rest of the evening, but they weren't trying
to hear it. Sammy pointedly reminded him that they had signed
a contract to make an appearance at the after-party. So he went
along begrudgingly, with his escort for the evening, the pretty
and single-minded Elise Kent.

He watched her now. She blended into the atmosphere of the
ballroom quite nicely. It was a dark place, just like Elise, he
thought. The prodigious room was decorated with maroon
walls, maroon carpet, and large, ornate chandeliers that hung
from high ceilings. There were tiny running lights twinkling
around the baseboards that gave the room a Christmasy atmosphere.

Elise worked the crowd like a pro, mingling from group to
group, never staying too long, but just long enough, Xavier
suspected. He still wasn't sure why he was with her. If it was
for a distraction, he'd be better off playing a video game.

The only thing Elise had managed to do since she returned
to his life was convince him that he was madly in love with
Destiny. Xavier propped himself up more firmly on the bar
stool. He had finally managed to get some time alone. Most of
the people at the after-party were local dignitaries, people he'd
met before. They had already taken their turns congratulating
him on a great performance.

All that deep admiration embarrassed him at times. And other
times it seemed to smother him. The only clear breaths he had
taken lately were when he spent time with Destiny. For the few
times she appeared to be attracted to him, she never lost her
sense of herself. Some of the women he had met more or less
forgot their own names.

"That will never do," he said out loud, just as Elise was
returning.

3 QUICK STEPS
TO RECEIVE YOUR "THANK YOU" GIFT
FROM THE EDITOR

Send this card back and you'll receive 4 FREE Arabesque novels! The introductory shipment of 4 Arabesque novels – a $23.96 value – is yours absolutely FREE!

There's no catch. You're under no obligation to buy anything. You'll receive your introductory shipment of 4 Arabesque novels absolutely FREE (plus $1.50 to offset the costs of shipping & handling). And you don't have to make any minimum number of purchases—not even one!

We hope that after receiving your books you'll want to remain an Arabesque subscriber. But the choice is yours to continue or cancel, anytime at all! So why not take us up on our invitation to receive 4 Arabesque Romance Novels, with no risk of any kind. You'll be glad you did!

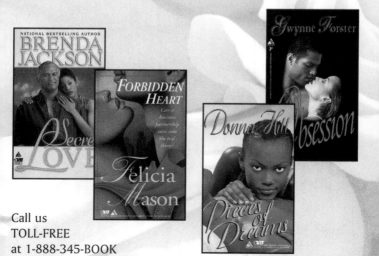

Call us
TOLL-FREE
at 1-888-345-BOOK

THE EDITOR'S "THANK YOU" GIFT INCLUDES:

- 4 books absolutely FREE (plus $1.50 for shipping and handling)
- A FREE newsletter, *Arabesque Romance News*, filled with author interviews, book previews, special offers, and more!
- No risks or obligations. You're free to cancel whenever you wish... with no questions asked.

BOOK CERTIFICATE

Yes! Please send me 4 FREE Arabesque novels (plus $1.50 for shipping & handling). I understand I am under no obligation to purchase any books, as explained on the back of this card.

Name _____

Address _____ Apt. ____

City _____ State _____ Zip _____

Telephone ( ) _____

Signature _____

Offer limited to one per household and not valid to current subscribers. All orders subject to approval. Terms, offer, & price subject to change. Offer valid only in the U.S.

AN120A

Thank you!

Accepting the four introductory books for FREE (plus $1.50 to offset the cost of shipping & handling) places you under no obligation to buy anything. You may keep the books and return the shipping statement marked "cancelled". If you do not cancel, about a month later we will send 4 additional Arabesque novels, and you will be billed the preferred subscriber's price of just $4.00 per title. That's $16.00 for all 4 books for a savings of 33% off the cover price (Plus $1.50 for shipping and handling). You may cancel at any time, but if you choose to continue, every month we'll send you 4 more books, which you may either purchase at the preferred discount price. . . or return to us and cancel your subscription.

ARABESQUE ROMANCE BOOK CLUB
P.O. Box 5214
Clifton NJ 07015-5214

PLACE
STAMP
HERE

"This party is exquisite," Elise purred like a cat being scratched behind the ears.

"Too bad we can't stay," Xavier responded, happy for the quick out.

"Why not?" Elise pouted. "People are still arriving." Elise gestured toward the entrance. "Besides, the important people are always fashionably late."

The important people indeed, Xavier thought. The most important person in the world wasn't even here. He surveyed the crowd to confirm his suspicions, and he was right. Destiny was nowhere to be found. He wondered what she and Davis were doing. He had given a specific invitation to Davis. He was trying not to imagine the worst, but it was too hard not to.

Davis had made it clear that he and Destiny were an item. The song tonight was the prelude to consummating their renewed relationship. According to Davis, he and Destiny had drawn closer together and tonight was going to be "the night." At that thought, Xavier recoiled on the bar stool.

"Are you all right?" Elise asked noncommittally.

Xavier, sensing a way out, responded quickly. "No. As a matter of fact, I'm not. I may be leaving early."

"Well," Elise said, sliding off of the bar stool, "Suit yourself. I'm sure I can find a ride."

I'm sure you can too, Xavier mused. He watched her long, pear-shaped frame sashay away. He had to admit that years ago they did have an affair like no other he had had before. She had been like a relief valve opened in him. But now, he needed much more than that. He needed nourishment, sustenance, medicine for his tired, hungry, and aching soul. He needed Destiny.

And then, like an answer to his eternal prayers, Destiny Chandler walked through the large ballroom doorway.

Nine

Everything had gone so fast, Destiny had to replay the last few minutes of the night in her head to catch up with herself here at Xavier's after-party.

She and Davis had left the concert in a hurry. She had no interest in being in the vicinity of Xavier and his *somebody that needs somebody,* Elise. Although she and Davis had made plans to attend the after-party, Destiny couldn't bear the thought. She knew that seeing Xavier with another woman would crush her.

And then it happened. The argument started. It was the first argument she and Davis had ever had. Even when he broke up with her years ago there were tears, yes, but no argument. So the experience was new and disturbing.

"I think we should go to the after-party," Davis said after driving most of the way to his condo.

Destiny stared at him. She couldn't believe what she was hearing.

"I'm sorry," she retorted.

"I think we should go to the after-party. I want to thank my boy for helping me out."

Davis was beginning to sound like a player who had just scored. Destiny was beginning to fume.

"I thought we agreed to go back to your place."

Davis drove with one hand and settled back into the white leather seat. "We did, but I changed my mind."

Now Destiny was furious. *"You* changed *your* mind? You are not the only one who deserves consideration here!"

"I'm sorry, Des." Davis's smug expression melded into a puppy-doggish plea. "I just need to say thanks, that's all. I think I owe my boy something for his effort tonight. I mean . . . he did jam."

Yes he did, Destiny reflected. Xavier had managed to *jam* up all her feelings. And now, she thought reflectively, they were colliding into this dispute with Davis. She would not allow herself to take her anger out on an innocent bystander.

"Okay," she heard herself say, "but, promise me we can leave soon after your thanksgiving."

Davis momentarily took his eyes off the road to look softly at Destiny. "I promise," he agreed. Destiny took a deep breath and released it slowly. She was silent the entire drive to the Ritz Carlton.

When they arrived, Destiny noticed that the room was filled with important-looking people. She even recognized some recording stars, Brian McKnight, Tyrese, and Toni Braxton, to name a few. She heard soft jazz playing in the background. Davis, who seemed oblivious to all the glitz and glamour, smiled, nodded, and meandered his way through the clusters of people until he led her to the guest of honor sitting alone on a bar stool.

Xavier's face lit up, and Destiny hoped against hope that it was because of her. When he and Davis exchanged high fives, her hopes were diminished. He was obviously happy to see his homeboy. Destiny remained silent during their greeting. Her mind was preoccupied with how ravishing Xavier looked. He had changed into a black silk shirt with a wide collar and matching pants. His arm and thigh muscles undulated beneath the soft material and made Destiny lick her lips.

Although he and Davis were well engaged in conversation, Destiny would swear that even though Xavier's eyes were looking at Davis, he was watching her.

"What are you drinking?" Xavier asked, signaling a server with a tray of champagne glasses filled to their brims.

"I don't know. What's in your glass?" Davis gestured toward the snifter beside Xavier.

"Orange juice and 7-Up," Xavier replied.

"Oh, I need something stronger than that. I'm celebrating." Davis took two champagne glasses from the tray and offered one to Destiny, who refused it. Ever since Rico's alcoholic episodes, she had promised herself that alcohol was out of her life for good.

"Aw, come on, Des. Have a drink with me."

"I'll have what he's having," Destiny responded, pointing to Xavier's juice-and-pop concoction.

Xavier smiled at the server, who had been gazing at him with goo-goo eyes the entire time she was in their presence. "Tasha, bring Ms. Chandler one of my special drinks."

Tasha winked at Xavier and crooned in sultry response, "Anything you say, Zay." She swished away in her black-and-white French maid's outfit. Destiny felt jealousy rearing its ugly head within her. And before she could prevent it, her feelings came abruptly out of her mouth.

"Damn," she snapped.

Davis and Xavier turned their attention from Tasha's walk-away to her.

"What?" Davis asked, dumbfounded. Xavier stood at his side looking slightly amused.

Destiny searched her mind for an honest response that wouldn't give away her jealousy.

"It's just terrible the way some women will throw themselves at men."

Davis laughed and patted Xavier on the back. "Zay gets that all the time. I'm sure he's used to it by now."

Xavier's expression changed from amused to more serious. "The day I get used to *that* is the day I should quit. It means I've developed some kind of callousness, that my feelings and connection to others have scabbed over. I've seen how taking your success for granted changes people, and it's repulsive. When that happens, you're dead, man. You're no longer part of the universe. I hope that *never* happens to me."

There he goes again, Destiny thought. *Saying things to make me fall for him.* Destiny reluctantly realized that whatever magic Xavier had was working on her like a mighty mojo—a super spell that could neither be erased nor recanted. She wondered if she would ever get over this man who had so shrewdly swept her heart into his hands. Maybe she did need a real drink after all.

"Davis, what are you going to do with that extra champagne?" Destiny asked, realizing that Davis had kept the drink he retrieved for her.

"He's going to give it to me," a female voice responded from behind her.

Destiny didn't need to look, but she did. And there, standing at least six feet to Destiny's five feet seven inches, was Elise. She was a vision in a short, cobalt-blue tux-dress that accentuated her creamed-coffee complexion. Her short hair was bone-straight and bounced when she did, which seemed to be all the time. Davis appeared more than impressed.

"Davis Van Housen, this is Elise Kent." Xavier's introduction sounded short and curt. The two shook hands. "And I believe you two have met." Xavier motioned from woman to woman. The two eyed each other sharply and then the piercing expression on Elise's face faded into a cloud of nothingness. "I don't believe we have," Elise said, extending her hand.

"Sure we have," Destiny said while taking the extra drink from Davis instead of shaking Elise's hand. *If this vixen wants to start something,* Destiny thought as thunderclouds of anger rumbled through her brain, *then I will damn well finish it.* Destiny took a long, slow sip of the champagne. "We met in Sammy Jam's church, remember? Xavier introduced us then."

Tasha returned with Xavier's special punch and more champagne. She looked from woman to woman and could readily sense what the men could not. Xavier took the special punch, and Elise took a glass of champagne. Tasha swished away and the women heard her faint sound of "Ummm" as she offered champagne to some new arrivals.

Elise took a sip of her champagne. "Oh, that's right," Elise conceded. "Now . . . what was it you two were doing in that church?"

"Nothing!" Xavier and Destiny replied in unison. Then Xavier spoke up. "Actually, we were delivering programs to Sammy's wife."

Destiny felt compelled to respond. "Yes, and then Xavier, uh, Zay, was kind enough to give me a tour."

"Really?" Elise responded, pushing the issue. "I could have sworn that I heard music when I pulled up." Destiny gulped down the rest of her champagne. Apparently this woman was determined to get under her skin. Tasha, who had been standing close by, came back with her serving tray. She took Destiny's empty glass and offered her another. Destiny accepted and readied herself for the imminent verbal battle. Davis took another glass of champagne from the tray before Tasha could saunter away, her short miniskirt going *swish-swish* behind her.

Destiny squared her shoulders. "The music—" she began, then was interrupted by Davis, who had already downed his second glass of champagne.

"The music was probably my man Zay on the or-gan. He probably wanted to show off," he offered, slinging an arm around Destiny's shoulders.

"Look, I was singing, but it was no big deal. Besides, this is a party. You people are bringing me down." Xavier looked from person to person in this little entourage, perplexed.

Destiny thought it was a good time to remind Davis of their earlier conversation.

"Davis, do you remember what you promised me?"

Xavier looked at Destiny, intrigued, and then turned his attention to Elise. "Elise, do you remember what you promised *me?*" Elise finished her drink.

"Yes, I remember." She slunk up to Xavier and gave him a

quick kiss on the mouth. Then she turned and walked toward the thinning crowd. "And I always keep my promises."

Davis trotted off after Elise. "I may have to break mine," he shot back. "I won't be long. I just want to meet some people." Before Destiny could respond, Davis had disappeared within the group of people mixing and mingling.

Xavier sat down, drink in hand. "I'm not sure what just happened here, but I know it was weird."

Destiny released a chuckle and sat down beside him. She could feel the warmth of his body radiating between them. She wanted so very badly to reach out and stroke his arm. Just to caress the muscles she had fixated on since she arrived would be a small piece of heaven.

And then she remembered that Xavier was with Elise, and worked quickly to divert her mind from thoughts of her and Xavier together.

"Thank you for the song tonight. You really are very talented."

If Destiny hadn't thought any better of it she would have believed that Xavier was self-conscious about her remark. His smile was childlike. "Thank you," he said, staring purposefully into her eyes.

"Davis is good people," he continued. "He deserves the best. Not that I'm speaking of my performance."

"Oh? What then?" Destiny asked eagerly.

"Zay!" A large man in a gray, three-piece suit shouted from across the room.

"Uh-oh," Xavier said under his breath as the man approached with wide arms. Xavier rose from his seat and the two embraced for what seemed like an eternity. The large man tossed Xavier back and forth. "My, my, my, it has been a while since I've seen you." He finally let go of Xavier and stepped back.

"And who is this beauty queen?" the man asked, moving closer to Destiny.

"This is Destiny Chandler."

"Destiny!" the man responded and enveloped Destiny in his

bulky arms. As he swooshed Destiny back and forth, Xavier finished the introduction. "Destiny, you are hugging Marvis Quatelbaum. He is head of the board of directors for my record label."

Marvis released Destiny and smiled brightly. "Nice to meet you Mr. Qua . . . uh—"

"Quatelbaum," he finished. "Do you like that name?" He grabbed a glass of champagne from Tasha's tray as she walked by. Destiny took another also. She wondered where Davis had gone off to.

"It sort of rolls right off the tongue once you get used to it," Marvis added, flashing a gold tooth. Xavier looked as though he were in pain. Marvis kept right on talking. "See, listen. Qua-tel-baum, Qua-tel-baum. Do you like that name, Ms. Chandler?"

Now how am I supposed to answer this? Destiny wondered. "It's a fine name, uh, Marvis."

Marvis moved closer to Destiny until his potbelly was practically touching her stomach. "If you like it so much, it can be yours if you marry me." Marvis's eyes sparkled with mischief.

Xavier quickly intervened. He put his arm around Marvis's wide shoulders. "You know, Marvis, I think I might know someone who would love to meet you." Xavier slowly turned Marvis away from Destiny and toward the crowd of people.

"Someone who wants to meet *me?*"

"Most definitely. Her name is Elise and she's gorgeous!"

Then Xavier whispered in Marvis's ear what sounded to Destiny like, "And she's some kinda lover, if you know what I mean." Marvis let out a deep, rolling laugh that made him sound like a mad scientist.

"And she wants to meet *me?*"

"I'm tellin' you, man, the way she's wearin' this deep blue dress tonight will make your toes curl."

By the time Xavier had finished his description of Elise and sent Marvis Quatelbaum to find her, Destiny had downed her fifth glass of champagne and was working on a sixth. She didn't ordinarily drink this much, but what the hell, she thought. To-night she was determined to enjoy herself, despite Xavier's date or his descriptions of her.

"S-so," she said, surprised by the slur in her voice. "Are you into the swapping thing?"

Xavier turned to Destiny with a curious look on his face. "What are you talking about?"

"Date s-swapping," Destiny slurred again. "Aren't you send-ing Qua-to, Qut-o, Qu—"

"Quatelbaum?"

"Uh-huh. Aren't you sending him after your girlfriend?"

Xavier smiled. "I don't have a girlfriend, Destiny."

Destiny smiled back. She was elated. That was the best news she had heard since the judge's verdict at Rico's trial. "Really!" she said, much louder than she intended. Suddenly, Destiny felt as if the floor were tilting beneath her, and she tumbled into Xavier. She felt his strong arms close around her and she decided she liked his arms much better than she liked Quatelbo's—or whatever his name was.

The smells of breakfast crept into Destiny's slumber and gen-tly awakened her. She turned to pull the covers more snugly around herself when she realized she didn't recognize her sur-roundings. Then a familiar voice calmed her.

"I thought I heard you stirring." Xavier's deep voice caressed her.

She was still groggy, still coming to. "I must be dreaming," she said aloud. She had had this dream many times since coming to Atlanta. Waking up in Xavier's bed was becoming an unshak-able scene in her nighttime fantasies.

Xavier laughed heartily, his deep, coarse voice chopping the air. "Wait until the headache sets in. Then you won't think it's a dream." He leaned up against the bedroom wall and watched her.

"What?" Destiny said, sitting up. When the covers fell from

her shoulders, she noticed that all she was wearing was her white laced camisole. She quickly looked up at Xavier, who was smiling intensely. Destiny gasped and covered herself with the sheet and blanket that had collected around her waist. That's when the pounding started.

"Oh my God," Deatiny moaned. She weakly cradled her head in one hand while holding on to the covers with the other.

"I thought so," Xavier said softly. He walked over to her and sat down on the edge of his king-size bed. "I figured you might need this." He held out his hands and offered her a pain reliever and a glass of water.

Destiny was careful to move slowly. She could tell that any sudden movement would cause the excruciating pain in her head to worsen. She took his kind offering and eased herself back down on the bed.

"Oh my God," she repeated. "What happened? And where's Davis?" Destiny thought she saw the slight smile on Xavier's face waver at the mention of Davis's name, but she was in too much pain to be sure.

"I'm not sure, actually," Xavier answered, rising easily from the side of the bed. "The last I saw of him, he and Elise were . . . well . . ." Destiny turned her head away and winced. Just the sound of the woman's name was enough to increase the throbbing in her skull.

Xavier noticed her obvious discomfort. "I think the best thing for you is to get something in your stomach. Let me bring you some breakfast."

Destiny groaned. "I don't think I can eat."

"What!" Xavier retorted, feigning insult. "No one refuses Zay's cooking." Destiny turned her head slightly. She could see Xavier backing out of the doorway.

"Just one taste," he said, rubbing his right thumb and index finger together, "and you'll be hooked for life." He retreated into the hallway and Destiny managed to smile without experiencing too much pain.

Destiny struggled desperately to remember how she had

ended up in Xavier's bed. The harder she tried to think, the more acute was the ache in her head, and now the rest of her body was beginning to join in the chorus of agony. She rubbed her temples as the reality of her situation sank in. She was in All-good's bed!

She sat up painfully and looked down at herself. She wondered if she and Xavier had been intimate. *Surely I would remember that,* she thought. She finished the water Xavier had left on the nightstand and turned to see him entering the bedroom with a tray of food.

He presented her with a large glass of cranberry juice, an English muffin, and a plate heaping with apples, grapes, and four medium-size sausage patties. Destiny smiled in appreciation. "At your service, Ms. Destiny," he said, setting the tray in front of her.

Destiny righted herself in the bed. She was going to attempt to cover her scantily clad body with the sheet, but it was obvious that Xavier had seen more than her cleavage and bare arms. Instead she took the napkin from the tray and placed it across her lap.

"Oh, I almost forgot." Xavier dashed out of the room and returned a few seconds later with a long-stemmed rose set in a crystal vase. He placed it on the tray and stepped away.

"Aren't you going to eat?" she asked, fork in hand.

"No. I'm not hungry." Xavier turned to go, and Destiny's heart sank. Before she could think better of it, she spoke her thoughts.

"Don't go, please. Stay with me." Xavier turned to her with an inquisitive look settling on his face. Destiny tried to find a way to justify her request. "I'm still foggy about what happened last night." Destiny speared a few grapes with her fork. "Can you fill in the blanks for me?"

She ate the grapes and apples while Xavier helped to clear the foggy memories in her head. He sat down in an oversize chair by the bed to reveal what happened. It seemed that she had had too much champagne last night. And Davis, for some reason, was nowhere to be found. So Xavier brought her back to his place. He didn't think she should be left alone considering her condition.

Destiny looked down at her attire once more, then up at Xavier with a question on her face. She couldn't bear to ask, but she needed to know. Xavier seemed to sense what she was thinking. "I know how to ask for what I want," he said, reassuring her. "And I won't take it if it's not given freely or coherently." Destiny breathed a sigh of relief and finished off her fruit.

Xavier watched her attentively. "You haven't touched your sausage," he commented.

"I know. I'm sorry, I don't eat red meat," Destiny responded.

"Neither do I. It's a special blend I make of turkey and tofu."

"Oh," Destiny said, smiling. She had already started to feel better. "Then look out!" she said, tearing into the patties.

Xavier laughed. "I hoped the food would make you feel better." Destiny relished the sausage, thinking that what was really making her feel better was being near Xavier. It took her breath away to think that the man sitting beside her, who had just cooked her breakfast, was the same man who was onstage the night before singing soul-stirring songs to hundreds of fans. Jacq would have a field day with this one.

And now Destiny was sitting half-naked in the bedroom of the man she had been lusting after for days. Hangover or not, if she didn't make a move now, Jacq would never forgive her. But more importantly, she would never forgive herself.

For years, Destiny had let Rico run her life. He had made all the major decisions and kept her away from all the things that made her happy. He prevented her from taking chances and stopped her from being impulsive. He had stolen her spontaneity. Well, she had a lot of catching up to do. And maybe she could start with a fling with Xavier. Besides, whatever Elise and Davis were doing, it sounded like they were doing it together. *So,* Destiny thought, *it's now or never.*

She finished the last of the sausage and handed the tray to Xavier. "That was wonderful. Thank you so much," she said.

"May I trouble you for just one more thing?" Destiny swung the covers back to expose her long mahogany legs. "Could you get me some towels," she said, sliding stealthily to the edge of the bed. "I'd like to take a shower."

Xavier stood silent for a moment. He looked as though he were consuming her with his eyes. "Your wish is my command," he said, and exited the bedroom.

Destiny stood at the side of the bed. She was a little wobbly but none the worse for wear. She glanced around the bedroom, noticing its intimate décor for the first time.

The bedroom was even more magnificent than her mind had imagined. The décor was rustic and unassuming. There were testaments to his love of music and culture everywhere.

There were percussion instruments placed strategically in the four corners of the room. On the walls hung handwoven tapestries in obsidian, bayberry, and cinnabar tones. His furniture was fashioned out of an aged teakwood with deep yellow hues in the grain. Where Davis's surroundings spoke of opulence and spectacle, Xavier's tastes felt like home.

By far the most prominent piece in the room was a large aluminum crossbow fastened to the wall above the bed like a magnificent headboard. There was a set of arrows crossed in an X formation on the adjacent wall.

When she heard Xavier's humming, she stopped her perusal, suddenly self-conscious of herself in nothing but a camisole. She didn't have time to dash back onto the bed and cover herself before he entered the room. She stood looking at him, hoping he liked what he saw. He came toward her, towels in hand.

"What are you humming?" she asked.

" 'You Are So Beautiful'," he answered, handing over the towels.

"I know," she quipped. "But what are you humming?"

Xavier took one more step and closed the distance between them. He ran his hand through the sisterlocks that outlined Destiny's face. She could feel the need inside her rising like red-hot lava. At just the mere touch of his hand, she felt the impending eruption and welcomed it.

"Destiny Chandler," Xavier said in low, murmured tones, "if you don't get into the shower right now, I may change my policy of always asking first."

Destiny couldn't move. She was riveted to the spot by the nearness of him. She looked up into his face with eyes she knew were silently pleading with him to take her now, before she went crazy with desire.

Xavier raised his arm and Destiny closed her eyes. But instead of feeling his embrace, she heard, "The bathroom is through there." Destiny opened her eyes to see him pointing toward a doorway at back of the bedroom. "I'll be downstairs. Your gown is in the closet. When you're ready, I'll take you to Davis's." With that, Xavier turned on his heel and marched out, leaving Destiny standing in the middle of the room forlorn, confused, and randy.

Xavier tried unsuccessfully to focus on clearing the breakfast dishes. He scraped the plates and skillet, then mindlessly set them in the dishwasher. When he heard the sound of running water coming from upstairs he could barely contain himself.

Right here, in his house, was the woman of his dreams. Not only that, but the thought of her naked in his shower was more than he could bear. The gentleman in him was rapidly losing the battle to the passion-consumed man who wanted, craved, absolutely had to have this woman.

Xavier turned on the dishwasher and thought about the promise he made to himself to remember that Destiny was off-limits. But after Davis's behavior last night, it was obvious that he and Destiny weren't the couple Xavier thought they were.

As the water in the dishwasher turned on full blast, so did Xavier's appetite for Destiny. Before he realized what was happening, Xavier was headed back upstairs and into his bedroom.

Once there, he removed his clothes like a man possessed. His muscles bulged in anticipation.

Xavier walked into the bathroom and for the first time regretted the size of the large room. The walk to the shower seemed to take an eternity. Before sliding open the beveled glass shower door, Xavier swallowed hard, put on a condom, and prayed he was doing the right thing. For it seemed his will was no longer his own. Some other force was driving him, a force unlike any he had felt before. And it was this he wanted to share with Destiny, a longing so deep and urgent that he couldn't tell where he ended and Destiny began. Xavier took a deep breath and slid open the shower door.

He heard a slight gasp escape from her lips and then she fell silent and didn't move. He watched the hot water strike her skin and ripple into currents down her body. Xavier wanted desperately to know her body like the water did. To flow over her on seen and unseen places. After taking in all the wondrous curves of her body, he looked deeply into her eyes. She appeared startled, but she made no move to resist him. Instead she stepped backward as he entered the shower.

He knew he had to take her slowly. The sadness he had seen well up in her eyes sometimes could not be shoved aside. It had to be gently pushed and coaxed until there was nothing left but faint whispers of a memory. He traced the patterns of the water on her skin—first with his hands, then with his lips, and finally his tongue. He heard faint moans escape from her lips and knew this was only the beginning of the pleasure he wanted to bring her.

He wanted her body to sing, to become a song and take them both to ecstasy on a crescendo of rising rapture. He felt her hands caress his arms, his back, his thighs. He had no choice but to reciprocate. Then, in one fluid motion, he scooped her up and turned her toward the water. Destiny tilted her head back and let the moisture surge down her neck and shoulders where Xavier's mouth was ready and waiting.

He pulled her closer, willing himself to hold on, and kissed her mouth wildly, then softer and softer. He felt Destiny's body go limp in his arms. At that he lifted her to him and entered her in one deliberate motion. Their deep moans broke the silence between them. For a moment, they remained perfectly still and gazed into each other's eyes.

Then Xavier felt the slow, soft undulations of Destiny's hips and matched her rhythm. Soon Xavier found himself lost, swept into a torrent of passion. All he could see was her. All he could touch, smell, taste, was Destiny. And as he let the rhythm of their lovemaking take him away, he realized she was all he would ever need.

He kissed and caressed every inch of her body—worshiped it. He made sure that every space on her body had been loved and loved some more. Before long, both their breathing quickened and the sounds of their enjoyment rose above the sound of the water. Xavier could feel Destiny's desire seeping into him. He felt her cling tighter to him and watched as two small tears pierced the veil of water on her face. Suddenly, he could hold back no longer. Everything he had wanted since the night he saw her singing on the staircase culminated in this moment of exchange. He felt his release and hers shatter throughout his body.

She buried her head in his chest, and he felt her gentle sobs. He held her tightly until her tears subsided. When she finally looked up at him, he kissed her intensely and knew that nothing in the world, not even Davis, would keep him from loving Destiny Chandler.

Ten

When Xavier Allgood was a small boy, Samuel "Sammy Jam" Webb stepped in and tried to fill his father's shoes after his death. Although Zay liked sports, he tended to be a loner and kept to himself. So Sammy introduced the boy to music—something he could do alone, but which also could be shared with others.

Sammy purchased a drum set and a small keyboard for the boy, and encouraged him to learn how to play the guitar his real father had given him. It had been in his family for four generations.

Being Pearson Allgood's closest friend for twenty years, Sammy knew that it was the only possession Pearson's great-grandfather Otis owned after slavery. The guitar had been passed down from father to son from then on. Since Zay had been the only son in his family, the heirloom had been passed to him.

The sky blue, handmade instrument was worn, nicked, and faded. It had played its share of happy harmonies, merry melodies, and sad songs. But the tune being played on it now had to be the saddest ever. Sammy went about his duties of cleaning up the church basement—one large expanse of room with a low ceiling and large black-and-white linoleum tiles on the floor. Tidying up was an old habit he hadn't seemed to break no matter how much the parishioners fussed. He listened attentively to

Zay's solemn playing and set about the best way to help the man with his problem.

"That song have any words, son?"

Xavier looked up from the strings, yet continued his somber strumming. The discordant notes weren't quite a funeral march, but they sounded awfully close. Too close for Sammy.

"Nope," Xavier replied, and returned his gaze to his fingers working steadily up and down the strings. The sounds were distant and hollow. Sammy was more than a little concerned.

The church had hosted a fund-raising luncheon earlier that day. Sammy gathered up the unused paper goods and utensils and put them in a large white cupboard. Then he began gathering the trash into large, clear garbage bags.

"Does it have a name?"

"What?" Xavier sounded off, slightly irritated.

Sammy continued his cleaning. "Your song. What's it called?"

"It's not called anything," Xavier insisted.

"Why not?" Sammy persisted, tying up the first garbage bag.

Xavier stopped his playing and stared at the older gentleman. Sammy continued cleaning and didn't look up.

"Because I'm just messin' with the music. Can't I just play?"

"Not with *that* guitar you can't," Sammy responded, picking up the garbage bag and carrying it over to the side door.

Xavier rested the guitar in his lap and looked at Sammy questioningly. "I've had this guitar since I was a kid. I almost broke it twice." Then Xavier smiled nostalgically. "I wrote my first top ten on her," he said, patting the belly of the instrument. "Now you gonna tell me that I can't just strum on it for the heck of it."

Sammy tied the second full garbage bag. "That's right."

Xavier shook his head. "Why the sudden change?"

"No change," Sammy answered. "It's always been that way." Sammy placed the second garbage bag beside the first. Then he reached over to where a push broom was propped against the wall. He swept the floor with a practiced arm.

"That guitar is the oldest member of your family. She was with you before you all had last names. She's helped put food on the table when your dad didn't think y'all would eat. She's been a pillow on dirt ground, and she's played a baptismal hymn when she was the only instrument this church had."

Xavier shifted on the edge of the table where he was sitting. "I know all the stories, Sammy."

Sammy stopped sweeping and looked at the man he had helped raise. He saw an unnecessary sadness lurking in his eyes. *It's a shame how he punishes himself,* Sammy thought.

"You know all the stories, huh? You don't act like it."

Suddenly, Xavier was up and on his feet. "Man, I came here to get quiet."

"You need to get smart," Sammy snapped.

"What are you talking about?"

"That guitar is the most valuable thing in your life, and you don't know how to treat it. You don't *play* with it, son. Not *that* guitar. It's all or nothing. You come to it, straight on. You don't hem and haw and pick and pluck. It deserves better."

Xavier took a deep breath and sat back down. Sammy returned to his sweeping. "Just like that little girl."

"What?" Xavier asked, surprised.

"Don't 'what' me. I ain't stupid." Sammy reached the far side of the church basement with his sweeping. He knew Xavier so well. This next question would tell the tale.

"Did you two . . . ?" Sammy let his voice trail off.

Xavier lowered his head but did not lie. "Yes."

It was as Sammy suspected. "You know I don't approve of premarital sex."

"I know, I know," Xavier admitted.

Sammy swept closer to where Xavier was sitting. "Felt the earth move, didn't you, son?"

Xavier raised his head and smiled like a cherub. "Like I was born again."

That's all Sammy needed to hear. "That little girl loves you."

"How can you be so sure?"

Sammy stopped sweeping again. "I've been married almost as many years as you've been alive. I think I know a little somethin' 'bout love."

Xavier laughed. And then his face was serious once again. "It's so hard, Sammy. Some of the women I've been with . . ."

"I know. I've met them."

"And I don't even want to replay the Elise vibe."

"Thank you, Lord."

Both men spied each other and then laughed. Sammy finished sweeping and sat down next to Xavier. "I got a feelin' you are about to add something more precious than that guitar to your life. And while you're sittin' here like a sad sack pickin' at this old guitar, can't you see, you're pickin' at her too. A woman is nothing to play with, son, especially that kind."

A spark of understanding lit up Xavier's face.

"So what are you telling me, old man?"

"And you, my son Solomon, acknowledge the God of your father, and serve him with wholehearted devotion and with a willing mind, for the Lord searches every heart and understands every motive behind the thoughts. If you seek him, he will be found by you; but if you forsake him, he will reject you forever. First Chronicles, chapter 28, verse 9," Sammy said, leaning on the broom. "If that woman is all you've ever wanted, then act like it. Don't stutter and pause before you get started. Jump into it full tilt."

"Just like that?"

Sammy looked over at Xavier Allgood, one of God's most precious gifts to him, and said, "Just like that."

"Des! Is that you? Girl, say something before I come down there to kick ass and ask questions later."

Destiny tried hard to compose herself. While dialing Jacq's number, she promised herself that she wouldn't cry. But something about hearing her friend's voice and knowing she was so far away had caused the dam to burst. Destiny's body shook with sobs.

"All right, that's it, damn it. I'm coming down there," Jacq's voice bellowed with conviction through the receiver. Destiny struggled with the demons willing her to cry, and won.

"No, Jacq . . . You don't . . . need to come down." Destiny took a deep breath and wiped the tears from her face. "I'm sorry," she said, starting to calm down. "I just lost it for a second."

"Girl, what's wrong?"

Just like before, Destiny wasn't quite sure how to tell her friend what had happened since they had last spoken.

"I love him, Jacq."

"Wow," Jacq responded. "So it's Destiny and Davis together again, huh? But girlfriend, those don't sound like tears of joy."

Destiny felt the tears welling up again and forced them back down. "It's . . . Allgood. I'm in love with him, damn it."

"Uh-oh," Jacq replied. "Des, I thought I taught you better than that. Never, ever fall in love. Especially with someone like Allgood."

For the first time, Jacq's unique perspective on matters of love made sense to Destiny. If she had just managed to keep her feelings detached, she wouldn't be in this mess. Destiny knew she was in for a scolding.

"Hit it and forget it, remember? And now we talkin' show business. That means he goes through women like Jerry Springer goes through wack guests."

"I know, I know. But he really doesn't seem like the type—"

Jacq interrupted. "They never do. Damn, Des. How did this happen?"

Destiny remained silent.

"No, don't tell me, let me guess. You gave him some and it was so good, you cried like a baby."

One solitary tear broke through Destiny's resolve and rolled down her cheek. "Jacq . . ."

"Uh-huh. That's what I thought. Look, Stella, it takes more than a good lay to get your groove back."

Destiny wept silently into the phone and couldn't respond. She heard Jacq take a deep breath on the other end.

"Look, Des," Jacq said softly. "Maybe the brotha cares about you."

Destiny perked up at that thought. "You think so," she muttered between sniffles.

"Well, there's only one way to find out."

"What's that?"

"Treat him like dirt."

"What!"

"Well . . . not that bad. But don't let him know that he got to you. Play it cool like they always do."

"What good will that do?"

"If you were just another conquest to him, then he won't have the satisfaction of seeing you hurt."

"But what if he cares about me?"

"If he cares about you, then he'll want you even more 'cause you ain't sweatin' him."

"Really?"

"Of course. You know how guys love a good chase."

Destiny wasn't so sure about Jacq's reasoning, but at this point, she was willing to try anything. "Okay," she agreed.

"Cool," Jacq replied. "When do you see him again?"

"Tomorrow. We're working on more ideas for the photo shoot."

"Then call me tomorrow night and let me know how it goes."

"Okay," Destiny said, not sure if she felt better or worse.

When she hung up the phone, Destiny made a promise to herself. She would put up a wall between herself and Xavier. After what she had experienced with Rico, she couldn't afford to be hurt again.

Davis walked out of the hotel quite pleased with himself. He checked his watch as he gave the valet the ticket for his car. Ten A.M. *Damn, I'm good,* he thought smugly. When the valet drove his car to the front of the hotel, Davis reached in his wallet, pulled out a twenty, and handed it to the young man. The young man was delighted. "Thank you, sir." He beamed.

"It's all right," Davis offered, getting into the car. He sped off toward home with a beaming smile of his own.

"That Elise is something else," he commented to himself. "Yep," he said, pushing the on button on his CD player and turning it up loud. He rocked his head back and forth to Prodigy's "Breathe." "I owe her one for this."

Davis thought he was the greatest corporate schmoozer in the world, but he had met his match last night. Elise had taught him some new tricks, like how to pretend you know all there is to know about someone while at the same time getting them to tell you exactly what you need to know. He had to admit that he didn't have the anatomy to obtain some of Elise's other networking inroads. The way she managed to show just a little more thigh or throw back her head and laugh at just the right time was a woman's advantage. But mingling through the crowded party with her had shown him more business tactics than he ever imagined acquiring in one evening. And now, with three brand-new accounts, he might have to hire an assistant just to keep up with the workload.

It was so simple, Davis thought, turning on to the interstate. And it went smoother than any business transaction he had ever made before. Certainly the liquor and Elise's physique had warmed them up, but he had sealed the deals. All because he had a hunch about Elise as soon as he saw her. When she wandered away from Xavier, he had to follow her. Something in her eyes said "come with me," and he went.

Elise maneuvered herself through the groups of famous and infamous like a pro. Wherever she stopped to talk, she was the center of attention. She only paused long enough to determine if those within earshot had anything to offer her. If they didn't, she skillfully moved on. Davis hadn't seen anyone as smooth as Elise in a long time.

"What's your game?" he finally asked.

Elise smiled elegantly and took another glass of champagne from Tasha, who just happened to be passing by. "Manhunt."

"I thought you and Zay—"

Elise wasted no time in interrupting. "Everybody does. A man is more likely to approach a woman if he thinks she's unavailable."

Davis laughed incredulously. "You've got to be kidding."

Elise took a sip from her glass and watched carefully as a short, plump man in a gray three-piece suit walked by. "I'm very serious."

Davis was flabbergasted. "You've got to be the most gorgeous woman *in here*. And your body is slammin'." Davis took careful inventory. "You must have men standing in line."

Elise finished her glass of champagne. "I'm looking for a certain *kind* of man."

Davis shook his head. "All women are. The problem is," Davis said, feeling warm from the champagne, "there are only ten of those certain kind of men on the planet. And all of you are fighting for the same ten men." Davis laughed at his own wit.

Elise, who didn't seem to be paying too close attention, had her eye trained on another group of people and walked in their direction. "I want to be taken care of—*well* taken care of," she admonished.

Throughout the course of the evening, Elise managed to locate every wealthy man in attendance and interview him for the position of her caretaker seemingly without his knowledge. In the process, Davis made invaluable contacts in the business world. He even persuaded four of his new contacts to meet that evening in one of the hotel rooms so he could pitch the services of his business. Davis left Elise, who seemed quite content in the company of a round man with a gold tooth.

When the men had assembled in the room, Davis took out his handheld computer, which always contained notes on his marketing strategy, and proceeded to make the biggest business pitch in his career as a consultant. By the time he finished, three of the businessmen were ready to sign on the dotted line, and the other one agreed to give him a call back within the week.

Unfortunately, it had taken all night and a good portion of the morning to download contracts from his minicomputer and answer all the businessmen's questions. Davis had lost all track of time and unfortunately he had lost all thought of Destiny. His tendency toward single-mindedness had gotten the best of him again.

When he emerged from his marathon meeting, the after-party had long since broken up. Davis felt terrible but knew that somehow, with all those do-gooders at the party, Destiny must have made it home safely. He checked with the front desk just to see if she had left a message for him. There was a message, but not from Destiny. The message was from Xavier:

> Davis,
> Destiny is zooted. Too much champagne.
> I'm taking her home.
> Zay.

Davis was somewhat disappointed concerning the events of the night. The tête-à-tête he wanted to have with Destiny didn't occur as planned. At the same time, he felt exuberant about his three new clients. With their accounts he could easily clear a quarter of a million dollars in revenue.

Just like always, Davis thought as he pulled into his driveway, *everything works out in the end.* Davis got out of the car and walked gingerly toward his front door. "When we finally do make that move," Davis said to himself confidently, "Destiny will be getting it on with a million-dollar man!"

The noise never stopped. Even at night, when any sane person would want to retreat into sleep, the sounds of controlled chaos surrounded him. Shouts, roars, screams, curses, banging, and nonsensical babbling went on incessantly. All manner of human utterances pierced the dark and entered Rico's eight-foot by ten-foot cell. Everything except crying. Crying meant death, or much worse.

Wimps . . . punks, Rico thought. "I will never, ever moan and howl like these imbeciles." Rico turned over on his back and looked up at the bunk bed above him. "Hey," he said, hitting the mattress on the top bunk with his fists. "I'm talking to you!"

"Yeah," a groggy voice returned.

"How can you sleep through this bedlam?"

"Through what?"

"Never mind," Rico responded, exasperated. Of all the inmates he could have been paired with, he had to get one who was the human equivalent of Scooby-Dumb. "Man, your name should be doofus, not Rufus."

"Man, *what?*"

"Nothing. Go back to sleep." Rico turned on his side, away from the cell-block noise. But the sounds could not be cut off. Rico replayed the events of his day to shift his mind from the pandemonium bombarding his senses . . .

The day had started out like all the rest since he had been on lockdown—officers screaming for everyone to wake up, the hard, rolling sound of metal doors sliding open, and the drone of male voices rising into a melee of discontent.

Boredom was too weak a word to describe the tedium of being in prison. Even the surprise search was an uneventful distraction. Rico watched impassively as twenty-five huge officers began their ritual shakedown. First, they conducted a thorough search of the inmates' personal property: books, clothes, and magazines. And then they began the degrading business of body searching everyone. At first, Rico found the whole process to be demeaning and horrific. But now, Rico was numb to it all.

And why shouldn't he be? Soon he was going to be transferred to the Hastings Correctional Facility. Apparently, the overcrowding was too much of a risk for the officers, so non-violent prisoners were getting relocated. Suddenly, nothing the system could do to him mattered.

And nothing the other inmates did mattered to Rico either. He surveyed the day room where most of the inmates gathered to watch *Ricki Lake*. Rico almost laughed out loud when for the first time he realized what a bunch of caricatures they all were. Cool Tony was the Billy Dee Williams of the group. He was stupid enough to think that he actually looked good in the state-issued orange jumpsuit. Neck Bone was a tall, thin throwback from the seventies with an Afro and overgrown sideburns. All he was missing, Rico mused, was platform shoes.

Nag shaped his criminal character from every prison movie he had ever seen. No one knew how many people he had killed, but Nag was always eager to increase the body count by one. And then there was Randall, the quintessential Don Knotts. Randall was down with everybody and constantly bit his nails. Rico's psychiatric training told him they were all malcontents suffering from bipolar disorder whose only salvation would be found in a prescription for megadoses of Prozac.

Rico moved through the day like a phantom. He hardly spoke to anyone. Instead, his mind fixated on his upcoming transfer and the process of going from one facility to the next. It was dinnertime before he allowed himself to be social.

"Rat!" he said, carrying his tray of beef stew, rice, bread, and Kool-Aid to a table. "Come here, man!"

True to his name, Rat was a small man with beady eyes and a nose that twitched uncontrollably most of the time. He took a seat next to Rico and several others.

"What chew wan', man?" Rat said with a mouthful of stew.

"What can you tell me about this transfer?"

Rat shoved a piece of bread into his tiny mouth. Rico was repulsed, but needed information. He waited patiently for the rodent-looking man to speak.

"I know wha chew know. They takin' some a y'all to Hastings."

Rico pushed his tray away. He was too wound up to eat. And watching Rat eat was enough to diminish anyone's appetite. He turned slightly so he wouldn't have such a clear view of Rat's gorging.

"Tell me about the process. *How* does the transfer occur?"

"What chew wan' know that for?"

Most of what was said in the Nebraska State Penitentiary was a lie, but there was one truth: Rat was the smartest brother on lockdown. He knew everything. Rumor had it that Rat had escaped several times and actually came back without anyone knowing it. Rat was a hard-rock, someone who didn't want to be on the outside. But he was also a genius. And Rico was after some of Rat's genius. He stared at Rat, who was sopping up the last of his beef stew. Rat returned his stare and smiled with that little rodent mouth of his.

"You gon' eat this?" Rat asked, helping himself to the food on Rico's tray.

"Naw, man," Rico replied. "You go ahead."

As Rat devoured his second helping of beef stew, he told Rico everything he knew about the transfer process, and promised to tell him other things as long as similar meal arrangements could be made.

Rico smiled as he finally drifted off to sleep. The harsh sounds of prison drifted in and out of his dreams, as did visions of fat rats leading him along a path out of jail and all the way back to Destiny Chandler.

"Des?" Davis's voice called from downstairs.

Damn, Destiny thought. She jumped up from sitting on the unslept-in bed and rushed to the cherry wood dresser. Since

Xavier had dropped her off, the only thing she had managed to
do was call Jacq and weep uncontrollably.

Destiny glanced at herself in the mirror. She was a wreck.
Sequin gown or no, her recent bout with tears left her drained
and distraught-looking. She couldn't let Davis see her like this.
He might ask her questions she wasn't willing to answer.
Quickly, Destiny slid under the covers and turned her back to
the wall.

"Des?" Davis called again more softly. She heard him push
open the door to the guest room. Destiny froze. She waited a
few moments and didn't hear anything. Frustrated that her plan
to keep Davis from seeing how pitiful she looked wasn't working, Destiny prepared to turn over when she heard the door
close softly.

"Whew," Destiny whispered. She remained still for a few
minutes longer just to be sure. Before long, Destiny drifted off
to sleep. When she awakened, it was seven o'clock in the evening. She got up and took a shower, and she had to admit that
the long nap did wonders for her disposition.

After putting on a pair of lavender sweats, Destiny headed
downstairs with hunger leading the way. It was her turn to call
out this time. "Davis?" Destiny paused at the bottom of the
stairs. No response. She headed toward the kitchen. "Davis?"
she called again. Still no response.

Destiny entered the kitchen gingerly, relieved that she might
have the evening to herself. Like the answer to her wishes, there
was a note for her on the refrigerator saying just that. Davis
apologized for getting separated from her last night. He promised to find a million ways to make it up to her. The note went
on to say that he was working at Integrated Marketing and to
call him on his cell phone if she needed anything.

Just like Davis, Destiny thought. She wasn't sure whether to
be angry or amused. "I guess you can't teach an old dog new
tricks," Destiny said—then proceeded to cook two of the salmon
fillets she found in the refrigerator.

When Destiny finished eating, she wandered into Davis's studio. It was a spacious room with large planning calendars and timelines posted on the walls. There were four medium-size worktables in the room. A computer sat on each one. At the far end of the room was a long table complete with a scanner, fax machine, and two printers.

Seeing all this technology didn't surprise Destiny. She had always known Davis to throw himself into his work. What she did find surprising was the grand piano sitting smack-dab in the middle of the room. It was enormous. Although there was more computational power in the space than any human could probably comprehend, the piano stood in the center of the room as the true testament of power and authority. Destiny wondered if Davis still played.

She walked over to the piano and ran her fingers across the keys. She had always wanted to learn how to play. The only song she could attempt to hunt and peck at was the tune from the Charlie Brown Christmas show. She remembered sitting on Davis's lap once while he played the bass chords and she struggled to find the keys for the melody.

"I love you," he had said unexpectedly. That was the first time Davis had declared his feelings for her.

"I love you, too," she responded, shocked and afraid of what those words really meant. And then he kissed her—her first French kiss. From then on, she and Davis spent a lot of time at his piano. They talked, kissed, and laughed at Destiny's futile attempts to learn even the simplest of songs.

Destiny pecked out a few notes of the Charlie Brown song on the piano. *I'm much better at computer keyboards,* Destiny thought as she moved from the piano to take a closer look at Davis's equipment setup. Each computer station appeared to be dedicated to a specific project. There was information about Davis's web site and Internet books near one computer. Another computer was surrounded by reports entitled "Converstion Project." Destiny stopped when she got to the third computer. There weren't any reports or thick computer books next to this one. Instead there was a mini-piano keyboard, a set of blueprints, the *Molten Hot Shop* CD, and three Zip disks labeled XAVIER ALLGOOD.

Destiny turned on the computer and put the disk entitled "Water & Breath" into the computer's Zip drive. As if in a dream, the music transported her back into Xavier's shower. She could almost feel his presence, feel his hands caressing her and his lips kissing her. Destiny sighed deeply. It was going to be hard for her to pretend their lovemaking was inconsequential, as Jacq recommended. But she had to know if he was serious or just using her.

The phone startled her away from her thoughts. Destiny walked over to the fourth computer table and picked up the phone that sat there.

"Van Housen residence."

"Hello, lovely." Destiny heard Xavier's voice and was at once exhilarated and tentative. "I just wanted to say good night and that I can't wait to see you tomorrow."

Destiny's first reaction was to utter an awestruck "Me too." But she remembered her promise to herself and thought better of it. Instead, she summoned all her strength to remain detached. "What time should I expect you?"

There was silence on the phone and then Xavier responded, "I was hoping we could get started around eight in the morning."

"Fine. I'll see you then." Destiny wished she could see him before then. Xavier must have read her thoughts. Instead of saying good-bye, he asked, "Do you miss me?"

"Why do you ask that?" Destiny replied calmly.

> *Rainbow in my soul*
> *I believe without seeing*
> *this inner constellation*
> *a state of new being*
>
> *Consumed by your eyes*
> *reborn defying death*

fed by your love-shine
like water and breath

Xavier sang along with himself in the background. Destiny could feel her heart melting and her stern resolve crumbling. She had to get off the phone or she knew words proclaiming her love would soon tumble uncontrollably out of her mouth.

"Thank you for the call, Xavier. I'll see you in the morning." Destiny set the receiver softly into the cradle and took a deep breath. One day down, she thought. Suddenly she felt that the quicker she could get this picture-taking business over with, the better.

Eleven

Destiny glanced at the clock on the dresser. It read 7:45. If she was going to step into this cold-shoulder role, she was going to play it to the hilt. She turned over in the bed and closed her eyes. *Maybe,* she thought, *I can actually go back to sleep.*

There was no mistaking it. The sound of Davis's "Ring My Doorbell" caught her attention. That could mean only one thing: Xavier was downstairs. Destiny felt the pace of her heart quicken. She wanted so much to race downstairs and jump into his arms. Just then she wished she had taken some of the acting workshops provided by some of the artists at the Arts and Humanities Council.

"Des!" came Davis's voice from downstairs. Destiny got up and walked to the doorway. She faked a groggy "Huh?" in response.

"The hardest-working man in show business is here!" Davis shouted.

"Okay," Destiny replied gruffly, hoping to sound sleepy.

She wrapped her blue chenille robe around her, put on her slippers, and ruffed up her locks. She walked down the stairs as if in a fog. Both men stared at her with odd expressions on their faces, Xavier's the oddest of all.

"Rough night?" he asked, watching her walk toward the kitchen.

"Sorry," she said, "I overslept." Destiny managed a slow

yawn and opened the refrigerator. "Do I have time to eat something?"

Both men looked at each other, then Davis broke the silence. "Dang, girl. You look toe-back!" He chuckled and slapped Xavier on the back. "You sure you want to be seen with her?"

"Yeah. I'm sure," Xavier said, looking in Destiny's direction. She was already putting two English muffins in the toaster.

"Man, I didn't get a chance to thank you for taking care of Destiny the other night," Davis said, sitting down on the sofa. He looked quite stylish in his long smoking jacket and silk pants. Destiny thought his attire was ironic since Davis didn't smoke. Xavier took a seat next to him within view of the kitchen.

"No problem," Xavier responded, shifting his attention to Davis. "Where were you anyway?"

"Yeah," Destiny chimed in. "I don't appreciate being left alone at a party where I don't know anyone." Destiny wasn't really mad. He had left her in good hands.

"I was doing my thang!" Davis said triumphantly.

"Uh-huh, but with whom?" Destiny quipped.

Davis looked wounded. "Destiny Chandler, you know me better than that. I was on a mission, negotiating three new contracts, together worth more than a quarter of a million in potential revenue."

Destiny and Xavier looked astounded. "You what?" they said in unison.

Davis patted his chest. "That's right . . . I'm bad." They all laughed at his boasting. Destiny spread strawberry jam on her muffins and realized that what Xavier said about Davis and Elise must have been a lie. They hadn't been together after all. *He must have said that to make it easier to get me into bed,* she thought.

The realization that Xavier could have lied to her sunk Destiny's spirits like a heavy load. She tried to finish the last English muffin, but found that she had no appetite. She tossed the dry bread in the trash and hoped against hope that there was a valid reason for Xavier's deceit.

"Where are you shooting today?" Davis asked.

"I thought we would go to Venn Gardens," Xavier answered.

"Isn't it late in the year for flowers?"

"That's exactly why I want to go there. The grounds will be in a state of transition." Xavier looked toward Destiny, who was still in the kitchen. "I want to make a statement about transformation in my next video."

"A worthy subject," Destiny commented, thinking Xavier should try transforming from a liar to an honest man. *Perhaps I won't be faking rebuff after all,* she thought.

"Just give me a few minutes to hop in the shower and get dressed." Destiny saw Xavier raise an eyebrow at the mention of the word *shower.* She pretended not to notice as she walked past the two men and headed back upstairs.

Destiny took a quick shower and dressed in her clothes recently shipped from Lincoln. Jacq was right on the money as usual. Everything she had asked for was in the box she received. Since she hadn't planned on working, Destiny left a lot of her camera supplies behind. The most important thing she needed wasn't a piece of equipment, however. It was her lucky vest.

Destiny had several photographs that she was extremely proud of. One was a picture of a young boy walking across a bridge. Something in the boy's gait suggested that the bridge was a symbol of a life crossing. She called the picture "Mid-Stride." Another photo Destiny was fond of was of her friend Ashiya wiping her tears on an American flag. She called this one "Dry Tears." But by far the photo she was most proud of was called "Outlook." One day while driving in Meadville, Nebraska, Destiny saw an overlook on the side of the road. She stopped, hoping to get a glimpse of the Niobrara River. When she walked over to the open area, she saw a young woman staring out over the river. The woman looked so at home amid the expanse of the lookout area that Destiny had to capture the moment. "Outlook" was Destiny's most widely published photograph.

Before long, Destiny noticed something in common about her photos. When she did her best work, she was wearing the same vest each time. Destiny didn't consider herself superstitious, but she liked the idea of having something that symbolized her mission to do good work.

She slipped the khaki-colored vest over her white turtleneck sweater and matching ribbed, cotton pants. The vest looked like something out of *Camper's Life* magazine. It had three pockets on each side, two large and one small. Then there were two deep pockets on the inside of the jacket. This allowed Destiny to keep most of her camera accessories close at hand.

Destiny loaded her pockets with the items Jacq had sent her, tied her locks back with a wide, khaki-colored ribbon, grabbed her camera, and headed downstairs.

When she got downstairs Davis and Xavier were no longer in the living room. Destiny followed the sound of their voices into Davis's study. They were sitting at the computer with the blueprints for Xavier's new studio. They were so engrossed with their conversation, Destiny didn't think they knew she was there. She was about to clear her throat to get their attention when Xavier turned his head in her direction. He looked at her intensely, like he wanted to say something but wasn't sure what.

"Looks like our fun's over," Davis said, noticing Destiny standing in the doorway. "Beware, Zay. I've seen her with a camera. She can be hell. Don't let her work you too hard."

"Don't worry," Xavier said, standing. "I think I can handle her."

"Humph." Destiny snorted. *You're not* that *smooth,* she thought to herself.

Davis walked them out and Destiny began to get a little nervous. It was easy to be cool toward Xavier while Davis was around. Davis was like a buffer between them. But now that she was alone with him, she hoped she could keep up the façade. Xavier helped her up into the Hummer. His touch on her arm sent electric currents surging through her soul. "This is going to be harder than I thought," she said aloud.

"No, it won't. I'm an easy subject."

Destiny frowned at Xavier. "I wasn't referring to that."

"Oh," Xavier said, backing out of Davis's driveway. "To what were you referring?"

Destiny shrugged her shoulders and looked away from Xavier. "Nothing really. It's not important."

They rode for a few moments in silence. Destiny wondered what Xavier was thinking. She also wondered why he lied to her. *Oh, well,* she thought. *I'll confront him with that soon enough. I just have to be sure.* Xavier's voice broke through her thoughts.

"Destiny, is something wrong?"

"No," Destiny replied, watching the road.

Xavier glanced over at her. She caught a glimpse of him out of the corner of her eye. He returned his attention to the road and probed further.

"Are you sure?"

Destiny looked away from the road and directly at Xavier. "I'm sure."

They rode the rest of the way to Venn Gardens engaging in small talk and not much else. Whenever Xavier's presence started to get the best of her, Destiny prayed that she was doing the right thing.

When they arrived at Venn Gardens, Xavier reached into the backseat of the Hummer and grabbed a straw hat. Its cream color accented the taupe pants and shirt he wore. Then he opened the glove compartment and took out a pair of RayBan sunglasses.

"Precautions?" Destiny asked, stepping out of the car.

"If I don't go incognito, we'll never be able to get any pictures taken."

As they walked toward the entrance together. Destiny wondered what it must be like to always be concerned about fans mobbing you in public. Again, Xavier seemed to sense what she was thinking.

"It's not as bad as you might think. At least not for me." Xavier paid their admission fee and they stepped into the grounds. "My music is popular, but I'm not a megastar. Yet. Some people I know can't leave home without a bodyguard."

"That must be awful," Destiny offered. "It almost makes you wonder if it's worth it."

"Well," Xavier said, stroking his chin pensively. "I can tell you how it is for me." He looked over to Destiny. She nodded in response. "Making music is like creating a balm for my soul. We all have demons, those things that ride us and torment our spirits. We all have important things to say—mostly to ourselves that help us become better people. Music rids me of my demons and tells me the things I need to hear about life." Xavier watched Destiny as they walked along the path. "About love.

"When I write a song, it's not about marketing, it's not about commercial viability, it's not about stage value, it's not even about the Top Ten. It's about keeping my soul honest and telling the truth as it is revealed to me."

Xavier took off his glasses for a moment and stopped. Destiny stopped beside him. "I can't *not* do what I do. So if, for whatever reason, people like what I do . . . it's worth it." Xavier put his sunglasses back on. "It's worth it," he repeated.

As they came into the main foyer of the gardens, Destiny was suddenly overwhelmed by color and fragrance. Venn Gardens was a large mazelike enclosure created with elaborately arranged flowers, plants, small trees, and well-manicured bushes. Destiny was delighted. For a moment, she forgot all about the photo shoot and wanted to go traipsing around in the twists and turns of the superstructure.

She could not hide her pleasure. She clapped her hands and then touched her hands to her cheeks. "A maze!" she blurted.

Xavier smiled at her and laughed. "Yes. It's a maze."

"Oh, wow," Destiny said, walking closer to the opening. "I've seen these on television. I've always wanted to walk around in one." She bent down to smell a lilac. The flower was a vivid purple with an aroma as strong and sweet as its coloring. "I always thought these contoured mazes were so . . ." Destiny caught herself before she could say the word *romantic*. She looked at Xavier, who was watching her with a raised eyebrow. She cleared her throat and finished her sentence. "Beautiful."

"Just like you," Xavier offered.

Destiny felt blood rush to her face. She stopped smiling and said "Thank you" without looking at him. She popped the lens cap off her camera and tilted her head in Xavier's direction. "Shall we go?" she suggested.

Xavier paused and looked at her questioningly. Then he shrugged his shoulders. "After you," he said, extending his arm toward the garden entrance.

Once inside, Destiny let the sweet aromas of the flowers envelop her. A constellation of daisies, chrysanthemums, tulips, gladiolas, and her favorite, sunflowers, surrounded her. Venn Gardens was an explosion of color carefully sculpted and shaped to exotic perfection. She twirled in delight, and then remembered why she was there.

"We've never really talked about this project in all its detail."

"Okay," Xavier said, watching her closely.

"Okay what? Okay we don't need to discuss it or okay we do."

Xavier smiled as Destiny touched various flowers. "Okay, what do you recommend?"

"Me!" Destiny exclaimed, taken aback. "You pose for promotional material all the time. This montage is a new concept for me."

"Me too," Xavier replied. "Why don't we learn together?"

They strolled a few more feet and came up to the first bend in the pattern. Destiny was not satisfied with his response. "You said you wanted a photo montage of where you are as an artist."

"Yes."

"Then the backdrop of each photo should speak to your growth process."

"Agreed."

Destiny stopped and let Xavier walk a few feet in front of her. She then tested the camera to see how he looked in the viewfinder. She took a light meter out of one of her pockets and began checking the light. It was a clear day full of sunshine. Destiny didn't foresee any problems there. "So tell me something . . . Why did you pick Venn Gardens? What does it say about you?" Destiny adjusted the camera from landscape to portrait view.

Xavier looked at the flowers surrounding them. "It doesn't really say anything about *me.*"

Destiny stopped looking through the viewfinder. She stared at Xavier incredulously. "This place doesn't have some special meaning for you?"

"Well, not until now."

Destiny walked up to Xavier slowly. "Then why are we here?"

"I thought you would like it."

Destiny was speechless.

"It's so beautiful," Xavier said, moving closer to Destiny. "It seemed to suit you."

"Suit me," Destiny said. "Isn't the whole point of this for people to get to know *you* better?"

Destiny glanced at some passersby—a couple nuzzled together the way that only new couples can. They walked together synchronously, oblivious to everything except each other. Destiny smiled. Seeing the happy couple gave her hopes that she would one day be like them—so love-silly that for a few moments nothing else mattered in the world.

"I think I should have the camera."

"Why?" Destiny asked, returning her attention to Xavier.

"Because just now I saw something magical move across your face. Whatever it was should be captured there forever."

Before Destiny let her embarrassment get the best of her, she decided to change the subject.

"You're trying to change the subject," she declared.

"I know. And there's a reason. I'm sort of melancholy about the other day. I keep thinking about us . . . together. We didn't get a chance to talk about it before I took you back to Davis's."

"Do we have anything to talk about?"

"I was hoping you could tell me."

If Destiny's heart could beat any harder, it would beat itself right out of her chest. She fiddled with the dials on the light meter to give herself a distraction, and also to hide her shaking hands. For one long second, she argued with herself over how to respond. In the end, Jacq's advice won out and Destiny stood her ground.

"I don't think we have anything to talk about. Maybe we should pretend that it never happened."

"Are you sure?" Xavier asked.

Destiny nodded, not trusting her voice, thinking it would betray her feelings.

"Okay," he said.

Was that disappointment she heard in his voice? Destiny wasn't sure. He was probably disappointed that he wouldn't be adding her to his list of triumphs he had planned. Unless, Destiny thought, he pursued it further. Destiny would wait and see. In the meantime, she had a job to do.

"So, if flowers aren't your thing, then what is?"

Destiny looked at Xavier, who seemed to be searching her face for something. Darned if she knew what it was. Then, after a few moments of silence, he responded.

"Bowling."

"Bowling?"

"Yeah, bowling."

"You mean like watching it on television?"

"No, I mean like going down to Casey's Bowl-a-Rama and knocking some pins over."

Destiny doubled over with laughter. Xavier rolled his eyes at her several times before she composed herself enough to talk.

"But look at you," she said, still laughing. "You are the king of suave, debonair, and cool. I can't imagine you in a bowling alley."

"My suave, debonair, and cool persona was created by a very highly paid image consultant. Her name is Carla Jones and she invented *Allgood*. I, on the other hand, am plain ol' Zay, and it's that side of me that I want people to begin to see."

Destiny shook her head. "Wow. Bowling, huh? This could be interesting."

"I was hoping you would say that."

Destiny scanned the perimeter of the gardens. She took in the beauty of the tulips, daffodils, hyacinths, daylilies, and amaryllis. Even though the gardens didn't hold much significance for Xavier, she thought that as long as they were there, they might as well take advantage of the opportunity.

"There's so much vibrant color here," Destiny said. "Before we go bowling, I would love to get some shots of you here."

"On one condition."

"What's that?"

"That you tell me what made you become a photographer."

"Oh, that's easy," Destiny said, squaring up Xavier in the viewfinder once more. When she saw Xavier stiffen and pose, she pulled the camera away from her face.

"No," she said. "Don't pose. Relax. Just walk through the maze, and I'll follow you. Do whatever you would do if I weren't here."

"Cool," he said.

Xavier began to walk through the maze, and Destiny began the story of how photography became the love of her life.

"I must have been about eight years old. I was visiting my great aunt Vivyonne. Aunt Viv had a small house in Independence, Kansas. Every summer my parents and I would go visit her and my cousins.

"My aunt Viv was a pack rat. She didn't throw anything away.

She would always say, 'Don't throw that away. You never know when it will come in handy.' " Destiny snapped a few pictures of Xavier, who had stopped to examine a small bud on a rose bush.

"Aunt Viv had stacks of old newspapers and magazines in her pantry. My dad said that her piles were a fire waiting to happen. I loved looking through her old magazines. She had *National Geographic, Reader's Digest,* and *Life.* Back then, *Life* magazine was tabloid size and I was always fascinated with how big it was."

Destiny snapped more pictures of Xavier walking along observing the flowers. He seemed quite reflective and genuinely interested in her story.

"One day, I was flipping through the pages of one of Aunt Viv's *Life* magazines, and I saw the most beautiful black-and-white photograph I've ever seen in my life. To this day, it's still my favorite."

Xavier stopped before a turn in the maze. "What was it?" he asked.

"It was a picture of a young Miles Davis. He was reclining in a chair, trumpet in hand." As Destiny recited the story, memories of the picture came back vividly. "He was the most beautiful man I had ever seen. He was stretched out in the chair like the maestro of cool. And the suit!"

Xavier chimed in at the mention of Miles's clothing. "Oh, my boy Miles could dress, now!"

"I know. Needless to say, I was in love." Destiny stopped focusing on taking pictures for a moment and let the full memory of her first experience of puppy love wash over her. "I was in love with Miles and I was in love with whatever, whoever created such an exquisite portrait."

Destiny knelt down to get a shot of Xavier from a different angle. "I found out later that the photographer was Gordon Parks. From that moment on, all I've wanted to do was to recreate that moment of awe for someone like Gordon Parks did for me."

"Have you always been a photographer?"

Destiny liked the way the sunlight hit Xavier's face at that moment and snapped a few close-ups. "Yes. I took pictures for my 4-H newsletter in junior high. In high school, I took pictures for the school newspaper and yearbook. My dad saw how serious I was about photography and bought me my first real camera when I was in high school."

Destiny stopped to reload. "Then I practiced by taking pictures of my friends. I would stage elaborate scenes with props and costumes. Every now and then, a picture would come out really good.

"Pretty soon, word got around that I was a camera bug. By the time I was a senior, I was doing portraits of my friends and making decent money at it."

"I'm impressed," Xavier said.

"I was impressed with myself back then. And the best part was when many of my friends asked me to take their senior pictures. That's when I knew I was legitimate."

Destiny and Xavier walked into a clearing in the maze. There were sculptured concrete benches and matching tables to sit at. They took seats beside each other.

"Okay," Destiny said, "your turn."

"What do you mean?" Xavier asked, surprised.

"Quid pro quo, Xavier. What called you into the music business?"

Xavier sucked in the sides of his cheeks and stroked his chin. "I don't want to bore you with my uninteresting stories."

"How about letting me decide whether or not it's boring? If it is, I'll let you know."

"You would, wouldn't you?"

"Yep. Now let's keep walking. Those women over there are staring in this direction. They may be trying to figure out if it's really you."

Xavier smiled and did as she suggested.

"I became a singer for a woman."

"I knew it!" Destiny quipped. "It must be true what they

say . . . that men get in the music business to get women." Destiny shook her head with disappointment. "I hoped that you were different," she admitted.

Xavier stopped walking. He turned to face Destiny. "You didn't let me finish. I said I got in the business for a woman. The woman is my mother."

"Oh . . . Xavier . . . I'm sorry for jumping to conclusions."

"Umm-hmm. You're bad," he said, giving her a sideways glance.

"All right," she responded, poking him lightly in the arm. "Don't rub it in."

Xavier faked being hurt and playfully winced as if her touch caused extreme pain.

"Oh, you!" Destiny protested. They both laughed heartily at their playfulness, and Destiny snapped a few more pictures of Xavier, capturing his warm smile. She was enjoying herself. Being with Xavier was like being with her complement. For the first time in years, Destiny felt like a whole person. She could listen to his velvety voice for hours.

"About this woman that you became an artist for, how did she encourage you to choose the music field?"

"Actually, she didn't."

"Mr. Allgood, you truly speak in paradoxes."

"Mr. Allgood?" he said, taken aback. Now he was up in her face, wiggling around. "Would Allgood do this?" Before Destiny could get her camera into position, Xavier stuck his tongue out at her several times. "Now," he said, inches from her face. "Call me Zay, please. All the important people in my life do."

Destiny could feel the effect of his words making her heart beat like a hummingbird's wings. But she was determined not to give in.

"I think I prefer Xavier for now. Especially since I'm your hired hand."

"In that case, you're fired!" They both laughed again as they approached an exit from the gardens.

"If you like, we can continue walking to other parts of the garden," Xavier offered.

"No," Destiny said, putting her light meter back into a pocket. "I'm eager to see you in your element."

Xavier smiled.

"It's just hard for me to believe that it's in a bowling alley."

At Destiny's comment, the two shared one more laugh before leaving the garden. They never noticed the two women taking pictures of them as they left.

Twelve

The loud sound of heavy balls rolling over the wood floors was followed by the crack of wooden pins being smashed into and knocked down. It sounded harsh at first, since Xavier hadn't been in a bowling alley since before his last tour. It took a few moments for him to become acclimated to the sounds again.

And just as he had expected, his surroundings became familiar. The smell of fresh beer, voices rising over the sounds of falling pins, and the thin haze of smoke that hovered deliberately over the smoking section brought back strong memories.

This was the hangout. The place his family went on Sunday evenings. No matter how much ruckus he and his five sisters caused during the week, things always settled down during family night. Something about being together simply to have fun and enjoy one another's company was enough to calm their hectic lives.

Xavier saw the flash from Destiny's camera go off beside him and remembered that he was on a photo shoot. "Let's go get our shoes," he suggested.

Xavier and Destiny got the shoes and took a lane at the far end of the alley. After putting on their shoes, they walked along the perimeter of the alley looking for balls with the proper weight for each of them. As Xavier checked the weight of each ball, he saw Destiny hanging back. "Aren't you going to look for a ball?" he asked.

"In a moment," Destiny answered. "Now remember. Act like I'm not here."

No chance of that, Xavier thought. It took all of his resolve to prevent himself from covering her with kisses from head to toe. Part of the reason he didn't was because Destiny seemed distant today. He wasn't sure why, but he was determined to find out. Being the only boy in the family taught him that sometimes the best way to find out what's on a woman's mind is to let her tell you in her own way and in her own time. He was prepared to wait as long as it took.

Xavier took a fifteen-pound ball and Destiny chose one that was eight pounds. "I haven't been bowling in ten years," Destiny admitted.

"It's been about ten months for me," Xavier said, placing his ball in the tray. "Can you keep score?" he asked.

"Nope. Besides, my job is to take pictures."

"All right," Xavier said, sitting down in the scorekeeper's chair. "Prepare to get mopped. You are about to see a master in action."

"Oh yeah," said Destiny. She had placed her bowling ball beside his in the tray and was aiming her camera at his feet. She snapped off a few pictures and then looked at him smugly.

"No, no!" he protested. "Not the shoes! My image consultant will go ballistic."

"You said you wanted your fans to see the other side of you. These red-and-white shoes will look great in your next video."

"I don't think so. The entire Allgood persona is built around the notion that I'm a cool bachelor type. My plan is to broaden the image gradually, not destroy it instantaneously."

"Okay," Destiny conceded.

"You can take pictures from afar in here, but I think close-ups on these shoes might intrude upon my rep."

"Enough said, Mister Cool."

"Thanks for understanding. Now let's get to the task at hand. You go first."

"No, you're bad. You go first," Destiny said, teasing.

"Okay. But don't say I didn't warn you."

Destiny stepped back and got her camera ready. Xavier picked up his bowling ball and stepped to the line. After a few seconds, he made his approach, swung his right hand back and then forward to release the ball. It went spinning down the lane and gradually veered left. Just as it was about to knock over its first pin, it plunged into the gutter.

Xavier was annoyed. He turned to Destiny and she quickly took a picture of his disappointment.

"I'm just warming up," he said, smiling. "I have my own shoes and ball at home. If I had them . . ."

"Uh-huh, Mister Master Bowler. Here, hold this," Destiny said, taking the camera from around her neck and handing it to him. "Now step aside and let me show you how it's done."

Xavier took the camera and stepped back. Oh, how he loved a woman with self-determination and conviction. Destiny seemed to have plenty of both. He watched her pick up her bowling ball and square up the lane. He paid close attention to her form in more ways than one.

When she released the ball, Xavier thought for a second she might have a strike coming. For a while, the ball rolled in the pocket, then, as if magnetized, it swerved off course and into the gutter. When Destiny turned to Xavier with pouty lips, he quickly snapped a picture of her.

"Hey!" she protested.

Xavier walked up to Destiny. He was so close he could smell her perfume. It was sweet and alluring. He handed the camera back to her and looked deeply into her almond-shaped eyes.

"I just couldn't resist," he said.

He thought he saw a spark of acknowledgment in her eyes, but as fast as it appeared, it was gone. She took her camera back and returned his stare.

"How about if I just take pictures of you while you bowl? It might go quicker that way, and then we can decide if we need to take more pictures tomorrow."

Xavier was disappointed. He couldn't understand why Destiny was pulling back. The only reason he could think of was that Destiny had feelings for Davis. After all, he did catch them deep in an impassioned kiss. Maybe their little tryst was just to get back at Davis for leaving her alone at the party.

Xavier was starting to feel sick about the possibility of Davis and Destiny together. He knew he had to think of some way to win her heart, but he wasn't sure how. For now he knew he was in the company of the woman he loved. And he would try to make the best of it.

"Let's *do* this," he said.

It only took one more try before Xavier was warmed up. Soon he bowled strike after strike. And Destiny took picture after picture. Xavier paused for a moment while Destiny reloaded the camera.

"You still haven't told me about your fascination with music." Destiny shut the camera and advanced the film. "How did you get started?"

Xavier stared into the return machine waiting for his ball to roll up. When it popped out of the hole, Xavier began his story.

"My father is the real musician in the family. My mother and sisters just loved to listen to him."

"Sisters?" Destiny asked. "How many sisters do you have?"

"Five."

"Wow. How many brothers?"

Xavier squared up the lane. "I'm the only boy. And," Xavier said, anticipating her next question, "I'm in the middle. I have three older sisters and two younger."

The ball found its mark again, creating another strike.

"My dad played the guitar. He used to play all the time when we were growing up. He had this old, beat-up guitar. Looked like it had been through ten hail storms." Xavier laughed fondly at the memory. "Well, one day, I must have been about eight, my sisters and I decided we were going to buy our father a new guitar. So we saved up our allowance money for weeks and went to a music store and bought him one.

"We got the best one we could afford. It was a shiny black

Martin acoustic guitar. On the day we gave it to him, we took that old, beat-up guitar and threw it in the trash. We put the new guitar in the old guitar case. Then we waited to hear the sound of our father whoop and holler over his new guitar."

"What a great idea," Destiny said, taking a picture.

"Not really. We heard a sound all right. It was the sound of our father's panic and angst. I remember being frightened and disappointed. I thought that he would be happy to get a new guitar. Instead, he had an angry discussion with my mother and then with us."

"Sarah! She's gone. The Blue Lady is gone!"

"Pearson, are you sure?"

"Am I sure? When I opened my case, I found this!"

Pearson Allgood held the shiny black guitar away from his body as if it were poisonous.

"I didn't take the Blue Lady, Pearson. It must have been one of the kids."

Pearson and Sarah Allgood proceeded to round up their children. When they had all gathered in the living room, Pearson interrogated them. He held out the new guitar and frowned accusingly at the children.

"Where did this come from?" he asked gruffly.

The children looked dumbfounded at one another. No one spoke.

"Someone in this house took the Blue Lady, and I want to know who it was!"

At that, Yolanda, the eldest daughter spoke. "Now that you have that new guitar, Father, do you really need that old raggedy one?"

"Oh, Pearson," Sarah Allgood said, placing a steadying hand on her husband's shoulders.

Pearson Allgood sat down with his children. An understanding smile spread across his face. "Let me tell you all a story," he said. "Once upon a time there was a beautiful young lady and an all right-looking young man."

Sarah chuckled softly beside her husband. Pearson continued.

"The young man was crazy about the young woman, but she wasn't too sure about him. He tried everything he knew to capture the young woman's heart, but she was too stubborn."

Sarah lightly smacked her husband on the shoulder. Pearson rubbed his shoulder, pretending to be wounded, and continued his story. *"One day, determined to show the young woman his love, the young man showed up at her doorstep with his guitar and sang her a song."*

The children looked at one another and smiled. *"The young woman came out of her house to listen to the young man's song. When he finished, he asked her to marry him and she said yes."*

Sarah leaned over and kissed her husband on the cheek.

"And they got married, had six children, and lived happily ever after," Pearson finished.

"So, kids, that guitar is not just an old raggedy instrument. It's magic. It helped me marry the most beautiful woman on earth. And without her none of you would be here now."

Smiling, Sarah shook her head and returned to the kitchen.

Xavier cleared his throat and spoke. *"We didn't know, Dad. We thought it was . . . well . . . we just wanted you to have something new."*

Pearson looked in the direction of the kitchen. *"I'm happy with what I got,"* he said.

Xavier got up from where he was sitting. *"I'll go get the Blue Lady, Dad."*

After finishing his story, Xavier sat down next to Destiny. "When I went to the trash to get that guitar, I was changed forever. Music was no longer just music. It had grown beyond mere notes and melodies. Like my father said, it was magic. It could make dreams come true. It had the power to make people live happily ever after."

Destiny was staring intently at Xavier. He stared back and thought he could see the universe sparkling in her dark eyes. He couldn't help himself. He brought her face to his and urgently claimed her mouth. It was moist and inviting and . . . gone. Destiny pulled away quickly.

"I'm sorry," he said, feeling awkward.

"Are we finished here?" Destiny asked.

"I just have one more ball to throw," Xavier said, rising. He picked up his ball from the bin and approached the line. When he was ready, he made his four-step approach and released the ball, and it went rolling down the lane. Another strike was imminent. Xavier was about to allow himself to smile when the ball pulled slightly to the right. It knocked over seven pins and left the one, three, and six pins.

Xavier shook his head and Destiny clicked a few pictures while he waited for his ball to return. When it did, Xavier picked up the ball and a wicked smile spread across his mouth. Destiny moved the camera slowly from her face without taking a picture and looked at him questioningly.

Xavier returned to the line, just to the left of dead center, in deep concentration. The thing he loved so much about bowling wasn't the strikes. It was picking up the spares. He smiled and thought to himself—bowling, the sport of second chances. In that instant, he allowed himself to believe that someday he would have a second chance with Destiny.

Xavier swung his arm back, then forward, and released the ball. It spun deliberately toward the three remaining pins and smacked loudly into them. They were instantly knocked over and within a few moments swept away by the reset equipment.

"Game over," he said.

"Are you hungry?" Xavier asked.

Destiny watched as the cars sped by. Her heart was in turmoil.

Somehow her plan to be the ice queen wasn't going well at all. She almost lost it a few moments ago in the bowling alley. And her stomach . . . could she eat?

"I'm starving, and if you don't mind, there's a place I'd like to take you. It has great food and it's, as you put it, part of my element."

Destiny felt strained and torn. She didn't know how much more of his presence she could take without giving in. She was about to suggest they call it a day when her stomach betrayed her. It groaned loudly with emptiness.

"I'll take that as a yes."

Destiny sat in silence as Xavier drove deftly through the Atlanta traffic. It occurred to her that she should be taking pictures of him behind the wheel. She took out her light meter and prepared her camera. After taking a few pictures, she wondered why Xavier seemed so at ease amidst the chaos of the highway traffic. Perhaps it had to do with this monster truck of a car, she thought.

"What made you get a Hummer?" she asked.

Xavier smiled and swiftly changed lanes. "It's like everything else in my life. I try to surround myself with things that will make me a better person." Xavier stole a quick glance in Destiny's direction, then returned his attention to the road. "This is a government-issued all-terrain vehicle. It can cross a thirty-inch stream, drive in two feet of water all day long, traverse a forty-percent slope and climb up a sixty-degree-grade hill. That means it is the most adaptable vehicle on the road. It can adjust itself to almost any situation.

"I call my Hummer Ali, 'cause no matter what, it always comes up swinging. A couple of years ago, we had a blizzard to end all blizzards. And here in the ATL, we ain't used to too much snow. A lot of folks were cut off, but you know, Ali handled it." Xavier merged the Land Rover into the exit lane. "That's the way I want to be, ready to take on whatever. Able to keep going even when the surface of the road I'm traveling goes through changes."

Destiny aimed the lens at Xavier once again. She saw a frown form on his face through the viewfinder. "Why don't we take a break from the picture taking?"

"Fine," Destiny replied. Without the distraction of picture taking between them, she would be forced to deal with Xavier directly. Destiny sighed deeply. Why couldn't she find happiness in the company of this man? she asked herself. Whenever she started to feel some sort of pleasure in being with him, her mind reminded her that he was a star who was probably just going through the motions with her. It was too bad. He seemed to be perfect for her in nearly every way. But then there was a time when she had thought the same about Rico, and Rico turned out to be a monster.

"I don't know what brought that expression on, but if it was standing in front of me, I'd pulverize it."

Destiny laughed. She found the thought of Xavier entangled in a duel over her quite amusing. It helped lift her out of her sullen mood.

"That's better," he said, entering a parking garage in downtown Atlanta.

"Actually, I know what would be better."

"What?"

"Food!" Destiny insisted.

"Okay, okay," Xavier said, parking the large vehicle that took up nearly two parking spaces. "Remember the sausage I gave you the other day?"

For a moment, Destiny's mind took a turn for the naughty. A wicked smirk materialized from the corners of her mouth.

"Mind out of the gutter, lovely," Xavier responded, waving his finger back and forth in the air.

"This is Chappy. Chappy, meet Destiny Chandler."

"What cha know good, Miss Destiny?"

"I know that I'm starving," Destiny said, eyeing the items on the old gentleman's open-air grill. On one side of the grill was a metal box where hot dog buns sat steaming. The other side was overflowing with condiments from melted cheese to onions and chili. Destiny watched as Chappy's hands worked the spatula and grilling fork quickly to turn over the sizzling sausages. His large knuckles looked swollen with arthritis.

"Give us two, Chappy," Xavier said.

Chappy whipped up the sandwiches like a magician performing sleight of hand. Destiny and Xavier took their food and moved to the other side of the grill where the condiments were.

"Where you been hidin'?" Chappy asked, plopping a sausage in a bun for the next person in line.

Xavier loaded his bun full of relish and sauerkraut. "I've been taking it easy."

"I see you took my advice," Chappy said, his toothless mouth working up and down.

Xavier quickly chewed through his first bite. Destiny looked back and forth from man to man, truly feeling like a fly on the wall.

"What's that?" Xavier said, swallowing.

Chappy filled another order, then there was a break in the line. He added more of the veggie sausages to cook on the grill.

"To get back on the horse," he said, motioning toward Destiny. "Besides, that other girly you had just weren't right. I can tell right off that this little filly here is worth riding into the sunset."

Chappy wiped his hands on his apron. He pulled a water jug from a container on the side of the grill and took a long drink. Xavier stopped chewing his food for a moment and looked cautiously at Destiny. Her eyes were wide with surprise and then she could hold it in no longer.

A blast of laughter shot out from deep inside her. She almost dropped her sandwich, but quickly steadied it in her hand. Xavier resumed chewing and stared sternly at the old man.

"See what I mean?" Chappy said.

"But," Destiny began, playing along, "you don't even know

me." Destiny took a bite of her sandwich and waited for Chappy to respond.

Chappy scratched lightly at his spiky white beard. "I don't have to know you," he said, turning his sausages. "I know *him*."

"I don't understand," Destiny replied.

"Y'ever notice how a dog can tell sometimes whether the people around you are good or bad? Some people they growl at, some they don't."

"Yeah," Destiny and Xavier said in unison.

"Well, it's not so much the other people that the dog picks up on, it's you—your reaction to the people and how you feel about them. That's what the dog senses." Chappy filled another order and looked at the two of them.

"People can be like that, too. So it's not you I'm picking up on, Miss Destiny. It's him. I've been knowin' him since he was a little squat. I can tell when he's worked up about something. And when that workup is a positive or a negative. And *you* are settin' up shop on the positive side."

"All right, Chappy, thank you," Xavier interrupted. "You don't see a black man blush too often, but I'm just about there."

Destiny finished the rest of her sandwich quietly and wondered if the things Chappy said were true.

"I'm sorry if Chappy embarrassed you."

Destiny took in the bustling sights of downtown Atlanta. She hadn't minded Chappy's comments at all.

"I thought he was sweet." *And I pray that he's right,* Destiny thought.

As they walked along one of Atlanta's many Peachtree streets, Destiny was overwhelmed by the number of people out. If she weren't on a photo shoot for Xavier, she would certainly have enough to fulfill her interest as a tourist. The picture she took of Chappy and Xavier together was more for herself than anything else. She planned on asking Xavier for the picture when she got it developed.

"He looks out for me," Xavier said. "Like a conscience. When you're in the business, it's a good idea to surround yourself with people that have your back."

Destiny thought about Jacq. She remembered a time when Jacq tried to help her see that Rico was a bad influence in her life. At the time, she couldn't see it.

"It's also important to listen to them," Destiny said.

"Oh, so you agree with Chappy?" Xavier beamed.

"Actually, I was thinking about my best friend, Jacq. I didn't listen when I should have and as a result, I got hurt." Destiny didn't want to go into any of the painful details, so she left it at that.

"I know what you mean," Xavier admitted.

They were nearing a park surrounded by numerous peddlers and street vendors.

"What's going on?" Destiny asked.

Xavier shrugged. "I don't know. But that's what I like about the ATL. There's always something."

Destiny and Xavier walked toward the gathering of people. They were all watching a group of clowns, jugglers, and tumblers. There were two people walking on stilts, and a tall man dressed like a ringmaster danced around holding a megaphone.

"Yes, ladies and gentlemen, it's hip-hop under the big top!" the ringmaster said. "Tonight at Turner Field, the UniverSoul Bigtop Circus will perform especially for you. We are the only black-owned circus in the world, and you can see us tonight at seven-thirty. Bring your parents, bring your children, but most of all, bring yourself! You don't want to miss the event of a lifetime!"

As the jugglers juggled and the tumblers tumbled, there was a series of applause from the onlookers. Destiny felt fifteen years younger just watching the all-black troupe of performers. After several minutes, Destiny looked at Xavier. The smile in his eyes probably matched her own, she thought.

Xavier glanced in her direction with a slaphappy grin taking up most of his face. "What are you doing tonight at seven-thirty?"

"You're going to what?" Davis asked from downstairs.

"A circus," Destiny answered. "We saw some of the perform-ers in the park today and they were great."

"A circus," Davis repeated as if he hadn't heard correctly.

"Yes," Destiny said, checking her makeup in the mirror. "And if this afternoon was any indication of their talent, it's going to be an awesome show." Destiny couldn't figure out for the life of her what was the most appropriate thing to wear to a circus. Looking at her vacation wardrobe didn't give her much to choose from.

At first she considered wearing a pantsuit. Even though it was a circus, it was an African-American circus. Destiny knew her people liked to dress. But then again, what was the sense of getting dressed up for clowns and animals?

She finally decided on a compromise. She chose a knit, forest green jogsuit. That was the casual. To dress it up a bit, she wore a black, tunic-length sweater vest over it. She slipped on black, cuffed ankle boots and was ready to go.

Destiny bounced jauntily down the spiral staircase, thinking she was ready for more than just the circus. Her entire day had been filled with a kind of magic—the kind that Xavier's father believed in. And if she could have that magic in her life for moments at a time with Xavier, then so be it.

Destiny was tired of her apprehensive approach to everything. Since Rico, she had been overcautious about everything, even her own future. Every day, she had to remind herself that Rico was in jail, and for the first time in years, she was free to live her life.

And Jacq, bless her heart. Jacq had been her rock. No rough water was too strong for Jacquelyn Jackson. She had been there, always weathering the storm with her. Destiny knew that Jacq had her back. And her advice to be careful was sound. But it was also restricting. And more than anything right now, Destiny needed to be free. And free sometimes meant disappointment, but Destiny found it hard to believe that the happiness that made her spirit fly today could ever disappoint her.

So tonight, Destiny thought, sitting on Davis's couch, *if Xavier says anything, behaves like anything or even hints like there's anything between us, I'll respond on the positive side.* "Heck, I might even start a little sumthin', sumthin'," she said out loud.

"What's that?"

Destiny heard Davis's voice coming from the studio.

"Nothing, Davis."

Pretty soon, Anita Ward sang the lyrics to her one and only hit. "I got it," Destiny yelled and sprang to the door. She opened it and Xavier stood before her in a black silk shirt that curved against his arm muscles in all the right ways. The black denim pants he wore clung snugly to his thick thighs. Like she, he wore a vest over his outfit. Destiny thought he looked delectable.

Impulsively, she stood on tiptoe and kissed him on the cheek as he entered.

Xavier cheesed widely. "Now that's what I'm talkin' 'bout," he responded.

Destiny stepped back confidently, ready to play. "Don't get too cocky, mister. I'm just saying hello."

"If that's hello, let's skip everything in between and say good night right now."

Just then, Davis emerged from the back room looking forlorn. He seemed oblivious to the chemistry and sparks flying in the room.

"It's official," Davis said, hanging his head. "Van Housen and Associates is really going to have some associates."

"That's great, man," Xavier commented.

"I'm proud of you, Davis," Destiny added.

"Yeah, well, hold your bets. I've been flying solo for so long, I'm not sure I can function with another person."

They were all silent for a moment. Destiny could tell that Davis was really struggling with the idea of hiring an assistant.

"But I guess I'm going to have to," he continued. "I'm not sure how much longer I can keep up these late nights. As a matter of fact, I just got a call from Integrated Marketing. I've got to go back there tonight."

"Man, look, you're going to kill yourself if you don't hire someone."

Destiny nodded. "Xavier's right."

"I know, I know. And I thought it would be nice to kick it with you two tonight at the circus, but I guess I'll have to take a rain check."

"No problem," Xavier assured him. Then he turned to Destiny. "Are you ready?"

"Yes," she said.

The two said their good-byes to Davis and were off to the performance. When they arrived at the circus, it was beginning to rain, but Destiny felt like a butterfly emerging from a cocoon. It was as if she were experiencing life for the first time. She wanted to try everything, see everything, touch everything. Being with Rico was so painful that she had dulled her senses to just about everything. But now, her nerve endings were on fire. Even the smell of the animals didn't bother her. She was excited by it all.

Xavier bought a program and gave it to Destiny. "Would you like some cotton candy?" he asked.

"Later," she said, preoccupied with the large clown seated on one side of the lobby. "Right now, I want my face painted."

"You what?" Xavier asked, astonishment lifting his voice.

"You heard me," she said, walking gingerly toward the clown. "I want my face painted."

Xavier followed her, laughing. "Are you serious?"

"Perfectly," she said, getting in line. "Do you mind?"

"No," he said. "Actually, I think it's kinda fly."

"Good," Destiny cooed and kissed Xavier's other cheek.

"If this is what the circus does to you, I will hire these guys to paint your face twenty-four seven."

Destiny laughed and moved up in line. Xavier leaned over and kissed her on the cheek. She felt a surge of excitement radiate throughout her body. *This man is in trouble tonight,* Destiny thought.

By the time Destiny reached the front of the line, her inner child had taken over. She stood there grinning and rocked back and forth on her heels. The clown chuckled heartily. "And what's your name, little girl?" he asked good-naturedly.

"Destiny," she said.

"Well, Destiny . . . would you like a heart, a lightning bolt, or a rainbow today."

"A rainbow, please."

The clown looked at Xavier. "I don't suppose she'll be sitting on my lap for this?"

"No, she won't," Xavier responded.

The clown painted a multicolored rainbow on the side of Destiny's face. Then she and Xavier went to the concession stand to get cotton candy and sparkling water. They were making their way to their seats when the sounds of James Brown's "Call Me SuperBad" came thundering through the loudspeakers.

Destiny thrilled as the traditional circus acts were set to an African-American beat. The ringmaster greeted his audience with high-stepping dance movements à la hip-hop and James Brown. He immediately pulled the audience in with his call and response. "When I say big top, you say circus!"

"Big top!"

"Circus!" the audience shouted.

Destiny's favorite part of the circus was the stilt dancers who wore the ritual garments of the stilt-walking shamans of West Africa and the clowns who presented a comedic tour of the history of blacks on American TV.

Just when she and Xavier thought they had seen it all, there were contortionists, aerial acts, and the King Charles Unicycle Troupe, which performed amazing feats on unicycles. Destiny and Xavier were saddened when the show was over. They promised to see it again one day.

Davis stared at the conference room wall. He had arrived several minutes early for the meeting and was enjoying the solitude. He had a lot on his mind. First, his new deals and what they would do to his time and his income. Second, hiring an assistant. He or she would have to be a precise fit. Davis could not visualize himself working with someone fresh out of college. He wanted someone a bit more seasoned, but not tainted with bad business habits either. He wanted someone who was open to new ideas, but experienced enough to make those new ideas work.

And last, there was Destiny. He and Destiny were passing each other like ships in the night. And Davis felt powerless to do anything about it. He wished Destiny could have chosen to visit at another time, when his plate wasn't so full. He had to admit that seeing Destiny again was doing wonders for his energy level. But the spark that he had expected to reignite between them was absent. He felt very close to her, yes, but closer than close was another matter. And even if Destiny was interested in rekindling their romance, Davis didn't see how that was possible. At least not right now.

If only he could get a chance to talk with her at length. Her photo project with Xavier was keeping her pretty busy as well. It seemed that now just wasn't the right time for them. And the sooner he resigned himself to that fact, he thought, the better.

"Well, this is the first time I've seen you sitting this still in . . . hmm . . . This is the first time I've seen you sitting this still! What's up?" Bill Goodman's long strides quickly put him at the table beside Davis.

"Man, can I talk to you for a second?"

"Sure." Bill sat down and folded his hands on the table.

"Man, I've got so many irons in the fire, I think I need to call the firefighters."

"I thought you liked it that way."

"I did. I do. It's just that lately, something's's falling through the cracks, and I'm not sure whether I want it to or not."

"Are you asking for juggling lessons or advice on how to recognize when you have too many balls in the air?"

"Hell if I know."

"Aren't you a project manager?"

"The best."

"I know this is your personal life, but how is this situation different from any other project you manage?"

Davis put his hand on his chin and leaned forward onto the table. While Bill talked, Davis mentally reviewed his activities and involvement over the past two weeks.

"Take today's meeting, for example. If you look on the agenda, we're having a project update meeting. That means all the project leaders need to report on the status of their parts of the project. Then the efforts of each team are coordinated into one joint effort to get our code to be error-free."

Davis could see where Bill was headed. He finished his analogy. "In order to determine which areas of the project received the most attention and resources, we prioritize and examine each area for its critical factors. The result of that analysis becomes the mission, the project."

Davis sat back, astonished. The answer to his quandary had been right there in front of him all along.

"So, what is your mission, Mr. Van Housen?"

"My goal is to make Van Housen and Associates the best computer consulting firm in the United States."

"What!"

"That's always been my goal. I guess I somehow got lost along the way."

"Well, I'll be. I thought we were talking about your lady friend."

"Well, we were, in a way," Davis said. He shifted in his seat.

"I mean, how can I even consider a serious relationship when my business is not in order? I'm president of Van Housen and Associates and I don't even have any associates. I've been in the business for years, but I feel like I'm just now realizing my potential. I'm still in the beginning stages. What woman would have me?"

Bill sat back in his chair. "What woman indeed?" he responded.

Davis picked up his Levenger pen and twirled it back and forth. "But all that is about to change." Several members of Davis's project team began entering the room. As they sat down, Davis leaned back in his seat with a grin on his face as wide as the Nile.

The rain had stopped. As Xavier and Destiny walked arm in arm to his car, Destiny's attention was diverted to a couple much farther down the street. They were arguing, and Destiny could just make out what they were saying.

"Oh, so now I'm BooBoo the Fool!" the man shouted.

"I didn't say that," the woman responded.

"Naw, you didn't say shit! You just sat there making me look like an idiot!"

The man grabbed the woman's arm and forced her a few yards down the street. She yanked away from him. "I'm not going!"

"What!" Destiny heard the man's voice clearer the closer she and Xavier got to them. Other couples and families were moving away from the skirmish. Many people just stood and stared.

A bolt of adrenaline shot through Destiny. She felt instantly angry and pushed over the edge. Desperate for something to grab on to, she bent down and picked up a discarded glass bottle from the curb. Destiny held the bottle by the neck and raised it over her head. Then, before Xavier could grab her, she made a mad dash toward the couple.

Xavier called out after her, but she couldn't hear his voice above her own screams. Just before she reached the man, Xavier grabbed her and knocked the bottle from her hand. She struggled furiously against him.

"No!" Destiny screamed. "Let me go! He just can't walk all over her like that! Let me go!"

The man, startled by Destiny's actions, stared at her wide-eyed. "What the hell is her problem, man?"

Destiny wrestled frantically against Xavier. "My problem! It's men like *you* that have a problem!"

The man had long since let go of the woman and was ushering her away from the scene. He shot back a warning toward Xavier. "Man, you better check your woman!"

Xavier looked at Destiny, who was finally beginning to settle down. Her anguished screams turned quickly to deep sobs. She held fast to Xavier and trembled with rage and exasperation. Then she shrunk against him, exhausted.

"Come on, baby," Xavier said softly. "Let me take you home."

Xavier placed Destiny on his bed and sat beside her on the mattress. She looked deflated and distressed. He wiped away the fresh tears still moist on her face and smoothed her hair with his hand.

"Let it go, baby."

She looked at him, fear welling up in her eyes.

"I'm here, lovely," he murmured. "Now, let it go."

All at once she was in his arms and clinging tightly. The sobs shook her body visibly and at times it seemed like she could barely catch her breath. Xavier cradled her in his arms and rocked her gently back and forth until her crying subsided.

When Destiny seemed calmer, he reached into his pocket and took out a handkerchief. He turned Destiny's face to his to dry her tears. He saw that her crying had washed away her rainbow. The sadness he saw in her face cut him deeply. He had to know what caused his woman this much pain. And he would do all he could do to stop it forever.

He cupped her face in his hands, furious with whatever it was that hurt her so. "Tell me," he said.

Destiny sat up and sighed deeply. "His name is . . . Rico," she said, sniffing. "Four years ago we were the happiest couple on the planet. We went everywhere. We did everything together.

"About a year into our relationship, Rico's attitude started to change. I thought it was just a phase he was going through. It wasn't. Pretty soon, Rico was drinking and smoking a lot of dope. But it wasn't a constant thing. It's like he went through cycles . . . like manic depression or something. After a while, we had a relationship of extremes. What was good was really good, and what was bad was horrid."

Xavier leaned back and took a deep breath as Destiny continued her story.

"I kept thinking during the good times that I had seen the last of the bad times. But that was never true."

Destiny stared deeply into Xavier's eyes. "Sometimes I can fool myself pretty good."

Xavier took her hands in his and waited for her to continue.

"During the bad times, he became a monster. He would rant and accuse me of all kinds of things. And the things he would say to me . . ."

Destiny's voice trailed off as more tears rolled down the sides of her face. Xavier could tell she was starting to falter. "Go on," he urged.

"I felt so isolated. For the last two years of our relationship, I had cut myself off from most of my friends. I couldn't let them see Rico the way he was. I was too embarrassed and too ashamed. When I couldn't take it anymore, I told him I wanted to end our relationship."

More tears trickled from Destiny's eyes. Xavier took the handkerchief and dabbed them away. Destiny released another sigh and closed her eyes. Xavier moved closer to her and kissed her forehead. "All of it," he said.

"Rico went berserk. I had to call the police in order to get him out of my apartment. Then I went to the courthouse and got a protection order. But that didn't stop him. He slashed my tires, broke windows in my car and apartment. And then he kept calling and sending me letters for more than a year."

"Damn," Xavier responded.

"The day you saw me dancing in Davis's house was the day Rico was sent to jail for three years for destruction of property and violation of a protection order. I was . . . celebrating."

Destiny managed a weak smile.

"Then tonight, when I saw that couple arguing, all the anger I've choked back for the last three years came rushing to the surface. I guess it's like you predicted. It overtook me."

There was so much pain in her face, Xavier ached to see her smile. "I'm just glad I was there to keep you from killing that guy!" Xavier waited, but there was no response. He decided to try again. "I mean, dang, my baby was gonna whoop some ass!"

At that, Destiny cracked a smile. He hugged her intensely, then pulled away. "Now, on a serious note," he said, inches away from her face. "When this guy Rico gets out, I'll be outside the jail waiting for him. And know this, he will never, *ever,* bother you again."

Destiny searched his face as if desperately desiring truth. She looked so alluring at that moment Xavier lowered his mouth to hers and kissed her with all the depth of his soul. It was a slow rolling kiss that led his mouth gradually to all the places on her face that had been wet with tears. Without thinking, he turned his focus to the nape of her neck, where he planted small, light kisses one after the other. In response, Destiny's arms slid around his neck and tender moans emerged from her lips.

Xavier made careful work of removing Destiny's vest and shirt. He took a moment to behold the beauty lying in his bed before he began a delicate massage of Destiny's succulent breasts. He moved his fingers closer and closer to their center and stroked her nipples until they stiffened to his touch.

Destiny parted her lips and licked them slowly. She reached up for him and he bent down to claim her mouth again. Then he gave each luscious mammary his full attention. Destiny arched her back and called out his name.

Xavier removed her pants and panties and his mouth continued on its journey to pleasure. He lingered over her stomach and savored her shapely thighs. When he reached Destiny's most tender spot, she screamed and called his name again.

"Oh, Xavier . . . ooh," he heard her whisper, and then he felt the force of her epiphany explode within her.

It was only after he had sent her hurtling over the edge again that he undressed himself. He reached into the drawer of his nightstand and retrieved a condom. As he was about to open the package, Destiny's sultry voice stopped him. "Let me," she said.

Destiny sat up and gently guided Xavier down on the bed. She opened the condom and set the wrapper on the nightstand. Then she slipped the condom into her mouth. Xavier was about to protest until he felt her mouth center warmly on his manhood.

Inch by inch, Destiny unrolled the condom over Xavier's firm organ. The sensations of her tongue and mouth were so overpowering, he could barely contain himself. From the center of his very being he called her name. She continued to move her tongue and lips over the condom in smooth pulses. Xavier could feel himself approaching release. At that moment, Destiny guided herself on top of him and together they moved in synchronous time. Until at last they ignited like two shooting stars against a black sky.

They lay there entwined and satisfied only for a few moments. Then Xavier got up and moved to the foot of the bed.

"Hey," Destiny said huskily, "aren't we supposed to be cuddling now? You know, basking in the afterglow?"

"I got something better."

Destiny sighed deeply and closed her eyes. "Nothing could be better than lying in your arms."

Xavier took Destiny's feet and placed them in his lap.

"What are you doing?" Destiny sat up.

Xavier gestured her back down. "Relax," he said. "Consider this the finishing touch."

Destiny settled back onto the bed, and Xavier began rubbing the sides of her heels. "Did you know that different places on your feet affect various parts of the body?"

"Is that so?" Destiny asked, closing her eyes again.

"Yes. The place on your heels that I'm rubbing now corresponds to . . . well . . . should I say a woman's sensitive areas?"

"Really?"

"As a matter of fact . . ." Xavier began walking his thumbs along the outside area of Destiny's heels.

"Oh, my," she purred.

When he finished his massage, Destiny was nearly asleep. He kissed her on the stomach. "Sleepy, baby?" he asked.

"I think I'm just very relaxed."

"Mind if I play some mood music?"

"Nope."

Xavier got up and walked over to a large wall cabinet. He pressed it lightly and the door to the cabinet swung open. An antique phonograph sat in the middle of it. Numerous sleeved 78s were stacked on the lower shelves. Xavier thumbed through the stacks before selecting a record to play. Then, he placed the record on the turntable, cranked the knob, and set the arm down.

At first the music of the band sounded hoarse and dusty. After a few seconds, it warmed in the rolling timbre of Billie Holiday's voice ascending from the aged megaphone.

> *If I belonged to you*
> *All the world would know*
> *And if I belonged to you*
> *My soul would be all a'glow*
> *I'd shout to the clouds*
> *Hey now look at me*
> *No more pinin', I'm shinin'*
> *This was truly meant to be*

And every day would be a sweet day
  This I tell you, true
  My heart and soul's complete day
  If I belonged to you

Impulsively, Xavier extended his hand and Destiny rose from the bed to join him. He enveloped her in his arms, never wanting to let go. As the radiance of the night streamed in through the windows, Xavier and Destiny gazed into each other's eyes and danced naked in the moonlight.

Thirteen

"Wake up, baby."

Destiny rolled over onto Xavier and huddled her body against his. "Do you know how peacefully I was sleeping?"

"Of course I do," Xavier replied, remembering their night of lovemaking. He had awakened more content than he had been in years. "Good lovin' will do that to you," he replied. He also felt more exhilarated, more alive than he had felt since his first CD went platinum. His senses were engaged in a way that he wanted to share with Destiny.

He stroked her arm while it rested on his chest. She looked so lovely. All his earlier hesitation was devoured by her beauty. There was so much he wanted to share with her, and so much he wanted to do with her. "Come on, lovely. There's someplace special I want to take you."

Slowly, Destiny's eyes opened and she looked up at him. The morning sun played warmly on her face, and she offered him a dopey smile. "You've already taken me to ecstasy and back again. Where else would you have me go, kind sir?"

His mood seemed suddenly buoyant. "Centershot Archery Range."

"Really?" Destiny said, sitting up.

"Um-hmm," he said, kissing her forehead. "You wanna go?"

"I'd love to," she said, examining the hunting bow on the wall above them.

Xavier sat up beside her. "I was hoping you would say that."

He cupped one of her exposed breasts in his hand and lowered his head toward the nipple already ripening to his touch. He traced the taut little orb with his tongue before enclosing it within his mouth. When he switched to the other breast, he felt Destiny's hands making soft patterns across his back.

Xavier pulled away gently and kissed her forehead again. "We better get ready to go."

"Oh!" Destiny stared at Xavier, mouth open and eyes wide.

"Don't worry, lovely. There will be plenty of time for that later. I promise." He bent down toward Destiny and kissed her deeply, then rose from the mattress and walked into the bathroom. A few moments later, he came back with a set of towels draped across his arm. "I'll shower downstairs, so we can save some time."

"Hmph," Destiny snorted playfully. "I wish you were as eager to get to me as you are to get to the archery range."

Xavier glanced at Destiny with a crooked smile and an arched eyebrow. "You are insatiable!"

Destiny slowly pulled back the covers and boldly exposed her full nakedness. "Really?" she asked, reclining on the bed.

Xavier could feel his blood beginning to heat with desire. He dropped the towels on the floor and walked back to where Destiny lay like a goddess on his bed. "You *are* beautiful," he said, lowering himself on her. She reached up to receive him and kissed him tenderly.

"Woman, what is this spell you've cast on me?" he whispered huskily in her ear.

"The same one you cast on me," she responded.

Just like the night before, he took her again and again, until they were both spent and content.

"Well, if we're going, we better go."

"Oh, *now* you're in a hurry," Xavier exclaimed, looking at all the empty condom wrappers on the nightstand.

"Yep," Destiny said, bounding from the bed. "I'll race ya!" she said, scurrying toward the shower.

"You're on!" Xavier said, picking up the towels from the floor and heading downstairs.

Xavier took his time in the shower, determined to let his baby win. When he returned to the bedroom with a damp towel wrapped around his waist, he expected to find Destiny showered and fully dressed, but she was still in the bathroom. He didn't hear the water running and assumed she was dressing in there until he saw her clothes still lying in the chair. Disappointed, he called to her in the bathroom. "I won."

"I don't think so," was her response. His jaw dropped as Destiny emerged from the bathroom fully clothed—in *his* clothes. She had gone into his closet and put on a pair of his white jeans. Tucked loosely into the jeans was a sky blue FUBU shirt. The ensemble was held together, and just barely, by a black leather belt. She had even found his RayBans from the dresser and sported them on the bridge of her nose.

"What do you think?" she asked.

Xavier smiled broadly. "I think the next words out of your mouth should be 'Throw your hands in the air and wave 'em like you just don't care!' "

Destiny laughed. "I don't care what you say. I like it." She pulled the sunglasses down even further on her nose. Her almond-shaped eyes softened like a doe's. "Can I wear the ensemble?"

Xavier wondered if he would ever be able to resist giving in to anything Destiny wanted. "Yes, you can wear it. Besides, I think it looks better on you than it does on me."

"Cool," Destiny said, posing like a five-star rapper. "So, as soon as you can break out in some gear, we can bounce!"

"Just give me a minute, Missy Elliott." As Xavier walked past Destiny on the way to his closet, he gave her a quick pat on the behind.

"Ooh," she cooed.

"Don't start," Xavier admonished from inside the closet.

* * *

"Destiny, I'd like you to meet the other woman." Xavier opened a camouflage duffel bag and pulled out a large, sleek-looking crossbow. "Her name is Satet. We've been together for ten years." Destiny examined the dark, shining crossbow. She held out her hands. "May I?"

"Be careful," Xavier said. "She's a delicate one."

Destiny took the crossbow in her hands. It must have weighed about eight pounds. Destiny could see along the sides of it where the wood had been worn and polished. It was obvious that Xavier took good care of it. She handed the weapon back to him. "Should I be jealous?" she asked in jest.

"Yes," Xavier said. "If anything could ever take me away from you, she could."

Destiny raised a quick eyebrow. "How so?"

"Whenever I need to unwind or think through something, I go to the archery range and just shoot. Something about the concentration helps me to focus on not just the target, but my life. Shooting helps me to put things in order."

"Satet?" Destiny said questioningly. "That sounds Egyptian."

Xavier smiled. "It is. Satet is the elephantine goddess of the Nile floods and fertility. The name Satet means 'One Who Shoots Arrows.' "

A very dark, large man sat behind the counter. He was so large his body covered whatever was holding him up. Destiny could only hope there was a seat beneath him. "Looka here, looka here," the fat man said. "If it ain't the songbird."

"Wassup, man?" Xavier responded, extending his hand.

The fat man closed his enormous fingers around Xavier's hand and shook it. "Same ol', same ol'. What about you?"

Xavier shook his head. "Ah, you know me."

"Yeah . . . still singin', huh?"

"It pays the rent, man."

The fat man rolled his rotund body in Destiny's direction. "Who's this?"

"This is Destiny. Destiny, meet Cha Cha."

"Nice to meet you," she said.

Cha Cha nodded and slid over to the cash register on whatever it was that was holding him. "You want the usual?"

"Yeah," Xavier responded.

"Thirty-five," Cha Cha said, extending his large hand once more.

Xavier paid him and turned to enter the range.

"What about her? Does she need a bow?" Cha Cha asked.

"She can use mine," Xavier replied. "I just want to show her the basics."

"Range rules say she has to have a *competent* instructor to help her."

Xavier said nothing. He simply stared at the man in silence.

"Go on, man," Cha Cha said, buzzing them back into the range.

After they entered the range, Destiny wanted to ask about Cha Cha's behavior.

"He's angry with me," Xavier said matter-of-factly.

Destiny sensed a small opening in Xavier's reflective demeanor and decided to enter. "Why?"

They walked along a path inside the range. The artificial bushes and trees made it look almost like the outdoors, but not quite. It looked like they had stepped into Sherwood Forest. Destiny half expected merry men in tights to appear out of nowhere.

"A long time ago I had a chance to be an archer in the Olympics."

"What happened?"

"Nothing happened. I just decided I didn't want to do it."

Xavier took a spot thirty yards in front of a large target with multicolored rings painted on the center and set down his equipment bag. "My passion is making music. I think it's what I was born to do."

Xavier assembled the pieces of his crossbow and Destiny watched in silence. Despite his closed expression, she sensed his vulnerability. "Cha Cha disagrees. He thinks I have some kind of gift for bow hunting. I do it because I enjoy it. It helps me power down and refocus. Cha Cha thinks I was a born archer."

"How did you get involved in archery?"

Xavier gave Destiny a half smile. "Cupid."

"Excuse me?" she asked, blinking in astonishment.

"You know . . . the mythological seraph that shoots people with an arrow and causes them to fall in love."

Xavier's dark eyes bore into Destiny's. She could feel them like hands moving over her body, caressing her. She tried to look away, but she was powerless against his intense gaze.

She managed to break the spell by forcing herself to speak. "Don't tell me you believe in Cupid."

"Why not? Some people call it fate, luck, karma, kismet, chance. I call it Cupid. And Cupid probably looks like a miniature version of Cha Cha with wings and a golden bow."

Destiny laughed heartily. "You believe in Cupid?"

Xavier looked at her with stern resolve poised on his face. Then he flashed her an electric smile. "I believe in Cupid," he said.

Xavier loaded an arrow into the crossbow and lined up the sight on the target. Destiny watched as his body relaxed and he became perfectly still. His breathing went shallow and then he pulled the trigger. The arrow shot from the crossbow and found its mark at the center of the target.

"Wow!" Destiny exclaimed. "Maybe Cha Cha's right."

"Not you too," Xavier said, reaching for another arrow.

"That was a heck of a shot, mister." Destiny watched as Xavier prepared to shoot another arrow. She fell silent, waiting for him to shoot.

"Talk to me, baby," he said. "It will help me concentrate."

"Are you serious?"

"Yes," he said, pulling the trigger. The second arrow took its place beside the first.

Xavier reached into his bag for another arrow. "I usually wear headphones, but today I was hoping you would help to keep me focused."

"Okay," she said. "What should I talk about?"

"Well, there are a couple of things I've been wanting to ask you since we met." Xavier eyed his target once again.

"What?"

"First," he said, smiling. "Are there more black people in Nebraska, or are you the only one?"

Destiny chuckled. "Silly! Of course there are more black people in Nebraska. As a matter of fact, there are quite a few."

"Do tell," he said, shooting the third arrow. It hit the target next to the two arrows already there. Destiny shook her head in astonishment. "Okay, you should really quit your day job."

Xavier smiled and kissed her forehead. "You just bring out the best in me, that's all. If you hadn't been here, I might have been off by as much as one sixteenth of an inch!"

They both laughed and gave each other loud smacks on the lips.

"But back to the Nebraska thing. I always thought that Nebraska was nothing but farmers, livestock, and cornfields. I never imagined any people of color living there."

"Wrong," Destiny replied. "Actually, Nebraska has good doses of Native American, Latino, and Asian populations and a rich African-American history. Most people forget that Malcolm X was born in Omaha."

"That's right," Xavier said.

"And the Underground Railroad had a major station in Nebraska City because of the abolitionist John Brown."

Xavier nodded his head and smoothed his fingers down his subtle facial hair. "Right, right."

"We were in Nebraska as early as the 1700s, when eastern Nebraska was no more than a trading post. The early African-

American homesteaders helped open the frontier to the west. You may have heard of the first African-American in Nebraska. His name was York. He was part of the Lewis and Clark expedition.

"And then when the Exodusters came in the 1860s, Nebraska became a permanent home for many African-American families. And we've been there ever since.

"You should come visit sometime. It's not as fast-paced as Atlanta, but I could show you a good time."

"I know you could," Xavier said. He set the crossbow on the table behind them and walked out to retrieve the arrows. Destiny fingered the crossbow.

"Okay, my turn," she said, as he approached her.

She picked up the weapon. Its surface felt smooth and hard in her hands. Xavier loaded an arrow for her and stood back. *It can't be that difficult,* she thought, aiming at the target.

Destiny pulled back the trigger and the arrow went sailing over the top of the target. Destiny sighed and lowered the crossbow.

"Try again," Xavier said.

"Oh, Xavier, I don't think so. I must not be good at this kinda stuff."

Xavier took a position beside her and explained how to hold the bow correctly. She could feel the warmth radiating from his body, and the smell of his manly cologne made her inhale deeply.

"Now," he said, "you load the arrow like this." He took her fingers and guided them along the shaft of the crossbow. "Got it?"

"Got it," she said. "Okay, look through the telescope and place the crosshairs in the telescope in the middle of the target."

"Got it."

"Now, concentrate on the sound of my voice. Archery begins with the feet, so you've got to align your center of gravity. I want you to relax. Take slow, deep breaths and bend your knees slightly."

Destiny felt herself calming to the sound of Xavier's voice. He spoke softly in her ear. "Take a picture of the target with your mind, keep breathing slowly in and out. Now, close your eyes. Keep breathing slowly in and out. Can you see the target?"

Destiny saw the target vividly in her mind, as if she had developed it in her own darkroom. "Yes, I see it," she said.

"Okay. Open your eyes, inhale, and squeeze the trigger."

Destiny opened her eyes and did as Xavier instructed. The arrow flew from the crossbow and hit the target dead center.

"Hey!" she said, smiling brightly. She triumphantly gave Xavier a high five. "Maybe I should quit my day job."

Xavier took Destiny in his arms. She felt like a breathless girl of eighteen. The very air around her seemed electrified and the nearness of him made her senses spin.

"You could, you know."

"I could what?" she asked as his compelling eyes quickened her heart.

"You could quit your day job and let me take care of you."

Xavier struck a vibrant chord in her. There was no denying that. But somewhere in her thoughts she was haunted by the demons of pain and love lost. Destiny returned Xavier's intense gaze and was about to speak when he covered her lips with his finger.

"Just think about it."

"I will," she agreed. Destiny felt a strong need to change the subject. "You said there were two things you wanted to know. I told you about Nebraska. What was the other thing?"

"It concerns you and Davis."

"Yes," she said, putting an arrow in the crossbow and lining the target in the sight once more.

"For the past few days I've been operating under the assumption that there's nothing between you and Davis except friendship."

Destiny pulled back the trigger and sent another arrow flying. She didn't make a bull's-eye this time, but at least she hit the target. She reached up and touched Xavier's shoulder. "Davis and I were high school sweethearts. Now we're friends."

Her mind drifted back to the nightmare she had several nights ago. She considered telling Xavier about the kiss she shared with Davis. But she wasn't sure if Xavier would understand that the kiss was just an impulsive reflex and nothing more. She decided against telling him.

"So you and he . . ."

Destiny finished Xavier's sentence. "Are buddies and that's all."

Xavier paid Cha Cha for another hour of range time, and he and Destiny spent part of the hour exchanging shots with his crossbow. After a while, Destiny just watched Xavier. He was amazing. "You are truly multitalented, Xavier."

"Not really," he said, shooting another bull's-eye. "I just know what I'm good at." With that, he stroked her chin and neckline with his finger. She felt a ripple of excitement move through her body, happy to be with the man she loved.

Several weeks had passed since Destiny arrived in Atlanta, and she was disappointed. She hadn't seen as much of the city as she had hoped. Most of her time was spent talking to Davis periodically or taking photographs of Xavier. Although Destiny didn't mind the male company, especially Xavier's, she wanted to take advantage of being in what appeared to be a wonderful city. She made up her mind to find out for herself.

It was obvious to her that Davis would be tied up with his projects and would not be able to devote a lot of time to sightseeing with her. Sightseeing with Xavier was an interesting prospect, but she was already spending so much time with him. So Destiny drove to the Atlanta Tourism and Convention Center and picked up some literature on the city and surrounding areas. Then she went back to Davis's and studied the many activities and attractions.

After a thorough examination of all the flyers, pamphlets,

and booklets, Destiny finally settled on an itinerary that would take her at least three days to complete.

Being a kid at heart, Destiny ventured off to ZooAtlanta first. Destiny strolled leisurely past the natural outdoor habitats. Some of the animals, like the gorillas, were difficult for Destiny to get a good look at because of the number of people walking and children in strollers.

But Destiny loved it all. The excitement. The look of awe on the faces of the kids, and probably hers too at times. She thoroughly enjoyed seeing all the rare and endangered animals like the Sumatran tiger, black rhino, and Komodo monitor lizards. Seeing these animals gave Destiny a fulfilling sense of hope for their survival.

Her favorite part of ZooAtlanta was seeing an old gorilla named Willie B. There were so many people around Willie B. that Destiny was enthralled. The crazy thing about it was that he seemed to know that everyone was there to see him. He would look around at the people and stare. Sometimes he sat quite still and then without warning he would raise his ancient body and slowly lumber closer to the visitors.

Before Destiny left the zoo, she got to see a wildlife show, an elephant show, and some of the animals being fed. It was truly an adventure.

When she left the zoo, she drove around for a while, just absorbing the sights. She decided to let chance be her navigator. With the architecture of the Atlanta skyline and the landscaping throughout the city, it was difficult for Destiny to resist the urge to gawk and stare at everything. She felt like the proverbial "goose in a new world" discovering her surroundings for the first time.

As she drove, the city whizzed by her, bright and shiny with possibilities. Even the trees were a different color than what she was used to. And the city sounds—the cars and trucks and people and sirens—went off at a greater pitch and were more jumbled and varied than in her hometown. Destiny's senses were heightened to a new and exciting level.

It was as if she were on the case of a great mystery and trying to solve it by looking for clues in places she'd never been. She had lost track of how many Peachtree streets she had encountered, but she was determined to drive down all of them.

By the time Destiny made her way back to Davis's condo, she had seen several buildings with the name Woodruff, driven through an area called Fayetteville, and seen America's largest concentration of African-American college students. *It's been a good day,* she thought to herself.

After wandering through the city wherever she fancied, Destiny decided on a cultural heritage tour for the next day's outing. For fifty-five dollars, she visited places that she imagined could keep her deep in photohistoric duties for years to come.

Her adventure started at 7:00 A.M. when a van full of twenty departed from the downtown Atlanta Hilton. It was an all-day tour that according to the brochure would provide visitors with an inspiring dose of African-American culture, Atlanta style. The price of the tour included lunch.

Destiny took a seat in the middle section of the van. She watched as the other tourists came on after her. There were two elderly couples, several families and one young couple that practically sat in each other's laps. Then there was one young woman who looked to be about Destiny's age. She plopped down in the seat next to her.

The woman wore a Tommy Hilfiger sweatsuit that coordinated quite well, Destiny noticed, with her shining auburn hair and deep red nail polish. The woman's silver sunglasses sat perched on top of her hair that was pulled into a tight ponytail, which swished from side to side. Destiny wasn't sure what perfume the woman was wearing, but it wafted around her with a heavy floral aroma.

The woman looked over at her while popping what Destiny imagined was a large wad of bubble gum. "Hi," she said brightly. "I'm Star."

"Hi, Star," Destiny said. "I'm Destiny."

"Nice to meet you," Star said, settling back into the seat. "Where are you from?"

"I'm from Nebraska. Lincoln, Nebraska."

"No kidding," Star said without missing a pop.

Destiny watched the remaining passengers board the van and then turned her attention back to Star. She waited for the all-too-familiar comment *I didn't know that there are black people in Nebraska.* Interestingly enough, it never came. "Where are you from?" she asked Star.

"I'm from here."

"Really?" Destiny said, intrigued.

"Yeah. I'm taking the tour because I want to go on vacation but I don't really have the time. So I decided to compromise and take my vacation in the ATL." Star stopped chewing for a moment. "Crazy, right?"

Destiny thought about that. It sounded reasonable to her. She might have done as much herself if she hadn't needed so desperately to get away from Lincoln. "Not at all," she said.

"Everybody always talks about how wonderful this place is. Since I've lived here all my life, it's hard for me to see what others see. Don't get me wrong. I like Atlanta. I just don't think it's *all that.*"

Even though Destiny and Star hit it off, they discovered they had many differences. Where Destiny was fascinated with history, Star's passion was in cosmetology. They both had bachelor's degrees. Destiny talked about her degree in cultural anthropology and Star spoke on her degrees in business and economics.

"You pursued a double major?" Destiny asked.

"My parents wouldn't have it any other way. I told them I was going to open my own beauty salon after I graduated from high school. They said they would give me the money if I earned a degree in business or economics before going to beauty school. When I earned both, my parents paid for my tuition at Clark's Beauty College, too."

"Must be nice," Destiny said, feeling lucky that she had gotten a scholarship to the University of Nebraska. Otherwise, she might not have been able to attend college at all.

"Sometimes it's best to beware of what you wish for. My salon keeps me so busy that it's hard for me to get away sometimes."

Destiny reflected on her own job at the arts council. Again she felt lucky that she was in a position to take a leisurely leave of absence, which allowed her to be here in Atlanta in the first place.

The van driver, who also served as the tour guide, introduced herself as Charlotte Perkins and welcomed them aboard. She reminded them that unlike the more scenic tours, the cultural heritage tour required that they spend most of their time off the van. The tall, slender woman with an ultrashort hairdo mentioned that she hoped all the passengers were wearing comfortable shoes. Destiny was glad she had read the tour brochure thoroughly and had put on her most comfortable outfit—a red-and-white striped sweater with red stretch pants and red tennis shoes. She brought her camera gear with her just in case.

The first stop for the group was Mind, Body, and Soul Enterprises, where lectures and seminars were given on the subject of holistic community development. Then it was on to the Afro-American Cultural Center and then to the National Black College Alumni Hall of Fame. After the hall of fame, the group continued to Trevor Arnett Library, which featured papers and works of prominent African-American literary figures, as well as works by modern African-American artists.

The tour guide commented on each place they stopped and allowed the group ample time to soak up the breadth of what each place had to offer. Destiny and Star became fast tour companions and walked together, sharing their reactions to what they saw and heard.

Destiny was all but overwhelmed by the sheer magnitude of the information and how well-documented the history of the area was. As they rode from one stop to the other, the tour guide relayed the details of the Civil War and how General William Tecumseh Sherman burned down the city of Atlanta during his famed march to the sea and forced J. B. Hood and his Confederate troops to surrender under a tremendous land assault. Destiny was captivated. Although she knew the events of the Civil War, she never knew them with such detail and had no idea about the important role the city of Atlanta played in the end of the Civil War and the freedom of her people.

Destiny wished she could summon some of the artists from the arts council to be with her on this tour. She knew they would thoroughly enjoy the cultural extravaganza she'd been treated to so far.

For lunch, the tour group went to Charlie Hall's, a soul food restaurant in the historic Sweet Auburn district. Destiny ordered greens, black-eyed peas, corn bread, and peach cobbler for dessert. She and the others on the tour remarked about how good the food was and were appreciative of the healthy portions they were served.

Star ordered a half slab of barbecued ribs, macaroni and cheese, and mashed potatoes and gravy. Destiny took one look at Star's slim figure and wondered where she was going to put all that food.

"Star, if I even smelled all that food, I'd gain ten pounds."

Star swallowed a forkful of mac and cheese and laughed. "I have a naturally high metabolism. I've always been able to eat as much as I want to." Star took a healthy bite of ribs and smiled.

"I wish I had that problem," Destiny remarked sarcastically.

The young couple that had been closer than close the entire morning caught Destiny's eye. They were smiling, laughing, and feeding lunch to each other. "How old do you think they are?"

Star followed Destiny's gaze over to the couple. "Early twenties. Very early twenties."

"Did you ever act like that when you were their age?"

"Destiny, I think the right person will make you act like that at any age."

Destiny thought about Xavier. He did have that effect on her. Since they had been spending time together, she felt blissfully happy and fully alive. Just being in his presence was a source of joy. "I guess you're right about that."

"Now," Star said, finishing off another bite of barbecue, "if I can just find the right person."

"Here, here," Destiny said, and the two exchanged a high five.

"What you need is to walk off all that food now," Charlotte said when they had finished eating. Charlotte signed for the check and the group headed back to the van. By the time they had finished their lunch, the sun was sitting in the middle of the sky. There were very few clouds and the breeze in the air was warm and constant. *Just like my feelings for Xavier,* Destiny thought as she got on the bus.

The afternoon was as impressive as the morning. They stopped at the Herndon Home, the former residence of Alonzo Herndon, a Georgia-born slave who founded the Atlanta Life Insurance Company. Destiny noted how the residence-turned-museum housed a permanent exhibit of the original family furnishings and decorative artwork.

Then they went on a quick visit to the *Atlanta Inquirer,* a weekly black community newspaper. From there they went to the APEX Museum, where Destiny found exhibits on African-American heritage specific to Atlanta. She spent time with the others in the group looking over the audiovisual presentations and other displays.

The favorite part of the trip for Destiny was the last stop before they returned to the hotel. They spent two hours in the Shrine of the Black Madonna bookstore. They spent the first hour just looking at the books and talking about the topics and authors. The second hour, the group attended a discussion and book signing by Amiri Baraka, one of Destiny's favorite poets.

With all their differences, Destiny and Star found that they had one important thing in common: a love of books. The two walked around the bookstore together and discussed the many books they had read and those they wanted to read.

"Who's your favorite author?" Star asked, flipping through an anthology of African-American short stories.

Destiny didn't have to think or hesitate. "James Baldwin."

"My sister!" Star exclaimed, replacing the anthology on its rack. "Go Tell It On The Mountain."

"If Beale Street Could Talk."

"The Devil Finds Work."

They continued to recount Baldwin's works in a call-and-response pattern.

"The Fire Next Time," they said in unison.

Their shared love of James Baldwin was the catalyst for the rest of their discussion in the bookstore. They browsed through rows of books, art displays, and magazines while swapping life stories. They managed to fill their time talking about the logistics of opening a new salon and the dynamics of archiving a people's history.

By the end of the tour, Destiny and Star were both tired and exhilarated. They exchanged business cards, and before they parted ways they promised to e-mail each other to keep in touch.

Destiny was on her own for dinner. She resisted the urge to call Davis and ask him to join her. She was determined to finish out the day with her independence intact. After shuffling through her tourist magazines, she decided on a place called Café TuTu Tango.

It was a restaurant that doubled as an artists' loft, where painters, sculptors, and musicians hung out and actually worked on their art as patrons were eating. Destiny found it had an avant-garde but pleasant atmosphere, especially the saxophone music played by a man named Billy T. After her full day, the appetizer-sized portions of food served at the restaurant were just what Destiny needed.

She drove back to Davis's condo full and content. She couldn't wait until the third and final day of her lone excursions.

The next morning, Destiny got an early start on the day. She wanted to get out while the city was still waking up. Since she hadn't really taken many pictures in the past two days, she decided to devote the majority of her time to that task.

When she told Davis about her plans to spend the day taking pictures, he suggested that she drive over to Piedmont Park. Now headed in that direction going east of downtown, Destiny thought of the simplicity of the streets in Lincoln. It was so easy to get around there. The streets ran east-west and north-south in nearly straight lines. But to Destiny, Atlanta seemed to be laid out more like a starburst of streets that emanated from somewhere in the center of the city and wiggled their way outward to the fringes. Twice Destiny had gotten lost only to find that she had missed her turn simply because she was expecting a predictable intersection with the street she wanted. Luckily, there was always someone around to point her in the right direction before she had gone too far out of her way.

Maybe people around here navigate on instinct, she thought. Xavier had called her Sojourner when she told him of her travels these past few days.

"You sound restless."

"No, not restless. Just eager to explore. I want to see what's out there, and I feel like going by myself."

After their conversation, Destiny realized that she was talking about more than venturing out into a new city. She also needed to see what possibilities were out there for her to regain some semblance of normalcy in her life. To be a whole human being again.

As she came upon the park area, Destiny was once again awed by the lush vegetation and rolling topography that seemed at times to just appear instantly on the Atlanta landscape. Here it was in front of her again. And she couldn't wait to get it on film. Her plan was to finish out her remaining roll and then meet Xavier for dinner. With camera in hand, Destiny headed toward where her artistic eye led her.

"Wait! Stay just like that," Destiny insisted, hopping out of bed. *I could get used to this,* she thought. She hurried over to where her camera bag lay at the foot of Xavier's bed. She had dropped it there along with the rest of her things. After spending all day taking pictures, and then having a late dinner with Xavier, they came back to his house exhausted.

Destiny didn't remember waking during the night either. The next thing she knew it was morning, and Xavier was awake with his head propped on his arm, watching her. She liked to watch him watching her. There was a light in his eyes these days that floated Destiny's heart on a cloud of happiness. If she could just capture that light, maybe she could make it last forever. The thought of being without Xavier was painful, but if their relationship should end, at least she'd have something to remember the happiness she felt.

She attached the flash unit to the top of the camera and turned around to face Xavier.

"Aw," he said, smiling at her in her T-shirt and undies. "I was enjoying the view."

"My thoughts exactly," she responded, and she aimed the camera toward Xavier lying on the bed. The champagne-colored sheet was swirled around his midsection, revealing part of a muscular thigh and well-defined stomach muscles.

Xavier held up a hand in protest. "Oh, no you don't."

"But, Xavier," Destiny said, focusing the lens on the camera. "You look so good lying there. Please let me take your picture." Destiny moved closer and continued adjusting the settings on her manual camera. First she focused on his muscular chest covered with crisp, fine hair, then down toward his caramel-rum-colored legs looking as firm as tree trunks. Destiny licked her lips. "Just one."

Xavier lowered his hand in concession. "All right, but you owe me. And you have to promise to pay up when I say it's time to pay up. Okay, Boo?"

"Boo?" Destiny replied, nearly satisfied with what she saw in her viewfinder.

"Boo, Shorty, Baby. They all mean you're mine." Destiny liked the sound of that. "So take your picture," he said. He watched her working the camera. Her locks and regal stance gave her the presence of an African queen.

"Umm, Xavier. There's one more thing. Can you pull the sheet back just a little? I want to give that massive thigh of yours some special attention."

Xavier did as she asked. "Just remember this when your time comes."

"I will," she said, snapping away.

"Hey! I thought you were only going to take one picture."

"Sorry, I got carried away."

Xavier got up from the bed and walked toward her. Destiny backed up and continued to take pictures of him as he came closer, wearing nothing but a pair of burgundy boxer shorts.

"Speaking of getting carried away," he said, scooping her up into his arms.

"Ooh," she said, holding on. He gently eased her down onto the bed.

"You won't be needing this," he said, taking the camera and placing it on the nightstand. Destiny felt her senses heightening. Her blood began to race throughout her body in anticipation of what Xavier would do next.

He lowered his head and took her mouth gently into his. His tongue slow-danced across her lips and made teasing ventures inside her mouth. Once there, the movements were as soothing as ocean waves, and Destiny moaned at the hypnotic sensation it caused. And then, quite abruptly, he stopped. Destiny gasped and opened her eyes. The light in his eyes was there, shining on her. It made her feel strong and vulnerable at the same time.

"Wait! Stay just like that," Xavier insisted, echoing Destiny's earlier line. He walked toward the door.

"Oh, Xavier, I . . ."

"Ah, ah, ah," Xavier said, pointing a finger in the air. "You promised."

Destiny felt her longing and need for Xavier rising. "Don't go now," she protested.

Xavier put his finger to his lips. "Shh," he said and left the room.

Destiny was outdone. Did he think he was just going to leave her hanging like this? Maybe she had it coming for asking to take his picture when he was half-clothed. And then she *did* take more than one. But to do *this*. Destiny could not imagine a worse punishment. Just as she was about to call out to him and say she was sorry, Xavier came back into the room carrying a metronome.

He set the metronome on his dresser and started it with a wide swing. The rhythmic pulse of the pendulum as it passed the center point reminded Destiny of her heart only a few short moments ago. Under the spell of Xavier's kiss, her heart could beat quite strongly.

Xavier took his place beside her on the bed. He ran his hand down the side of Destiny's face and across her chin. The sensation sent small detonations to all the sensitive areas on Destiny's body. "What's the metronome for?" she asked softly.

The light in Xavier's eyes ignited once again. "I am going to play your body like an instrument." He kissed her on the lips. "And you, with the help of that pacesetter, are going to keep time."

"What?" Destiny responded, opening her eyes wide.

With each beat of the metronome, Xavier placed a small kiss along her neck and shoulders. "Remember your promise."

"I remember," she said, and cooperated with Xavier as he removed first her T-shirt, then her underwear.

"I'm going to tell you a story," he said, kissing Destiny's

hand and wrist. "Do you know why the drum was the first instrument ever invented?"

"No," she said, feeling her body tingle wherever Xavier kissed it. Then Destiny relaxed completely as Xavier told her the story of the drum. Mingled throughout the story were kisses and caresses that made Destiny wriggle with passion.

"The first form of communication ever was a man trying to tell the woman he loved how he felt." Destiny felt Xavier's strong hands explore the soft lines of her back, her waist, and her hips. "The only way he could think to explain himself was to pound his chest or pound the objects around him, the rocks, the wood."

Xavier returned his attentions to Destiny's shoulders, then carefully worked his way across them, kissing, caressing, stroking, and then down where he lingered lavishly on each breast. His tongue made a path down her ribs to her stomach while his hands searched for her pleasure points and found them. "Because that was the sound he heard his heart make whenever she was around."

Xavier was a sensual virtuoso. He let his fingers eagerly roam her body, strumming, tapping, and rolling back and forth over each erogenous zone.

By the time he finished the story, Destiny's need was exquisite. Xavier removed his boxers, put on a condom, and placed himself carefully inside her. Instantly, she surrendered to the sleek caress of his body.

They began their joining slowly, and then Destiny's passion became more and more urgent. Just as she felt herself about to be swept away in the current of their lovemaking, she heard Xavier's voice in her ear. "Remember your promise," he whispered.

"I remember," she said, and she slowed her rhythm to match that of the metronome. But just as before, Xavier's kisses and soft caresses took her to the brink of ecstasy. And again he whispered in her ear. "You keep your promises, don't you?"

"Y-yes," Destiny moaned and slowed her rhythm. Xavier held

Destiny's hands as they lay on the pillow above her head. "Do you keep other promises too?" he murmured and kissed her on the forehead. "Do you promise to be mine?"

"Y-yes."

"Do you promise to let me make you happy?"

"Y-yes," Destiny whimpered. She could feel her love for Xavier so intensely she could hardly contain herself. His body imprisoned hers in a web of growing arousal. She held on to Xavier's hands tighter and tighter. Instinctively, she arched her body toward him.

"Nope, not yet, baby," he said, probing her mouth with his tongue.

And then she felt the wall of her resolve burst into a million rainbows in her soul. Destiny cried out his name in release.

"Hmm," Xavier said, using his tongue to pluck delicately at a place on her neck that made her gasp. "I think you should do that again."

"But, Xavier . . ." she began.

"Shh," he whispered. "Do you remember your promise?"

Destiny was too spellbound by Xavier's lovemaking to speak, but her body communicated a slow and rhythmic "Yes."

Destiny sorted through the pictures she had taken of Xavier. She had them spread out all over the bed in Davis's guest room. She had to admit they looked good. Xavier looked good. She especially liked the pictures she took of him in the subway. Even in a crowd, his presence was captivating. Pictures of him walking among streams of people, and then alone. The picture of him leaning against a concrete wall was exceptional. The contrast between Xavier's well-groomed and chiseled features and the raw, cracked cement was both startling and intriguing.

In some of the pictures he looked eternally youthful, almost boyish, and Destiny had worked hard to capture the radiant smile that warmed her heart so. In other pictures, his sensuality was smoldering and nearly vaporized the photo paper it was printed on. Destiny traced her finger across Xavier's thick eyebrows, over to his sideburns, and down to the cleft in his chin. Like a schoolgirl, she couldn't resist the temptation, so she picked up the picture and kissed it. Her lipstick left a rose-colored impression of her lips on the side of Xavier's face.

Destiny continued sorting the pictures. She set the ones aside that she knew would work for his montage and collected the others in a pile. She noticed that in some of the pictures, Xavier looked solemn and pensive, as if he were thinking about something painful or sad. Whatever it was, Destiny wanted to remove it from his thoughts forever.

She heard the phone ringing and was expecting Davis to answer it when she remembered that he was at work. She walked over to the other side of the bed and picked up the phone.

"Van Housen residence."

"Hey, baby."

Xavier's melodic voice wrapped her in its tenderness. Destiny felt her spirits soar. "Hey," she said.

"I'm in the car headed to the studio and suddenly I got an urge to call. So . . . whatchadoin'?"

"Actually," Destiny said slyly, "I have a delicious-looking man on my bed."

"You better be kidding," Xavier said, bass thundering through his voice.

"I'm very serious," Destiny replied, trying not to laugh.

"You're trying to make me crash my vehicle, aren't you?"

Destiny couldn't hold back the laughter anymore. "Of course not. The man on my bed is you, silly. I'm looking at the pictures we took. They turned out nicely."

"Really? When can I see them?"

"Well, ordinarily I would put them into a grouping that sort of tells a story, so that my client can get an idea of the portfolio's full potential."

"Sounds good to me. When can you have it ready?"

"Well, as a matter of fact, I was looking at a tentative arrangement when you called. I like it, but I think something's missing."

"What could be missing? Woman, you have taken more pictures of me than any other photographer in the history of my short music career."

"Any experienced photographer takes lots of pictures. You're just mad because I won't let you have your way in the poses."

They both laughed. "So what's missing, camera lady?"

"You, singing. No matter what, you're a singer. So to do justice to this montage, somewhere there should be shots of you performing."

"I was afraid you were going to say that. I don't have another concert scheduled for a while. I'm supposed to be spending this time working on songs to record soon."

"Will you be working alone?"

"Some of the time. And some of the time, I'll be trying things out with the crew. Experimenting with new tracks, getting the kinks worked out before I actually record."

"Perfect," Destiny commented. "I can go with you to the studio one day and shoot a couple rolls of film. That is, if you don't mind."

"Well . . . no, I guess I don't mind."

"Uh-oh," she said. "You sound hesitant."

"I know. I think it would make me nervous to have to perform in front of you."

"But, Xavier, you perform in front of hundreds of people. And besides, you've already performed in front of me, remember?"

"That was different. I was on a stage and the fans gave off so much energy, it took the pressure off me trying to impress you. But if you're going to be right there and I don't have a hundred fans to vibe from . . ."

"Why, Xavier, if I didn't know better, I'd accuse you of stage fright. What about the time in the church? There weren't any fans then."

"I know, but I wasn't performing or rehearsing. I was venting, sort of."

Destiny wasn't sure what to say to allay his concerns. And then he conceded.

"Okay, okay. After today, I'm due at the studio in two days. Will you be ready at nine?"

"Have camera, will travel!"

"You know I consider you the toughest audience I've ever had."

Destiny looked down at the pictures on the bed. "I know what you mean. I've been going through these photographs hoping that you'll like them."

Destiny twirled the phone cord between her thumb and index finger. She felt giddy and wondered if at some point her natural high would end. After Rico, the last thing she needed was to come crashing down from a relationship with someone else. If she had used her better judgment, she would never have become involved with Xavier in the first place.

She remembered picking up the pictures of him at the photo developers. Destiny was lucky enough to find a company that developed photos by hand. The woman at the counter went over each shot with her to make sure Destiny was satisfied with the quality.

"Is this who I think it is?" the woman asked.

"If you think it's Allgood, the answer is yes."

"Oooo," the woman said, flipping through the photographs. "He is so handsome. And I love his music. He really is a star."

A star indeed, Destiny said to herself. What was she thinking? Could he possibly care about her, really? After all, she was just a Nebraska girl. Elise Kent seemed much more outgoing and sophisticated.

"You didn't hang up on me, did you?" Xavier's comment brought Destiny out of her thoughts.

"No, I'm still here. I've just got some things on my mind, I guess."

"Hmm. Something I can help with?"

"I don't know, Xavier. I don't think you can. I just need to work it through myself."

"Well, whatever it is, I don't like it. You sound too distant. What's up?"

"N-nothing. Really. Nothing at all." Destiny didn't feel comfortable sharing her insecurities with Xavier. She wasn't sure at this point if they were real insecurities or merely residue from a bad relationship. Until she could figure out which, she thought it best to keep her feelings to herself.

"You're sure it's nothing."

Destiny couldn't lie to Xavier, but she wasn't ready to tell him what was on her mind, yet. "I'm sure it's something that I have to resolve on my own and nothing for you to worry about."

When Destiny and Xavier arrived at The Sky Set, the band was already warming up.

"Where you been, big guy?" Tyrica asked, loudly popping her gum.

Xavier looked at Destiny and smiled broadly. Then he sucked his cheeks in and pushed out his lips. "We . . . ah . . ."

Destiny helped him finish his sentence. "We got . . . ah . . . stuck in traffic." She looked up at him. The ardor in his eyes caught her breath. She truly loved this man.

"Good lord, you two. Does he have any energy left to sing?" Sammy scratched his head. "Getting stuck in traffic can be, ah, strenuous."

Xavier watched as Destiny headed toward the sound room. "I've got more energy than I know what to do with. So, are we gonna do this?"

As Destiny walked past Tyrica, Tyrica whispered in her ear. "Girl, did you do it in the car on the way over or what?"

Destiny just smiled. She knew she was probably giving herself away, but she didn't care. She was too happy. Tyrica's words traveled into the sound room with her. "Ah, sookie, sookie, now."

Brian was tapping lightly on the drums and watching Tyrica. "Girl, you need to stay outta grown folks' business."

"Oh, she's all right," Destiny replied.

"Well, if she gets outta hand, you let me know."

"Hey, y'all," Shade said from behind her keyboard. "Are we ready?"

Destiny stepped into the sound room. She was grateful for the closed session and wanted to let them warm up before she started taking pictures. That way, she figured, if they were really into it, she would not be as much of a distraction. And she could still get some really good shots.

Destiny sat quietly and resisted the temptation to push, pull, or turn something. There were so many levers, buttons, and knobs on the mixing board in front of her, it was amazing to her that anyone could figure out how it worked. *This is worse than being in an airplane cockpit,* she thought.

After some discussion over music sheets, and numerous half starts and pauses, Xavier's band finally started playing. The song was upbeat but not too fast. It was just funky enough to make you want to move your head to the rhythm.

She didn't know how he had done it, but Xavier managed to weave together several distinct styles into one hot stroke of musical genius. Dutch's lead guitar was reminiscent of heavy metal, Sammy's bass guitar sounded like old-school funk, Brian played percussion seasoned with Latin salsa, and Shade at the keyboard held it all together with undertones of gospel.

Unlike his other songs, which were famous for their full-bodied lyrics, this one was primarily an instrumental. Periodically, Xavier would harmonize with his background singers, LeRoy, LeRon, and Tyrica.

> *Why fly when you can soar*
> *Ever more?*
> *Heaven's where you explore*
> *Ever more, ever more, ever more*

Just like exercise, Destiny thought, *this was an easy warmup.* Something snappy yet not too strenuous that tuned the instruments and vocal cords until they were synchronous. It got the blood flowing, like a good stretch, and prepared them for the workout to come.

Destiny watched them and plotted out shots in her mind. She decided that she would have to adjust the lighting, but once done, she would stand near the entrance and the windows where the light would favor Xavier best. She watched him poised at the microphone. He seemed so comfortable there despite his reservations of performing in front of her.

Xavier smiled at her periodically, but mostly he looked full of concentration as he attended to the band's playing and his singing. Xavier had told her he had made a special arrangement with his record company so that the band he recorded with was also the band he toured with. This was not always the case, especially for relatively new artists. But the record producers had agreed, and thankfully so had the musicians.

Destiny wanted that element to show through in the pictures. The band's camaraderie and sense of family was an important aspect of Xavier's life. If this montage was going to be an honest portrayal of Xavier's life, she owed it to him to try and capture it.

"Stop, stop," Xavier's voice came loud and clear into the sound room. The music halted into a trailing off of discordant notes.

"Something's not right here and damned if I know what it is." Xavier motioned to the man considered to be Jimi Hendrix's alter ego. "Dutch, give me the refrain again." Dutch did as he was asked.

"Okay, cool. Shade, now you."

Shade moved her fingers across the keyboard as if they were gliding on air. "All right, now both of you together."

The two band members played their parts together and the other band members recoiled slightly. Xavier shook his head. "Found it."

"Oh, lord," Sammy responded. "Now he's gonna make us lay tracks individually."

"Never happen," Xavier countered. "Here's the deal. The message of this song is to expect the best, in each of us, but especially ourselves. I want to punch the song during the second refrain so that we . . ."

Xavier was interrupted by his crew, who finished his sentence for him. "Take it to another level."

Destiny could feel that they were in sync now. She removed the lens cap of her camera and stepped out of the sound room.

Shade was ripping notes off her keyboard. Xavier was nodding his head and smiling. "Now that's the level I'm talkin' 'bout. Let's take it from the top to see if the rest of us can catch up with you."

The musicians began the song again, and just as Xavier had wanted, it was obvious that they had all ascended to the next level. The music was an eclectic blend of cultures and influences and the vocals were uplifting and powerful. Destiny took picture after picture. Some of Xavier alone, but most of Xavier singing, playing the tambourine, and dancing around to each band member. As the rehearsal continued, Destiny took pictures from various angles. For some, she sat or lay on the floor. For others, she stood on tables and chairs to get special angles and interactions between band members. She also experimented with different amounts of light, from no artificial light to turning on every light in the studio. Before Destiny realized it, she had taken six rolls of film. While the band members wound down from the short but intense session, Destiny wound down too.

She hoped she captured the magic through her lens—the magic she felt in the church, the magic she felt at the concert, and the magic in her heart at that very moment when Xavier smiled at her from behind the mike and she knew she was the luckiest woman on earth.

Fourteen

Destiny was tired. She was glad that her *client* was giving her the day off. With the exception of her three-day tour, she had spent nearly every day taking pictures or talking about taking pictures or planning to take pictures or having the pictures that she had taken developed. Sometimes she wondered if Xavier really needed all these pictures or if he was just using the montage as an excuse for them to be together.

But Destiny soon proved that she was willing to simply spend time with him without the intrusion of the camera. When he asked if she wanted to just hang out one day at his house, she jumped at the chance. Her heart had spoken so quickly for her. "Xavier, that sounds wonderful!" She hoped she didn't seem too eager. She didn't want him to think that she was starstruck. He had smiled so sweetly and sighed after her response, as if he was experiencing his own eagerness.

She was sitting on the floor of Xavier's living room. It was decorated in an almost pristine white, from the carpet to the furniture to the walls. In the borders on the walls and accents on the furniture were flecks of hunter green that broke up the sheer bright white in the room.

Destiny made herself comfortable in the living room while Xavier made a phone call in the den. She had taken her shoes off and was running her hands across the plush-pile Berber. It was bumpy and silky smooth. She watched as the fibers moved

under her fingers and spread into patterns where her palm left
a trail.

"What I wouldn't give to be that carpet right now."

Destiny turned to see Xavier coming toward her. He looked
marvelously comfortable in a pair of loose denim shorts and a
snug tank top.

"What were you thinking just then?"

"I was thinking that I'm glad I've finally got a day off. My
latest client has been _so_ demanding," she teased.

Xavier walked over to the fireplace and lit the logs piled in
the hearth. "Oh, really. Tell me about this _client_ of yours."

Xavier sat down behind Destiny and stretched his long muscular legs on the outsides of hers. Destiny felt a tingling sensation in the lower part of her stomach as he scooted in behind
her and wrapped her in his powerful arms.

"Well, first of all," she said, cradling his arms in hers, "he's
narcissistic."

"What!"

Destiny chuckled silently. "Yeah. I can't tell you how many
pictures I've taken of him, and no matter how many I take, he
wants more."

"Uh-huh."

"But it's okay, because he's kinda cute."

Xavier put his chin on Destiny's shoulder. "So you like him,
then?"

Destiny was thoroughly enjoying their role-play. "I'm not
sure," she said, chuckling loudly this time.

"What!"

"I mean, he's all right."

Xavier planted tiny kisses along the base of Destiny's neck.
"What would it take to make you like him better?"

"I don't know, maybe . . ." Destiny's voice trailed off as his
massive hands encircled her breasts and kneaded them delicately.

"How about that?" he asked. "Does that convince you?"

"Maybe," she said, wanting more of him.

He curved his body toward her and kissed her mouth passionately. Destiny's need for him started on its slow, familiar ascent. She reached out for him and pulled herself close. Xavier pulled himself away gently. "Do you like him better now?"

"Yes!" Destiny said, twisting herself around. When they were face-to-face, she returned Xavier's passion-filled kiss with one of her own. Then, slowly, she painted a trail of kisses down the side of his neck and onto his chest. She pulled his tank top out of his shorts and slid her tongue lightly across the fine curly hairs on Xavier's lower abdomen. He moaned deeply.

"Destiny," he murmured.

She continued her careful descent of his body until she found the place where the hairs on his stomach thickened.

"Destiny, stop."

Now it was her turn to be astonished. "Why?" she asked as she sat back.

Xavier reached up and touched the side of her face. "I want you so badly right now," he said.

"I hear a *but* coming," she said, disappointed.

Xavier's eyes searched hers for understanding. "But I don't want you to ever believe that that's all there is between us. There's more to what I feel for you, and there are other ways to express it besides making love."

"That's the nicest rejection I've ever had." Destiny took a deep breath and released it slowly.

"It's not a rejection, lovely. It's just me wanting to experience all of you." Xavier circled one of Destiny's hardened nipples with his finger. "Not just your beautiful body."

"Okay," she said and sank into his arms. "So what shall we do today since we're just hanging out here?"

Xavier snuggled up closer to Destiny. "Well, we could watch videos, listen to music, or . . ."

"What's that?" Destiny was curious about the rectangular wood carving on the wall above the fireplace. It was painted with bold swatches of copper, as if it were splashed over in a frenzy. And there were small, gnarled-looking lobes clustered

on the outside of the piece. On the inside were multicolored
bits of jewelry, buttons, feathers, and other small objects. The
piece reminded her of the work of an artist in Lincoln.

"My sister Martí made it," Xavier said. Destiny could hear
the pride flowing through in his voice. "She's not an artist, but
every now and then something comes over her. The next thing
you know, she's sending us all something from her latest fascination." Xavier pointed to another wood carving on the opposite
wall. "She made that one, too."

"And you say she's not an artist."

"Well, she's the one that actually says that. The rest of us
just go along with her until we get something else from her
that's wonderful."

Destiny settled back into his embrace. "Tell me about your
family, Xavier. We've never talked much about them."

Xavier cocked his head to the side. He looked up as if fetch-
ing a memory. "Let's see. My sisters are Yolanda, Roxanne,
Morgan, Ashley, and Martí, in that order."

"And you're in the middle?"

"Yep. Right between Morgan and Ashley."

"What was it like growing up in a house full of women?"

Xavier smiled. "Loud. If you wanted something, like new
clothes, a toy, or to stay out late, sometimes it was simply a
matter of who had the loudest voice."

"In other words, the one who got on your parents' nerves the
most."

"You got it." Xavier rose and walked to the fireplace. The
logs were burning too quickly. Xavier stoked the fire with a
black iron poker and then added another log. He returned to
where Destiny was sitting, and both of them stretched out on
the carpet beside each other.

"Most of our activities centered around church. My parents
were very religious."

"Were?"

"Yes," Xavier responded, lowering his head slightly. "My

father died when I was ten and my mother when I was twenty-five."

"I'm sorry," Destiny said, seeing the sorrow in Xavier's eyes. "My father was a diabetic and went into a diabetic coma. He never recovered. I think my mother missed him so much that as soon as she felt that Martí, the baby, could take care of herself, she went to join her husband."

Destiny could see that the pain in Xavier's eyes was beginning to dissipate. "What about you?" he asked. "You haven't told me much about your family either."

"My parents live in Lincoln. And it's just me, myself, and I. You don't have to worry about shouting matches when you're an only child. But you do have to find ways to entertain yourself."

Xavier turned over on his back and Destiny turned toward him, lying on her side. She fought an urge to kiss him, and lost. She gave him a quick smooch on the cheek and continued. "My mom and dad were in their forties when they had me. They had tried for twenty years to have a child.

"I come from a religious family too, and when other people said that my parents should adopt, they believed that God would bless them with a child.

"One day my mom went to the doctor because she wasn't feeling well. The doctor ran some tests and told her she was pregnant. When she went home and told my dad, he held her in his arms and said he knew they were destined to have a child. It was at that moment that my mom says they decided to name me Destiny."

Xavier reached up and pulled Destiny to him. He gave her a kiss on the cheek. He tried to imagine what it would be like to have parents again. Then he hoped Destiny's parents would accept him as their son-in-law because he was determined to marry their daughter. Just then he sat up. "I've got something for you," he said and sprang from the floor.

He returned with a wallet-sized box wrapped in blue and gold paper. A small gold bow was set in the middle.

Destiny sat up and took the box. She worked carefully to open it without ripping the paper. Finally she uncovered the small white box and opened it. At first, Destiny's mouth gaped open, and then it melted into a smile that lit up the entire room. She reached into the box and took out the watch encrusted with tiny chipped diamonds.

Just like at the bazaar, Xavier saw the reflection of the diamonds sparkling in her eyes. The sight was beautiful and moving. He hoped that expression on her face meant she still liked it.

Destiny threw her arms around him and covered him with kisses. Before he could get his balance, the two of them toppled over. That didn't dissuade Destiny. She still continued to smother him with kisses.

"Does that mean that you like it?" he asked, giving Destiny's lips free reign over his body.

Destiny paused her onslaught of affection. "I adore it, Xavier. Thank you."

She spent the rest of the day styling and profiling her watch. Xavier was glad it made her happy. If she liked diamonds, there was one in particular he had in mind. But he wondered if he might be rushing things.

They spent the afternoon playing all kinds of games. First it was spades, then blackjack, gin rummy, and hearts. After that, they played dominoes and Othello.

They played checkers and chess many times over. Then they played backgammon. After several games, they found that they were evenly matched.

"You were an only child," Xavier exclaimed when Destiny beat him at acey-duecy. "How did you get so good at these games?"

Destiny grabbed a handful of peanuts and shook them in her hand. "My best friend Jacq is a game fanatic. We play all the time."

"Who is this Jack? This must be the third time you've mentioned him."

"Jacq and I go way back. *She* and I have known each other since junior high."

"Whew. For a moment I thought I had some competition." Xavier was relieved. He couldn't help himself. He felt a hard twinge of jealousy whenever he thought of Destiny with any other man.

They finished their day by cooking a large dinner together and eating outside on Xavier's patio. They sat under the stars and talked some more about their families. When they finally went inside, they put the dishes in the dishwasher and had just enough energy to take themselves to bed.

"Do you mind getting up early in the morning? I've got to go down to my manager's office. He left me an urgent message. Apparently there's something going on that can't wait, but he didn't say what it was."

"Oh, Xavier, you know how I like to sleep late."

"I know, but I couldn't track him down earlier today, and I know he'll be in his office tomorrow."

"Can't I just stay here?"

"Well, you could, but I've got another surprise for you."

"Really?"

"Yep, my homeboy Brian McKnight is giving a concert tomorrow and he's got some tickets for us."

"I like Brian McKnight."

"Then it's a plan. I'll take you to Davis's tomorrow morning and you can do all those things women do to get ready for a night out on the town. In the meantime, I'll find out what's got my manager bent outta shape."

Xavier lay down on the bed and opened his arms. Destiny crawled right into them and they spent the night together holding each other in a blissful sleep.

The aroma of freshly baked manicotti hung heavily in the air, but Destiny was too excited to eat. During the past few days, she and Xavier had spent inordinate amounts of time together.

They behaved like the new lovers they were—hanging on to each other's every word, gazing deeply into each other's eyes, and attempting to satisfy their insatiable cravings for each other.

Xavier became Destiny's chauffeur and took her to the Coca-Cola plant and Centennial Olympic Park. But by far her most memorable experience as a tourist was visiting Martin Luther King, Jr.'s gravesite. His tomb lay majestically in the middle of a manmade pond. The scene was tranquil and serene. Then they visited the King museums and birthplace. Destiny bought lots of souvenirs for Jacq, who was an MLK devotee.

That night they were going to hear Brian McKnight sing at Hairston's. Destiny had gone off on an all-day shopping excursion looking for the perfect outfit. She settled on a simple, knee-length black dress, which she accented with silver earrings, silver shoes, and a shimmering silver shoulder wrap.

She checked the time. It was 7:00 P.M. If she and Xavier were going to get to the concert by eight, he had better come soon, she thought. She paced back and forth in Davis's living room, too excited to sit. She checked the clock again. Seven-ten. Then seven-twenty. Destiny was getting worried. "Please, God," she whispered. "Don't let anything have happened to him."

She had walked over to the phone to call him, when Davis emerged from his studio with someone she didn't know. Davis had the beginnings of dark circles under his eyes. There was stubble on his usually baby-smooth face. And where there would normally be a fresh press on his Corneliani suit, there were wrinkles and creases.

"This is Sylvana Reed. She's interviewing for the assistant position. This is Destiny Chandler." The two exchanged greetings and Davis showed the job candidate out. When she was gone Davis slumped against the door and rubbed his hand down his face. "Now I know why I'm so marketable. If I want a decent systems analyst, I'm going to have to commandeer some robotics equipment and build one from scratch."

"That bad?" Destiny asked.

"I'm so desperate, I might just have to hire the next person who walks through the door."

Davis walked into the kitchen to check the casserole. "So, what are you all dressed up for?"

"Xavier is taking me to the Brian McKnight concert."

"Uh-oh," Davis said.

Destiny didn't like the sound of Davis's response and followed him into the kitchen "What?" she asked.

"I've been so busy interviewing today I forgot to tell you. Zay called this morning, but you were zonked out. He said that he had to leave town unexpectedly, but he would call when he got back."

Destiny felt her excitement fade as if it were spiraling down a drain.

"So, I take it you're still working on his portfolio," Davis said, retrieving the piping-hot dish from the oven.

Destiny was barely paying attention. Most of her thoughts were on the disappointment of not being with Xavier tonight.

"Y-yes," she said, taking her earrings off. "I'm going upstairs to change."

"Okay," Davis answered. "I'll fix you a plate, so hurry back."

Destiny dragged up the staircase, forlorn and dejected. She wondered why Xavier had to leave so suddenly. She hoped everything was okay. She quickly changed into a henna-toned knit skirt and matching blouse. She hung the black dress up, hoping that Xavier would one day get to see her in it. When she returned downstairs, Davis had set the table and was serving up heaping portions of manicotti on gold-trimmed plates. Destiny took her food and sat down in the dining room. Davis joined her with his own plate and a bottle of sparkling cider.

They said grace and dug in. The pasta was stuffed with just the right blend of cottage and ricotta cheeses. "This is great, Davis."

"Thanks," he said. "Programming isn't the only thing I do well."

They sat in silence for a while, then Davis picked up the

remote control and aimed it at his wide-screen TV. The surround sound blared through the speakers.

"Sorry," Davis said, turning the volume down hastily. Then he began what Jacq called the macho mash. Destiny watched as Davis flipped through the stations in rapid succession. "How many channels do you have?" Destiny asked.

"Two hundred, I think."

Davis continued to flip mindlessly through the channels.

"How can you tell if a station has interesting programming if you don't stay there long enough to find out?"

"Men can tell," Davis proclaimed and took a sip of his cider. "No wonder he couldn't go to the concert with you."

"What?" Destiny said, placing a forkful of food in her mouth.

"Check it out," Davis said, motioning toward the television.

There on the fifty-six-inch screen was Xavier. He was wearing brown pants and a tan shirt open to the navel, with a coordinating brown vest. He was walking suavely from a limousine and down a red-carpeted sidewalk. A crowd of screaming fans flanked each side of the walkway, and periodically he waved at them. But mostly what he did was hold the hand of the woman walking beside him.

"I see Elise got her hooks back into Zay after all."

Destiny stared at the television screen, willing it to change. But no matter how hard she wished, the view was still the same. Xavier and Elise were together, holding hands, looking like the happy couple. Destiny suddenly felt tired.

"I wonder what this is," Davis said, pressing the menu button on the remote. After a few moments the words "Ninth Annual Stellar Music Awards" were displayed on the screen.

Destiny was fuming. *So,* she thought, *I'm good enough to go to bed with, but when it comes to being seen in public, you put the midwestern filly back in the stable.*

The phone rang and Davis answered it. "It's for you," he said.

Destiny took the receiver and tried to remove the anger from her voice. "Hello?"

"Hey, girl, it's Jacq. Are you watching TV?"

"I'll have to call you back," she said and handed the phone back to Davis. She was too upset to talk or think coherently. Davis placed the receiver in the cradle.

"Do you mind if we watch this?" Davis asked. He finished the last of his food and drained the remaining cider from his glass.

"No. Let's watch," she said. Maybe somehow she could determine what the hell was going on. The Stellar Music Awards ended up being a show featuring musical tributes to legendary performers. Each year they picked a genre of music and honored several artists within that genre. Last year country music was featured. The year before that was dedicated to folk music. This year the focus was on R&B.

Destiny watched closely as Earth, Wind and Fire; James Brown; and Aretha Franklin received awards. Once, Destiny sucked in her breath as the cameras panned the audience and showed Xavier and Elise sitting near the stage.

The next presentation was a contributor's award in the male category. The host of the show, Kenneth "Babyface" Edmonds, caught Destiny's full attention as he announced, "Here to pay tribute to Prince, singing 'Diamonds & Pearls,' are Shanice and Allgood!"

The curtain rose to strong applause and Xavier stood center stage. He was backed by a full orchestra. The familiar tones of his singing flowed into Destiny's ears and touched her very soul. *How could he do this?* she wondered. She watched him extend his arm as Shanice joined him on the stage. Their harmony was in perfect pitch.

They traded phrases back and forth in a musical call and response, then blended their voices together, holding one long note between them. The audience applauded wildly.

After their performance, they received a standing ovation and the audience continued its ovation as Prince came to the stage to accept his award. He stepped behind the lectern and adjusted the microphone. "People always compare him to me and now

I know why." The audience laughed. "That was great, man, thanks. And Shanice . . . what can I say? You were wonderful."

"That had to be one of the greatest duets in history," Davis said. "You want some ice cream, Des?"

"No thanks. I'll pass."

"I've got butter brickle, your favorite," Davis teased.

"Maybe later," she said. While Prince made his acceptance speech, Davis served himself a large bowl of ice cream and returned to the dining room. "I wondered if those two would get back together."

"Who?" Destiny asked, whipping her head around to where Davis sat.

"Zay and Elise. I heard they had a hot love affair—molten hot according to his CD. Supposedly, he wrote the entire *Hot Shop* CD about their liaison." Davis smacked loudly while eating his ice cream. Destiny had forgotten how much he liked frozen treats.

"When I met the brotha, he was still toe-up," Davis went on. "Elise left him without so much as another whiff, and he had trouble dealing with it. If he hadn't made that CD, I hate to think what would have happened to him."

As Destiny listened, she could feel her stomach twisting into thick knots.

"But now I know why lately he's been mackin' around here like a rich dada. He got his lady back."

Destiny was devastated. Jacq was right, she thought. Never fall in love. It was not worth it. Giving your heart to someone came with risks. Destiny had opened up her whole being and revealed the most intimate parts of herself. The memories of the way she spilled her guts to Xavier about Rico were enough to make her ill. She made up her mind to leave Atlanta as soon as possible.

She rose to go upstairs to pack her things. The sound of Xavier's voice came through the speakers once again. Destiny turned to see that the post-award ceremony had begun and reporters were interviewing some of the presenters and winners.

"So, Allgood, we're sure all the ladies want to know who the beautiful woman is on your arm."

"She's someone very special," he said, smiling at Elise and patting her hand, which rested securely on his arm.

Another reporter shouted a question from the background. "Should we remove your name from the most eligible bachelors' list?"

Xavier smiled whimsically. "I am definitely taken."

Destiny had heard enough. She picked up her dishes and walked into the kitchen. She scraped the remaining food on her plate into the trash and placed the plate and glass into the dishwasher.

"I think I'm going to go to bed."

"Already?" Davis questioned.

"Yeah," she said, ascending the staircase. "I don't feel well."

"Then it's a good thing you didn't go to that concert tonight."

Destiny rubbed the center of her forehead where a headache was beginning to form. "It sure is," she replied.

Fifteen

The rain was heavy and cold. Periodically, the sky would open up and crashing thunder would shake the air. With no jacket or umbrella, Rico stepped out into Atlanta's inclement weather. He looked up into the gray expanse of sky. The rain poured down his face and clothing. He hadn't allowed himself to feel free until this very moment. And now, his Destiny was so close, he could almost smell her in the air.

"Ay, mon!" a man shouted from the inside of a yellow car. "You be needing a lift?"

"Yeah." Rico's voice barely cut through the sound of the pelting rain.

"Hop in!" the man said.

Rico walked nonchalantly to the cab and got in.

"Where guan?" the man asked, putting the cab in gear. Rico pulled the address from a long memory and the driver headed the cab away from the bus station.

"What were you tryin' ta do back dere? Catch ya death?"

Rico ignored the man's question and stared up at the small contraption hanging from the interior light in the cab. It looked like a makeshift mobile made with matchbooks, all different colors and sizes. It was held together by multicolored threads, which connected one matchbook to the other.

"Dat's my tribute t'all da cool places I been," the cab driver said. "Some people got a memory book. I got a mobile. Each matchbook is from a restaurant or a hotel I stayed at while . . ."

Rico tuned the cab driver out. But he continued to stare at the hanging contrivance. It reminded Rico of how he got to be here in this cab. Connections, he said to himself. It's all about connections. His connections, Rat's connections, Destiny's connections. Connections were paramount when you were inside the joint. If you weren't hooked up with someone, you were as good as dead or punked out. On the outside, people were so selfish it was impossible to make connections.

The cab driver droned on and on. Only a few words made it to Rico's consciousness. Words like *power, danger, control,* and *lost.* The rest were just garbled blurs of sound. Rico's thoughts were fixed on more important matters: the woman who would never leave him again.

When they were together, he knew that sifting through Destiny's so-called private things would tell him things he needed to know. Useful tidbits he may have to refer to later. Her address book, journal, and old letters kept him occupied whenever she was away from home. Some things he committed to memory, like the phone numbers of all her relatives and the addresses of old boyfriends. He figured that if Destiny ever got out of hand and tried to leave him, he could find her using that information.

He had hoped that when he got out, she would be at work and he could surprise her there. But the receptionist said that she was out of town indefinitely. A little more prying and Rico soon found out that she was in Atlanta. It didn't take much to put two and two together.

"How much longer!" Rico demanded.

"You got at least another tirty minutes, mon. You might as well lean back and relax."

Rico pursed his lips together and blew hot air through them. The clothes he wore were sopping. A small puddle was starting to collect under each foot. "Rat," he said softly.

"What's dat?" the cabby asked.

"This guy I know . . . Rat. He got some friend of his to give me these clothes."

The cabby looked up into the rearview mirror for a few seconds, then looked back at the road.

"He got me these shoes, too. And the damn bus ticket down here."

"Must be a nice guy," the cabby said.

"Nice, huh. The punk charged me two tousand dollars."

"You paid two tousand dollars?"

"Yeah, I got connections."

"Listen. I've been drivin' cab for over five years. I've heard all kinds a stories. Anytime a guy does somethin' crazy like dat, dere's usually a woman involved. Am I right?"

"You damn skippy."

"I knew it!" the cabby exclaimed. "Two thousand dollars? Dat's big love, mon. She worth it?"

"And then some. And then some."

Just as the cabby had estimated, the ride to Rico's destination took thirty minutes. Rico reached into his rain-soaked pocket. Instead of the money he expected, Rico pulled out the page he had torn out of a tabloid in Lincoln. The headline read SOULFUL SINGER SEEN WITH SEXY SEDUCTRESS. Rico read the article about a singer and his mistress at Venn Gardens in Atlanta. There was no mistaking the woman in the picture. It was Destiny Chandler. His suspicions were confirmed.

Rico reached into his pocket again and retrieved a few crumpled twenties. It was the last of his stash. Relinquishing his money made Rico realize he had paid for a one-way ticket.

The cab driver pulled away and left Rico standing in the pouring rain. He waited a few moments before heading toward the condominium. *This guy better know where Destiny is,* Rico thought.

Rico walked up to the door and was about to knock when the door swung open. This man had to be Davis, Rico thought to himself. Rico carefully examined Davis's ecru suit. With him was a young guy who Rico thought looked fresh out of college.

"I'll be in touch," Davis said as the young man walked past Rico.

Rico watched him as he walked away, then turned his attention toward the man in the doorway.

"I'm sorry," Davis said. "I wasn't expecting anyone after five. Did you have an appointment?"

Rico frowned. "No."

"Well, that's okay," Davis said. "I like a fellow with initiative. Come on in." Davis checked his watch.

Rico smiled and entered Davis's condominium. Davis closed the door behind him. "I've gotten this interviewing thing down to a science. I won't take up too much of your time. Especially since you came out in the rain."

Rico shook off some of the rain that collected on his clothes and slipped his hand into his pocket where a .45-caliber pistol had rested ever since he left Nebraska.

Despite her better judgment, Destiny changed directions and headed toward Xavier's house. She and Davis had said their good-byes between his interview sessions, and Destiny packed her belongings in the rental car bound for the airport. When she had driven halfway to the airport, she felt compelled to tell Xavier just exactly what he could do with his music and anything *lovely.*

She was so angry she pulled over to the side of the road. The rain was coming down furiously. Even if she hadn't been angry, it would have been a good idea for her to pull over. Many other motorists followed suit. *It's too bad he's not in town. I'd tell him what a jerk he is to his face.*

As the rain continued in its torrential fashion, Destiny decided to write down her feelings in hopes of dispelling the anger she felt. She took a small scratch pad from her purse, and before she knew it she had filled nearly every page. The more she wrote, the better she felt. By the time she had finished, the rain had slowed enough for her to continue driving.

Destiny checked the clock on the dashboard and impulsively decided she would take her writings and drop them off in Xavier's mailbox. *At least I'll have the satisfaction of having the last word,* she thought.

She drove the car up into the long driveway and killed the engine. Destiny looked up admiringly at the majestic place. Just two days ago she was inside with Xavier drinking tea on the floor in front of his fireplace. They had turned off all the lights and sat there talking until 4:00 A.M. They were almost like children fighting sleep. It was as though they were trying to avoid anything that would come between them, even dreams.

Sucker no more, Destiny thought, dashing out of the car and into the rain. She ran up on the porch and slipped the pages into the mail slot on the door. Quickly she got back into the car and started the engine. She put the car in reverse and turned around to back out as Xavier's large, black Hummer pulled up behind her.

Destiny's heart leaped, momentarily forgetting Xavier's transgression, and then she remembered why she was there at his house. Fuming, she stepped out of the car. "Let me out!" she demanded.

Xavier rolled down the driver's side window. "Hey, baby," he said, smiling.

Now Destiny was furious. *He thinks he can come back and pick up right where he left off,* she mused. "Let me out!" she demanded again. Xavier said nothing and stepped out of his car with a look of concern on his face.

"Baby, I'm sorry I had to leave town like that," he said, seemingly oblivious to the rain coming down. "I was enjoying myself so much with you that I had forgotten I had a prior commitment. My manager was trying to track me down to—"

She interrupted him vehemently. "What about your commitment to *me?*" Destiny shot back.

"What?"

"Xavier, I saw the awards ceremony."

Xavier lowered his head. His deep sigh could be heard over

the sound of the rain. As he was about to speak, a loud clap of thunder went off above them. Destiny waited for his response. She wanted to hear what possible explanation he could have for his actions.

"Let's go inside. I can explain everything."

"I don't think so. I have a plane to catch. So if you have something to say, make it quick."

Xavier walked closer to where Destiny was standing and chose his words carefully. "I had promised to take Elise to the awards ceremony long before you and I started seeing each other."

"And the fact that you and I were seeing each other didn't prevent you from going out with her?"

"Listen, Destiny, Elise thinks I owe her something for my success. And maybe in a way, I do. If it hadn't been for her, there would probably be no *Molten Hot Shop*. A few weeks ago, she asked me to take her to places where she could meet some eligible men, some eligible *rich* men. She said that would make us even. So I agreed to take her to the after-party and to the awards ceremony."

"Is it true that you and Elise had a relationship in the past?"

"I'm not sure what we had, but it wasn't a relationship. I wanted one at the time, but she didn't."

"I still don't understand how you could make a date with me when you knew all along you were planning to be with Elise."

"Wait, let me finish explaining."

"Explaining what? I saw you two on television. You looked quite dapper with that decoration on your arm." Destiny paced in the driveway. "Why didn't you tell me you weren't available? Or that you weren't serious about us? I would have never gotten involved with you."

Xavier grabbed on to Destiny's shoulders and stopped her in her tracks. Destiny wrenched herself away. "Don't touch me! Just move your tank; that's the only thing you can do for me!" The rain was coming down in sheets now.

Xavier stiffened as though she had struck him. "I can't believe you. All this time we've spent together and you don't know anything about me." Xavier's mouth thinned with displeasure as Destiny walked back toward the direction of her car.

Xavier moved in front of her, blocking her path. "I hope you don't think you're going to accuse me of some dirt and then just run." A muscle flickered angrily in his jaw.

"I'm not sure how much you keep up on current events, but on any video show or entertainment report or in any newspaper or magazine article, have you ever read, heard, or seen anything about me bowling or shooting a crossbow?" Destiny folded her arms across her chest and set her chin in a stubborn line.

"Hell no! I don't reveal my personal interests to just anyone, but I revealed them to you. Now, as for Elise, have I ever given you a reason not to trust me? Have I ever? Naw! Now *you* on the other hand."

"What about me?" Destiny's voice exploded above the thunder. Her eyes flashed with outrage.

"What about you? Where do you want me to start? How about you and Davis swappin' spit in your room?"

Destiny dropped her arms to her sides. "You saw that?"

"Yeah, I saw it. And something else. Sometimes you spend the night at my tilt, and sometimes I take you back to Davis's house. What's up with that? If we're supposed to be together, then why can't you just stay with me? What's at Davis's house that you need?"

"Oh, now you're being ridiculous. I'm visiting Davis. It would be rude for me to just up and leave like that."

"Why? He does it to you. In fact, he's been doing it to you since you got here."

Destiny pressed her lips together in anger. "Look, this conversation is dysfunctional."

"Dysfunctional? I sang a song to *you* from *him!* That's how I spell dysfunctional." A sudden thin chill hung on the edge of his words. "You just don't want to deal with the truth. You *had* to know that Davis was trying to get with you."

Destiny stared at Xavier with haughty rebuke. "He was not."

"Yes, he was. At least in the beginning. But I'll bet you never talked about it, did you? Uh-uh. You just let him think that maybe there was a chance for you and him to get together."

"I did not."

"Yes, you did. All the while, you were seeing me. If anyone has some trust issues here, I think it's me."

The steady beat of the rain was drenching them both, and neither seemed to notice. "But I heard you on television. You said you had a relationship with Elise."

"I admitted to having a relationship." Xavier lowered his voice. "I meant with you."

At the sound of those four words, Destiny felt her will faltering.

"Look," Xavier said, walking toward his vehicle. "It's obvious that you don't trust me. I can't be in a relationship with someone that doesn't trust me. So I guess we don't have any more to say to each other." Xavier ran his hand over his dreads, pushing them from his face. "But you need to talk to Davis. You really need to talk to the brother. Either you wanna be with him or you don't, but you should at least tell him what's up."

Destiny watched as Xavier got into his vehicle and backed it out of the driveway. Then slowly she got into her rental car and did the same.

Maybe Xavier was right, she thought. She looked at the clock on the dashboard. It read 3:05. If she hurried, she could talk to Davis before he went to work and still catch her flight back to Lincoln.

The weather in Lincoln was turning cold. Jacquelyn turned on the heater as soon as she got into her car. As she pulled out of the driveway of her apartment, she smiled, grateful that she would only be spending half a day at work.

She was happy that Destiny was returning home. But she was sad too. Destiny had had her share of bad relationships. Recently, it seemed she was having more difficulty than ever, what with that crazy Rico. And now this singer fiasco. She hoped her friend wasn't too hurt by it all. Fine or not, Jacq thought, Allgood obviously wasn't about anything real.

Jacq took the Interstate 80 on-ramp and headed toward Omaha. Living in one city and working in another didn't bother her. As a matter of fact, she preferred it. She had held so many jobs in Lincoln, it was refreshing to go someplace new and different to work.

She checked the time on the dashboard. It read 7:00 A.M. She had gotten her drive to Omaha down to a science at an amazing forty-five minutes. She made a game out of clocking her trip each day. It helped her pass the time. She had measured the distance in landmarks, Platte River State Park, Mahoney State Park, The Nebraska Crossing Outlet Mall, and finally Sapp Bros. Jacq checked the clock at each point along the journey. So far, she was right on schedule.

Eventually, Jacq drove into the employee parking lot of First Data Resources. She had been working there for just over three months. Her probation was up and she got an exceptional review. The trouble was that she was bored, as usual. She knew she would have to look for a new job soon.

The security guard was sitting in his customary position behind the front desk. He was a small, caramel-colored man. Jacq suspected he was from Louisiana because she could hear the bayou loud and clear in his accent. He always flirted with her and she with him.

"Mornin', Miss Jackson."

"Morning, Julian," she said, swiping her ID card in the electronic card reader.

When the small red light on the reader turned green, Julian buzzed Jacq into the building.

"How come you're always so sunny?"

"Thinking of you just makes me glow, Julian."

"Have a good day, Miss Jackson."

"You too!"

Jacq waited for the elevator with three other employees. They were talking in exaggerated tones. The elevator doors opened and they all got on. The three were still talking excitedly about something.

"If it had been me, I would have headed straight for Canada."

"Yeah, right. You can't even find your way to Iowa."

"How long has he been gone, anyway?"

"Three days."

"Did you see when they interviewed some people from the hood? They were all saying Freeman is a free man."

At the mention of that name, Jacq perked up. She had to find out what they were talking about.

"What's going on?" she asked as they exited the elevator.

"Oh, we're just talking about the jailbreak."

"Someone escaped from jail?"

"Three guys escaped. They caught two, but one is still at large."

"Oh, no," Jacq said.

Suddenly she had a strange feeling at the pit of her stomach. Instead of going to her office, Jacq went to the employee break room and turned the TV to the twenty-four-hour local news channel. Instantly, a mug shot of Rico Freeman appeared on the screen.

"Damn," Jacq said, staring at the TV. She caught the last of the news broadcast about the jailbreak.

"The man police are looking for is five foot ten, weighing approximately 170 pounds. He has brown hair and brown eyes. He was last seen headed east toward Iowa. If you have any information regarding Rico Freeman, please contact the authorities at 555-STOP."

Jacq felt like she was going to be ill. She walked into her work area and found her supervisor. "Tom," she said.

Her supervisor looked up from his desk and frowned. "You don't look so hot, Jackson."

"I'm sure I feel worse than I look, Tom."

"Well, whatever you've got, none of the rest of us want it. You better go home."

"Thanks, Tom. I'll call you tomorrow to give you an update."

"Go get well, Jackson."

Instead of driving all the way back to Lincoln, Jacq drove to her mother's house in Omaha. Once there, Jacq took out the spare key she kept and unlocked the door.

"That you, Jackie?"

Her mother's familiar voice came out of the kitchen.

"It's me, Momma. I need to use the phone."

"You know where it is."

Jacq bounded up her mother's stairs to use the upstairs extension. She dug in her purse for her address book and picked up the receiver.

"Hello?" the deep masculine voice answered.

She knew it was Allgood as soon as he answered. "This is Jacquelyn Jackson. I'd like to speak to Destiny Chandler, please."

"She's not here," the voice responded. "How did you get this number?"

"Des gave it to me. She said I could use it to reach her in an emergency and this is an emergency. Do you know where she is?"

"I hope she's at Davis Van Housen's house."

"Nope." Jacq responded. "I called. There was no answer. Do you think she might be at the airport already?"

"I think I talked her out of that."

"What!"

"Look, Miss . . ."

"Jackson."

"Miss Jackson, maybe if you tell me what the emergency is I might be able to help."

Jacq paused. She wasn't sure how serious the two of them had been. She didn't want to give out her homegirl's business. But if he could help . . . "How close did you and Destiny get?"

"I don't see what that has to do with anything?"

"Does the name Rico Freeman mean anything to you?"

"I know I got something for him when he gets out of jail."

"Well, whatever you got, get it ready 'cause he's out now."

"What? I thought he was in jail for three years."

"He broke out and he's been on the run for three days."

"And you are just now calling!"

Jacq could hear the concern in his voice. Maybe he cared for Destiny after all. "I just found out half an hour ago."

"Is there any way he could find out that Destiny's here? Do you think he would try to come to Atlanta?"

"Knowing that crazy mother, anything's possible."

"Thank you for calling, Miss Jackson. I'll take care of it."

Jacq heard the tone of his voice change as if it had suddenly been put on ice. "If you find Destiny, tell her I called. And make sure—"

"Miss Jackson," Xavier interrupted. "I'll take care of it."

"Thank you," Jacq said and hung up the phone.

Sixteen

Rico stroked the photograph in his hands. It was bright and glossy, and in it Destiny had a look of stunned surprise on her face. He imagined he would eventually see that look, but not today.

The guy on the floor said that Destiny was on her way back to Lincoln. At first, Rico didn't believe him. But even with a gun pointed at his groin, the man insisted that Destiny was headed toward the airport. Rico found this disturbing. He hated to have sacrificed everything, *everything* to come here and then have his Destiny slip by him.

When he shot the fool, Rico had been merciful. He could have dismembered him in a most unpleasant way. But instead, he shot him in the stomach. Rico liked what a good gut shot could do. It didn't kill right away, but it bled a whole hell of a lot. *It's too bad the idiot had to pass out,* Rico thought, stepping over Davis. *I could use a distraction.*

Rico walked into the living room. There were photographs everywhere. Rico had thrown them at the wall in a fit of rage. The photos were mostly of the punk Rico saw Destiny with in the tabloid. He resented that they had Destiny's unmistakable creativity all over them. She hadn't done anything this creative for him, he mused.

He deliberately stepped on a photograph of the man standing among flowers. Rico's action left a footprint on Xavier's face.

But the pictures he rescued from the jumble on the floor were the ones taken of Destiny herself. In one, she hung her head slightly and looked downward. In another, the smile on her face was enough to light up the heavens. He rubbed them against his body, wishing they were the real thing. And then, consumed by another fit of rage, he ripped them to shreds.

Destiny pushed on Davis's door and found it locked. *That's unusual,* she thought. She rang the doorbell. Imagining the sounds of Anita Ward echoing throughout the house made Destiny chuckle. Then she heard a voice that sent the sensation of flying ice splinters through her body.

"Glad to see you in a good mood."

Destiny was about to run when she saw the gun in Rico's hand.

"Hup, hup, hup. No running," Rico said, smiling. Then he grabbed her arm and held her while he planted a big sloppy kiss on her cheek.

"Auh," Destiny moaned. She turned her head and wiped the side of her face with her free hand. Rico's eyes darkened dangerously.

"I came all this way, on the wings of a Rat, and this is the thanks I get?" Rico yanked on Destiny's arm. "Get in here!"

Destiny reluctantly entered the house and Rico closed the door behind her. Once inside, she let out an ear-piercing scream and rushed to where Davis lay on the floor. She knelt beside him, her fear absorbed by anger. "What have you done, you sick bastard!"

"Watch it, or you and your boyfriend will be in the same predicament."

"He's not my boyfriend, Rico," she said, getting up. Her head was spinning but she knew one thing. Davis was still alive and in need of medical attention.

"I'm calling an ambulance." Destiny walked toward the phone on the coffee table. As she reached for the phone, Rico fired the gun several times. The bullets exploded into the phone and sent pieces of it flying in all directions.

"You're not gonna do a damn thing except what I tell you. Got that?"

"Rico, he could die!"

"Why do you think I shot him?"

"You're crazy. What did I ever see in you?"

"Now that's the question of the hour, isn't it?" Rico perched himself on the kitchen table. He rocked his leg back and forth and laid the gun in his lap.

"See, I think if we can just identify what that is," he said as he let out a small sigh, "then we can get back together and you'll be mine again like you're supposed to be."

Destiny sat on the floor next to Davis. She could smell the liquor on Rico's breath. He must have gotten into Davis's bar, she thought, noticing a bottle of Crown Royal on the table in the dining room. She prayed he'd pass out.

"Don't touch him," Rico said.

"I thought you were so brilliant," Destiny said.

"That's it, keep talkin'."

"It must be true what they say."

"And what's that? And I must say, you look ravishing."

"That in the mind, genius and madness sleep in the same bed. The thing is, wisdom keeps them separated. And that's the one quality I assumed you had. But I was wrong. I mean, you tracking me down here, I got to give it to you on that one. But if you think I'm going to get back together with you, you're insane."

Destiny thought it was ironic that she never had the courage to speak to Rico like this when they were together. But now, after she'd been through so much, she could keep her peace no longer. And if she was going to die, then she would die with the truth and a clear conscience.

Rico walked over to where Destiny was sitting and circled her. "I bet you wouldn't say that to your boyfriend." He picked up one of the strewn pictures and threw it at her. This time Destiny was silent.

"Oh, so he's the one, huh?"

Rico picked up some of the pictures of Xavier and gathered them in a pile. He reached into his pocket and took out a lighter. "I know you think he means something to you, but he really doesn't. And to prove it, I want you to burn these pictures."

"Rico—"

"Burn them!" Rico pointed the gun toward Davis's head. "Or I'll take him out."

Destiny flicked the lighter and touched the flame to the edges of the black-and-white photos. In seconds the glossy paper ignited and the photos began to curl and melt. The flames rose higher as the number of burning photos increased. The room began to fill with smoke and the pungent smell of burning chemicals.

"Put that shit out!" he ordered.

Destiny jumped up and ran into the kitchen. She filled a large bowl with water and ran back to the living area. She doused the fire and wisps of smoke filled the room. A few seconds later, the smoke alarm went off, but only for a moment before Rico shot it and it whined into silence.

"I need a drink," Rico said, walking toward the dining room.

"You've had enough."

"No, I haven't," he said, pouring a shot of Crown Royal into a glass. "Can't get enough of this," he said, saluting the bottle of liquor. "And I can't get enough of you." Rico picked up the glass, looked at it, then put it back down. "Oh, what the hell," he said. He picked up the bottle of Crown Royal and turned it up to his lips, taking the liquor in large gulps.

"Jesus!" Destiny said, watching the spectacle.

Rico yanked the bottle from his mouth and clutched his chest as he went into coughing spasms. After a few moments, he regained his composure.

Despite the barrage of bullets the phone took, it started to ring. Rico swung the gun wildly in the direction of the phone and pulled the trigger several times, but nothing happened. Rico smiled at Destiny. "Must be time to reload," he said.

Destiny tried desperately to figure out how she could get away from Rico and call the police. If only he was a little more drunk, she might be able to knock him down and make a run for it. But now, he still had most of his faculties. If she tried anything, he could still overpower her and possibly even shoot her. Destiny decided to wait until he was a little more inebriated.

"I know you got that fool's music around here somewhere," Rico said, loading his gun. "Let's hear it."

"I don't know if—"

"No lies. Or we'll search this house from top to bottom. And if I find something by him, wonderboy on the floor gets his stuff blown off. You dig?"

Rico followed Destiny into the studio. She selected Xavier's CD from the pile of Zip disks.

"I knew you had it in you."

The two of them went back into the living room and Destiny noticed the bloodstain beneath Davis. It had gotten larger since she got there. Davis was bleeding badly. She had to think of some way to gain control of this situation.

"Let me play it," she said, reaching for the CD.

Rico staggered toward the stereo. "Hell no. You think I can't do it. I know how to play a CD," Rico slurred. *Same old Rico,* Destiny thought.

As he bent over the stereo equipment, Destiny grabbed a lamp from the end table and hit him across the back as hard as she could. Then she turned and ran toward the door. She was almost to the door when she slipped on one of the pictures on the floor. She fell forward and scrambled to get up when she heard Rico's gun cocking in her ear.

"I love you, Destiny, but if you do anything like that again, I'll shoot you."

Destiny's hopes fell. She sank to the floor and wondered what would happen next.

"You know life without you has been, oh, how shall I put

it"—his expression clouded in anger as he searched for words—"extremely difficult," he finished.

"How do you breathe without breath? How do you see without vision? How do you live without life?" The expression on his face bordered on mockery. Rico circled her position like a noxious animal. Icy fear and cold rage twisted around Destiny's heart.

"What do you want, Rico?" She heard her bitterness spill over into her voice.

His tone was cold and exact. "Why, you, of course."

Destiny fought to keep herself from flipping him off.

"Come here," he said, hoisting her up from the floor. He twirled her around and ordered her to sit in Davis's overstuffed chair. When she did as he instructed, Rico sat down on the floor in front of her. *Too bad you're not close enough for me to kick you in the face,* Destiny thought.

"I just need to know one thing; then all this will be over and we can return to living our lives the way we should." She heard a possessive desperation in his voice.

While Rico talked, Destiny set her mind on trying to get out of the situation. The last attempt almost cost her her life. She would have to be more careful this time. She used her peripheral vision to scan the room. There had to be something here that would help her. Then the bottle of Crown Royal caught her attention.

If Rico were more inebriated, she might have a chance of overpowering him or at least knocking the gun away. Destiny felt her adrenaline surge. She couldn't believe her own courage. She had never been this resourceful when they were together. If she had, she would have ended their relationship the first time he came home in the middle of the night in a drunken stupor.

A ready strategy came to her mind. She knew if she suggested that he have another drink, he would suspect something. But if she asked for one, he would probably give her one and hopefully pour one for himself. Considering that he was so close to the edge now, one or two more drinks and he should plunge half-seas over.

Rico droned on and on about something incomprehensible. His voice sounded like an echo from an empty tomb. Destiny watched closely as the man who normally talked animatedly with his hands struggled as his arms cast about in slow motion. One more drink, Destiny thought.

"But no matter what," Rico slurred, "I still love you."

"You say you love me, but you haven't even offered me a drink. What were you doing, trying to keep it all to yourself?"

Rico rose awkwardly from his position on the floor. "Of course not, my dear." He staggered over to the kitchen table and poured her a glass of whiskey. Destiny's prayers were answered when instead of returning the bottle to the table, he turned it up to his lips and drained the last of the liquor from the bottle.

"Ah," he said, placing the bottle on the table. He wiped his lips with the back of his hand and stumbled toward Destiny. "Ooh," he said, righting himself. He paused momentarily while lifting the glass of whiskey in one hand and the gun in the other. "These two things, and that thing between your legs, are the most powerful forces in the universe," he said. And with that he tipped the glass to his lips and proceeded to drink the whiskey he had poured for Destiny.

Destiny's eyes widened. "Oops, I'm sorry," he said, coughing. Then he shot her a twisted smile and reached over to touch her cheek. Destiny shrank back but not far enough. His fingers clumsily grazed her face. The sensation was like a hundred tiny spiders crawling across her chin and jaw.

"You can pretend not to like it all you want," Rico whispered harshly. "I still love you."

Davis felt searing hot bolts of pain shooting through his torso. It seemed to start from his navel and burst directly in his brain, exploding in a prism of fireworks and bright lights. Davis fought hard to steady his panic against the agony. *No one knows*

I'm lying here, he thought. *Please, God, don't let me die. Please, God.*

Davis felt a small ray of hope when he heard his doorbell ringing.

"What the . . . ?" Rico said and looked out the window. A man in a suit stood at the door, adjusting his tie. Rico watched the man fidget for a few minutes, then ring the doorbell again.

"Who is it?" Rico asked, standing unsteadily behind the door. He looked at Destiny and put his index finger up to his lips, with his gun drawn at his side.

"It's Lenny Krammer. I'm here about the systems analyst position."

Davis summoned his failing strength. If he could holler for help, he might have a chance. Otherwise . . .

He pushed as hard as he could from his lungs, but instead of a scream for help, blood and mucus bubbled up and out of his mouth. After that, there were no more colors in his head.

Rico lowered the gun and took a deep breath. Destiny's hopes of overpowering Rico vaporized as she saw the enormity of the situation begin to sober him up. "Sorry," he said, almost laughing. "That position has been filled."

"Oh," the man said. "Are you sure?"

"What? W-what?" his irritation beginning to rise.

"Are you sure? I thought the ad said the position would remain open until the end of the week."

Rico wiped away the small droplets of sweat beading above his upper lip. "Look, man, we already hired someone."

"We?" the man responded insistently. "I was under the impression that this was a one-person consulting business. Is that right?"

Rico tightened the grip on the gun. "Look, fool. There *is* no job! Now get outta here before I call five-oh."

"Call them," ordered a calm voice from behind Rico.

Rico whirled around to come face-to-face with Xavier All-good.

"Xavier!" Destiny's tearful voice cried out.

"Who the . . . ?"

Before Rico could finish his sentence, his gun flew from his hand—knocked away by an arrow from Xavier's crossbow. The arrow made a thwang sound as it pierced a wall.

Rico watched intently as Xavier crept into the living area like a panther in stalking mode. He carefully loaded his crossbow. "Mr. Tabloid," Rico said.

Xavier called out to the man outside. "Lenny, I can handle it from here."

"No sweat, man. Thanks for the autograph."

"Xavier, Davis needs an ambulance!" Destiny screamed.

Xavier followed the terror in Destiny's eyes to where his friend lay on the floor. The tan carpet around him was stained bright red.

"Oh, Jesus!" Xavier ran over to Davis and knelt down next to his sprawled body. Just then, Rico leaped for his gun.

"Xavier!" Destiny screamed.

Xavier stood and drew his crossbow but it was too late. Rico had the gun and was pointing it at Destiny.

"You wanna put that medieval contraption down, or do I add a new orifice to this beautiful woman's face?"

"I can't let you do that, Rico."

"So, Destiny's been talking about me, huh? I hope it was all good." Rico laughed maniacally. He pulled Destiny to his side. "I said put that thing *down!*"

Xavier closed his eyes, and Destiny saw him relax and let his breathing go shallow. *Oh my God,* she thought and held her breath. Instantly she heard the thwang of Xavier's arrow as it pierced Rico's chest. Rico dropped the gun and clutched the area were the arrow had entered. Destiny saw Rico's eyes roll backward in his head as he fell forward. The force of the fall sent the arrow through Rico's body. Destiny turned her head as she saw the head of the arrow push out of Rico's back.

Immediately, Xavier was at her side. "Are you all right?"

"Y-yes," she said, shaking.

"Then call an ambulance," Xavier said, walking quickly to where Davis lay on the carpet.

Seventeen

"Hold still!" Jacq insisted.

"I would if you weren't trying to kill me," Davis replied.

"Oh, buck up, mister programmer." Jacq applied the last of the tape to the bandages on Davis's stomach. When she finished, she rose from the edge of the couch where Davis was lying.

Davis pulled his shirt down carefully over his bandaged abdomen. "You just wait until these stitches heal, Jacquelyn. Then you'll be in trouble."

"Yeah, yeah," Jacq said nonchalantly. But Destiny saw the smile curling mischievously on her friend's lips. She knew Jacq's flippant behavior to be a telltale sign. The girl was definitely on a mission. And Davis was the goal.

Destiny thought that Davis and Jacq would make a great couple, but she wasn't going to jump to any conclusions. Jumping to conclusions had gotten Destiny in trouble before. She had jumped to the conclusion that Rico would change his vile ways. She had jumped to the conclusion that she and Davis could rekindle their old fire. She had even jumped to the conclusion that Xavier had betrayed her. Each time, she had been utterly wrong.

Rico was Rico until the bitter end. She and Davis had outgrown their childhood fascination to discover a wonderfully strong friendship, and Xavier Allgood was not at all interested in Elise Kent. As a matter of fact, he had introduced Elise to Marvis Quatelbaum, to whom she was now engaged.

According to Davis, Elise only wanted to be seen with Xavier so she could size up all the eligible, *rich* bachelors. It didn't take her long to discover that Marvis was extremely wealthy and more than willing to make her his bride. And to top it all off, Xavier was scheduled to sing at their upcoming wedding.

It seemed that Davis had confirmed everything that Xavier had said to her during their argument in the rain. And now Destiny felt as though her insolent presumption had lost her the most important person in her life.

"I like the way he says Jacquelyn," Jacq whispered in Destiny's ear.

"I see you in there whispering," Davis shouted from the living room couch. "Des, I know she's talking about me. What's she saying?"

Before Destiny could answer, Jacq was already shouting a response back. "You just worry about your stomach. Now that you can eat, you think you can *run* things. You ain't running things here, mister flowchart. You better be glad that I'm helping Destiny take care of your ol' sorry butt."

Destiny smiled. The two of them had been going at it ever since Jacq had arrived. Destiny didn't know how Jacq had managed it, but she had caught a plane and shown up at Davis's door just as the ambulances were taking Rico and Davis to the hospital.

Destiny didn't ask any questions, but apparently Jacq had left her mother's house and flown down to try to stop Rico. When she saw what had happened, Jacq kept her and Xavier company through the long hours of Davis's surgery and the grueling questions of the police investigation.

When it was all said and done, Rico had been killed in self-defense, Davis would be fine with healing and extensive therapy, and Destiny saw Xavier less and less. But again, through another trauma in her life, Jacq was there. And she had more or less taken over the duty of nursing Davis back to health.

Over the past week since Davis's release from the hospital, Destiny had watched the two of them together. She had never seen Davis this attentive to anything except his work. And Destiny could scarcely recognize her friend sometimes. She was so good at dressing Davis's wounds and working his body through his home-therapy exercises that Destiny could see why Jacq was never satisfied with her other jobs. She was obviously meant to work closely with people and not group benefits or company policies.

Once when Destiny was in Davis's studio, she had returned to the kitchen and found them in a serious lip lock. She crept back into the studio and never mentioned her accidental discovery. She knew Jacq would tell her about it in time. Destiny was happy that Jacq and Davis were hitting it off.

One of the most difficult heart-to-heart talks Destiny ever had was with Davis Van Housen. After the effects of Xavier's fervent words sunk in, Destiny realized she had been playing a game of avoidance for a long time. Somewhere in the back of her mind, she knew Davis had some interest in her, but she fooled herself into believing she was so busy with the montage and he was so busy with his projects that she could ignore it.

She had learned the hard way, first with Rico and now with Davis, that trying to ignore a problem sometimes made it worse. And one thing was for sure, no problem would ever be solved through ignorance.

Through her silence, she had actually contributed to Davis's continued interested, when what was called for was a firm stance on her part to set the record straight regarding her feelings and her intentions.

She even remembered thinking, *Maybe it's my imagination. He's just being his usual flirtatious self.* However, deep down inside, she knew there was more to it. The problem was that after Rico, dealing with a man whose attentions she didn't want brought to mind a whole set of painful memories, which Destiny tried to bury by coming to Atlanta.

The ironic part about the entire situation was that when Destiny offered her apology, Davis had his own confession to make. It seemed that he was so blinded by ambition that it was his own career development that was driving his interest and not love. But he admitted that the more time they spent together, the more he was reminded of what made him fall for her all those years ago—the way she brought out the best in people, her intelligence, and her willingness to give. And out of respect for those qualities, he revoked his selfish aspirations.

They both realized how wrong they had been and agreed that their friendship was too important to be tarnished by their ridiculous actions.

Davis and Destiny finished their conversation on a positive note by promising to be straight with each other from that moment on. Destiny really felt good about getting through their talk. But somewhere in the back of her mind she knew her most difficult heart-to-heart was yet to come.

Watching Jacq and Davis together also made Destiny a little sad. She was glad her friends were getting along so well, despite what might pass for outward disdain. But since the argument they had had in the rain, she and Xavier hadn't been able to reconcile their differences. The funny and new relationship developing between Davis and Jacq reminded Destiny of the cavernous rift in her relationship with Xavier.

He had been over a few times that week to visit Davis. He and Davis spent most of the time in the studio. Even against his doctor's orders, Davis spent at least thirty minutes a day working. When Xavier came over, he and Davis would leave her and Jacq alone while Xavier and Davis briefly discussed the final plans for Xavier's automated recording studio. She and Jacq would always find something to talk about, but it never held her concentration. Her thoughts were always in the other room with the man she loved. The man who had saved her life.

"You really should call him."

Jacq's voice brought Destiny back to the present. "I have

called him, Jacq. There's never an answer." Destiny fidgeted with the book she was reading. It was a romance novel by her favorite author, L. M. Harrison. "I even called Sammy. I left a message at his record company. No one knows where he is. It's as if he's dropped off the face of the earth."

Jacq reached over and took the book out of her friend's hands. "Destiny, I was wrong before. That man loves you. And girl, if you can't see that, then all the romance novels in the world won't make a difference if you don't give yourself the chance to experience the real thing.

"Up until now, he's been pursuing you. He's been after you. If you want him, maybe it's time you went after *him*."

"What do you think I've been doing?"

"All you've done is make a couple of phone calls."

"Well, what else am I supposed to do?"

"Go get him!" Davis shouted from the living room.

"Are you eavesdropping on my conversation?" Jacq shot back.

"Actually I was trying to get some rest. But you were talking so loudly I couldn't help but overhear."

"So you just had to put your two cents in, huh?"

"I'll put fifty cents in if I want to. I'm Des's friend, too."

"Shut up before I come over there and rip off those bandages!"

The three of them laughed at Jacq's retort. And then Jacq resumed their conversation. "Now think, Des. We know he's not on tour 'cause he was here just a couple of days ago."

"And when he left, he said he'd be back in a couple of days to check on me again," Davis added.

"So where do you think he would go?" Jacq asked.

"Yeah," Davis responded. "You two spent so much time together, you probably know his habits better than anyone. Where could he be?"

Davis's remark triggered a memory in Destiny's mind. "Davis, may I borrow your car?"

"Of course."

Destiny ran upstairs and grabbed her purse and the car keys from Davis's dresser. She came back downstairs and headed toward the door. Jacq was seated on the edge of the couch next to Davis.

"Don't hurry back," Jacq said as Destiny opened the door. Then Jacq bent down and kissed Davis on the cheek.

"Oh, lord," Davis murmured, rubbing his stomach tenderly. "You really *are* trying to kill me."

It's a good thing the music business is lucrative, Xavier thought as he shot the latest in a succession of target rounds at the range. Spending hours here could get expensive, he mused.

Another arrow went sailing through the air. Although he had been slightly off beat recently, this arrow went straight into the center of the target. Xavier loaded the crossbow with another arrow and heard the swoosh and thwack of someone else's arrow as it cut through the air and landed in his target. Xavier looked up, annoyed.

Standing quite close to him with a crossbow in her hands was Destiny. She looked more lovely than his heart had dared to remember. The days without her had been tasteless and colorless. And now, with her standing before him, his senses shifted into overdrive. He could smell her perfume, and the white tank top and jeans she wore made the golden undertones in her skin dance in the sun. The very idea of kissing her again made him dizzy. But then the thought of their rainy encounter fell like a shadowy curtain between them. He wondered what she wanted.

She walked slowly toward him. "Cha Cha said you've been here for a while."

"For once in his life," Xavier said, lining up the target in his sight, "he's right about me."

Xavier pulled the trigger and sent the arrow flying to its mark. He was tired of being hurt by women. He hoped that whatever Destiny was there for she would make it quick so he could get on with the process of getting over her. "What do you want, Destiny?"

"With everything that's happened, I never got the chance to

thank you properly for saving my life. I-I'm not even sure how you thank a person for that. But I just . . ."

"You don't need to thank me." In spite of everything that had happened, he still wanted Destiny Chandler more than anything. He thought about the ring box in his pocket. On the day he got back from the awards show, he had gone out shopping for a ring. He found a magnificent five-carat diamond set in a braided gold band.

He had been rehearsing his proposal all the way home from the jewelry store. When he pulled into his driveway and saw Destiny there, he almost popped the question right then. But Destiny had accused him of doing something he wasn't capable of doing—betraying her trust and her love.

Xavier was hurt beyond measure. But something he didn't understand kept Destiny in his thoughts every day. And since then, he had kept the ring box with him, not willing to take it back even though he believed that what he had with Destiny was over. *And now here she is saying how much she wants to thank me,* Xavier thought. *Well, if she thinks she can come traipsing back into my life that easily . . .*

"Xavier?"

"Yes. What?" Xavier said, snapping back to reality.

Destiny sighed. "I'm sorry," she said. "I guess coming here was a bad idea." Xavier stared at her in silence.

"Before I go, will you answer me one thing?"

"What?"

"Do you still believe in Cupid?"

Xavier was taken aback. "What?"

"Cupid. You said you believed in him. Do you still?"

Xavier set his crossbow on a table. There wasn't much he believed in lately. And coming here to the range wasn't helping to clear his head the way it usually did. "I don't know," he said wearily, crossing his arms in front of him.

"Xavier, what I said to you that day in the rain . . . that was wrong. I was wrong. I didn't give you a chance to explain. I just jumped to conclusions and went ballistic." Destiny walked closer to Xavier. "It was residual anger left over from my relationship with Rico. Somehow, I released it on you. And I shouldn't have. I'm sorry."

Xavier walked closer to Destiny, his wall of resolve broken down forever. "I'm sorry, too. I should have explained things to you, but I was afraid of getting hurt again. So that made it easy for me not to tell you about my promise to Elise. If I had told you, that would have meant that my nose was all the way open. And open means the possibility of pain."

"Please forgive me," they said in unison, each stepping forward to close the remaining gap between them.

Xavier set Destiny's crossbow on the table and took her hands. His heart was pounding so hard he felt as though it must be beating for the both of them. He looked deeply into her eyes and found himself again. In her beautiful, beautiful eyes were the answers to all his questions, except one.

"I bought you something," he said, reaching into his pants pocket. He pulled out the black velvet-covered ring box from where it had been for much too long. It was warm, just like his love for Destiny.

She was so quiet when he gave it to her, he didn't know quite what to think. Then she opened it and tears spilled down the sides of her cheeks.

"I love you, Destiny."

"I l-love you, too," she said through her tears.

"Marry me, Destiny. Be my wife." Xavier swallowed hard. "Will you do that?"

"Yes!" she said.

Xavier bent down for the kiss he had been waiting a lifetime for. All the passion, longing, and desire he had bottled up during the past few weeks overtook him and their embrace lingered for what seemed like an eternity.

When they released each other, both of their faces were wet with tears of joy.

Eighteen

The summer was kind this August day. Although it could easily be sweltering, the temperature was a modest eighty degrees. The sun was playing peek-a-boo with the clouds that puffed up in the sky like fresh cotton.

And inside the First Baptist Church on Fifth and Driscal, Destiny Chandler stood smiling in front of a full-length mirror. The gown she wore was ivory with pearls stitched in a simple pattern on the bodice leading up to the plunging neckline. She turned to her friend Jacq, who had been fussing over her all morning.

"I feel beautiful, Jacq."

"You look beautiful, girl. Now what about me?" Jacq whirled around. The lavender dress she wore fit snugly to the hourglass-shaped contours of her body. "Ain't I the best-dressed hottie you've ever seen?"

They laughed together. "But seriously, Des, do you think Davis will like it?"

"I think he'll love it."

Verle Webb poked her head into the dressing room. "Oh, Destiny, you look radiant." She dabbed at the tears beginning to form in her eyes. "They're ready for you, baby."

Destiny closed her eyes and held her breath. Xavier was wrong, she thought. This had to be a fairy tale because she felt just like a princess and all her wishes had been granted. Then she opened her eyes. "Thank you, Mother Webb. We're coming."

* * *

"All I've got to say, man, is you *better* have the ring."

Davis stood in front of the mirror frantically brushing his hair. "I got the ring, man. I got the ring," he replied, dropping the brush.

"If I didn't know any better, I would think it was you who was getting married, not me."

"Chill out, man. I'm just a little nervous, that's all."

Xavier shook his head. "Don't tell me you've never been in a wedding before."

"Actually, I haven't." Davis turned from the mirror to Xavier. "I know you wanted Sammy to be your best man. I'm just honored that I could step in to fill his shoes."

"Just don't trip over them, all right?"

Davis picked up the brush. "It's a deal."

The twins, LeRoy and LeRon, came into the dressing room. They were dressed identically, even down to the earrings in their ears. "Show time, my brothers," LeRon said. LeRoy threw an arm around Xavier. "Let's get you married, dog."

Xavier watched Davis. He was picking away imaginary lint from his tuxedo. "Check him," he said to the twins. "Make sure he's got the ring."

Almost all brides have shudder stories to tell about their weddings. There's always something that doesn't go quite right: the cake is late, the ring bearer trips, the singer suddenly gets laryngitis, it rains, or worse, the minister gets stuck in traffic. Destiny Allgood would have no such story to tell.

Her wedding to Xavier Allgood was as perfect as the diamond on her finger. Shade played "Overjoyed" by Stevie Wonder on the organ while Destiny's attendants and their escorts walked to the altar. Her two closest friends, Jacq and Davis, were maid of honor and best man. Tyrica, who had one of the most beautiful voices Destiny had ever heard, sang "The First Time Ever

I Saw Your Face" by Roberta Flack. Best of all, her parents were there watching the ceremony with tear-filled eyes.

The highlight of the wedding ceremony was when Dutch, whom Destiny had never heard say more than two or three words at a time, sang "So Amazing" by Luther Vandross and "You Were Meant For Me" by Donny Hathaway. The Reverend Samuel J. Webb performed the ceremony, and Destiny was happier than she had ever been in her entire life. By the time she said, "I do," she was softly crying. When Xavier lifted her veil for his kiss, Destiny could see fresh tears glistening in his eyes, too.

During the reception, it was no surprise who caught the bouquet. Jacq was right there. And even if she hadn't been, Destiny knew Jacq would have toppled whomever she had to to get at the flowers.

Some of the guests at the reception appeared to be having an exceptionally good time. Cha Cha's wide face beamed as he took turns dancing with each one of Xavier's sisters. Destiny was inspired by his agility. Chappy, the sausage vendor, looked twenty years younger as he circulated from group to group. And Jacq was the ultimate southern belle, whisking herself around as if she owned the world.

Even Destiny's newest friend, Star, was wearing a smile a mile long. And she had every right to. Somehow Star had managed to coif the hair of Destiny, Jacq, and Xavier's five sisters. Their elegant hairdos could have been featured at a hair design conference.

Throughout the reception, Destiny's feet never touched the floor. She was floating on a cloud of bliss and joy. She was surrounded by people that she cared about, and married to the man of her dreams. Destiny couldn't imagine anything more exquisite until Davis tapped her on the shoulder while she was chatting with Mother Webb.

"Yes," she said, beaming.

"I need you to come with me," Davis said, fidgeting with the buttons on his shirt.

"Why? Is something wrong?" she asked, alarmed.

"No, no," he quietly replied. "Zay wants you."

Destiny's face lit up like a child's at Christmas. "Oh, well, in that case."

Davis led her to a chair in the middle of the room. He then bowed to her like a knight in the queen's court. "Your throne, ma'am." Davis gestured for her to be seated, and she obliged. Somewhere in the background, underneath the hum of voices, she heard a guitar playing. Then the unmistakable sound of Xavier's singing quickened her heart. She turned in the direction of his voice and watched as the crowd parted as he approached her. She clasped her hands in front of her and brought them to her chin. She sat, childlike, in awe of what she saw and heard. Her Xavier was serenading her.

> *Found you*
> *when I wasn't looking*
> *'cause you share my own heartbeat*
>
> *Saw you*
> *in all of love's splendor*
> *knocked me straight up off my feet*
>
> *Your eyes*
> *show me my tomorrow*
> *Your smile*
> *lights up my today*
> *Your hands*
> *push aside my sorrow*
> *Your soul*
> *saved my yesterday*
>
> *Now, I wanna live*
> *my whole life long*
> *singing Destiny's Song*

I just wanna live
my whole life long
singing Destiny's Song

From this moment on
I'm living a brand-new day
Love has brought a rainbow
And cast the rain away

And I'm gonna live
my whole life long
singing Destiny's Song

The song was beautiful, and the way he played that blue guitar struck her like magic. She felt her heart might burst with delight.

When Xavier finished his song, there wasn't a dry eye in the house, including his own. Jacq and Davis held on to each other tightly and everyone in the room seemed to have moved closer together. Destiny rose from her seat and threw her arms around Xavier.

She held him dearly and knew that from that moment on she would never again be afraid to love with her soul and her spirit. She had found the man who could safeguard her very being, who would nurture her, heal her, and defend her with his life. He was the song in her heart. And she would let the music play forever.

Epilogue

Sharla Waters twisted in her seat. She crossed and uncrossed her legs, trying to get comfortable. No matter what she did, she still felt slightly out of place.

She examined her surroundings. The room could easily seat one hundred people. However, there were only fifteen present, all women.

Various black-and-white portraits of women hung on the walls. Some of the photos were close-ups and some were full-length, but in all, the women stared ahead as if pondering the answer to some ancient question.

Sharla had been asking herself a question lately. Several of them actually. Why did she let Dennis treat her so badly? And why for so long? Right now the question she asked herself was, did she do the right thing by coming here? Sharla shifted in her chair once more. The answers were not forthcoming.

She noticed however that the expressions on the women's faces in the room almost matched the expressions in the photos exactly. She wondered if hers did as well.

No one in the room seemed to know one another. Only two women were engaged in conversation. Their posture and gestures suggested that they didn't know each other either. The woman next to Sharla handed her a sign-in sheet, the top of which read OASIS WOMEN'S RESOURCE CENTER. Sharla had gotten a referral to the center when she obtained a protection order against Dennis. The secretary at the Office of Protection

Orders said that the woman in charge of the education programs for the center was a wonderful person. According to the secretary, the woman had experienced what Sharla had experienced and since then was instrumental in helping other women get out of abusive relationships.

Sharla signed her name and passed along the sign-in sheet. As she did so, a woman entered the room and walked to the front. Sharla thought she was very pretty and very pregnant. She listened intently as the woman introduced herself.

"Good evening, ladies. My name is Destiny Allgood. I know that some of you may not want to be here. Some of you may be scared. And some of you may just be curious. But believe me, I know what you're all going through and I'm here to tell you, you can, *and you will,* get through it." Then she paused and placed her hand carefully on the place where a miracle was happening inside her.

"Welcome, ladies, to the first step into your new life."

Dear Reader:

I hope you enjoyed reading Destiny and Xavier's story as much as I enjoyed writing it. We hear so much about domestic violence, and most of us associate it with the physical manifestations of this horrendous situation. But domestic violence can occur without either party ever striking a blow. In writing this story, it is my desire to take action against this kind of abuse.

On a special note, I want to thank you, the reader, for reading Destiny's story and validating the music of her love song. Let me hear from you. My Web site is www.kimlouise.com. My e-mail address is mskimlouise@aol.com. Or you can write me at P.O. Box 31554, Omaha, NE 68131. Please include a self-addressed, stamped envelope if you would like me to reply.

Until next time,
Kim Louise

ABOUT THE AUTHOR

Kim Louise is a resident of Omaha, Nebraska, where she lives with her son, Steve. She has a degree in journalism from the University of Nebraska at Omaha, and is currently a graduate student at Drake University, where she is studying Adult Learning and Development. Kim's articles and poetry have been published in numerous regional and national publications. She is also the winner of several writing contests, slogan contests, and a poetry slam.

In her "spare" time, Kim enjoys card making, calligraphy, surfing the net, writing poetry, and public speaking. Her second romance novel, *A Touch Away,* is due for release by Arabesque Books in July 2001, and she is currently at work on her third.

COMING IN JANUARY FROM
ARABESQUE ROMANCES

__PRIVATE PASSIONS
by Rochelle Alers   1-58314-151-0 $5.99US/$7.99CAN

Successful journalist Emily Kirkland never expected that her long-time friendship with gubernatorial candidate Christopher Delgado would ignite a dangerously irresistible desire—and result in their secret marriage. Now, with scandal and a formidable enemy threatening all of their most cherished dreams, Emily must uncover the truth, risking all for a passion that could promise forever . . .

__A SECOND CHANCE AT LOVE
by Janice Sims   1-58314-153-7 $5.99US/$7.99CAN

Author Toni Shaw has it all: two grown daughters on their own, a hot new novel in stores, and a gorgeous man in her bed. It's been three years since the father of her children entered her life, and things between Toni and Charles Waters are better than ever—until he pops an unexpected question: Will you marry me?

__GOOD INTENTIONS
by Crystal Wilson-Harris   1-58314-154-5 $5.99US/$7.99CAN

Minutes before she was about to marry Chicago's most-desirable catch, bride-to-be Ivy Daniels realized she needed time to sort out what *she* really wanted. With the unexpected help of handsome stranger Ben Stephens, she promptly bolts the "wedding-of-the-year"—only to discover a scandalous, surprising passion.

__TRULY
by Adrienne Ellis Reeves, Geri Guillaume, Mildred Riley
      1-58314-196-0 $5.99US/$7.99CAN

It is a day of hearts by surprise—and promises forever kept. Spend a glorious Valentine's Day with three of Arabesque's best-loved authors and discover love's most passionate delights.

Call toll free **1-888-345-BOOK** to order by phone or use this coupon to order by mail. *ALL BOOKS AVAILABLE JANUARY 1, 2001.*

Name _____

Address _____

City _____ State _____ Zip _____

Please send me the books I have checked above.

I am enclosing $_____

Plus postage and handling* $_____

Sales tax (+in NY and TN) $_____

Total amount enclosed $_____

*Add $2.50 for the first book and $.50 for each additional book.

Send check or money order (no cash or CODs) to:

Kensington Publishing Corp., Dept. C.O., 850 Third Avenue, New York, NY 10022

Prices and numbers subject to change without notice. Valid only in the U.S.

All orders subject to availability. **NO ADVANCE ORDERS.**

Visit our website at **www.arabesquebooks.com.**